# GIRL

## IN THE ARENA

# GIRL
## IN THE ARENA

A NOVEL CONTAINING INTENSE PROLONGED
SEQUENCES OF DISASTER AND PERIL

LISE HAINES

BLOOMSBURY

NEW YORK BERLIN LONDON

Published by Bloomsbury U.S.A. Children's Books
175 Fifth Avenue, New York, New York 10010

Library of Congress Cataloging-in-Publication Data
Haines, Lise.
Girl in the arena / by Lise Haines.—1st U.S. ed.
p.    cm.
Summary: In Massachusetts, eighteen-year-old Lyn, who has grown up in the
public eye as the daughter of seven gladiators, wants nothing less than to
follow her mother's path, but her only way of avoiding marriage to the
warrior who killed her last stepfather may be to face him in the arena.
ISBN-13: 978-1-59990-372-9 • ISBN-10: 1-59990-372-5
[1. Gladiators—Fiction. 2. Marriage—Fiction. 3. Sex role—Fiction.
4. Fame—Fiction. 5. People with mental disabilities—Fiction. 6. Family
life—Massachusetts—Fiction. 7. Massachusetts—Fiction.] I. Title.
PZ7.H128126Gir 2009        [Fic]—dc22        2008055013

First U.S. Edition 2009
Designed by Donna Mark
Typeset by Westchester Book Composition
Printed in the U.S.A. by Quebecor World Fairfield
2   4   6   8   10   9   7   5   3   1

*To Sienna*

*They became too powerful to live among us,*
*too self-concerned, too visionary, too blind.*

—JEFFREY EUGENIDES, *The Virgin Suicides*

# GIRL

## IN THE ARENA

# PROLOGUE

## A HISTORY OF THE
## GLADIATOR SPORTS ASSOCIATION

In 1969 there was a young widower named Joseph Byers who lost his only child, Ned, to the war in Vietnam, when Ned tried to dodge the draft. Ned was a serious asthmatic whose condition became aggravated by any small contact with cats. So he borrowed nine of his friends' tabbies and minxes and Persians and drove around in his VW Bug with the windows rolled up. The cats laced in and out of Ned's lap, moved along the back of his seat, nudged the stick shift, and tried to rub against the foot pedals. The plan was to drive around the city and pull right up to an emergency room, and then 4-F all the way. He just couldn't find a hospital in time. The coroner said that Ned miscalculated the number of cats he needed in the car.

Joe Byers introduced neo-gladiator sport into American life to involve teenage boys in a new form of athletic competition that would be exhilarating while releasing aggressive energy in a safe, clean way. He hoped there would be less need for war over time, especially for useless, savage wars like Vietnam.

Byers purchased plastic shields at a toy store. He whipped up balsa wood swords on his band saw and lathe, and tipped them in soft rubber. He bought swim goggles to protect their eyes, the kind of shin guards Ned had used to play soccer, bicycle gloves and football helmets, and a few catcher's face guards. Then Byers cleared out his backyard, built a wooden platform, put sand down on top of this, and coaxed his son's friends over to his house with the offer of a barbeque, television sports, and a chance to honor the dead. Despite some awkward moments and stupid jokes, the boys took to the sport, and soon began inviting more friends over. Weapons were modified so no one would get seriously injured, but it's possible this concept put him in league with the scientists who worked on atomic energy and didn't foresee Hiroshima, Mon Amour.

Joe Byers had a cousin, Craig Winsome, who started his own neo-gladiator chapter. He was a tool manufacturer, and came up with a retractable sword and spearhead that made it appear that one's guts were being sliced or impaled, a small reservoir of artificial blood in the weapons breaking on contact. Craig's wife, Anna, wrote out the Gladiator Rules as Craig dictated them. Later she penned the original 28 Bylaws, which were expanded to 128 and governed the social mores, attitudes, and conduct of the gladiator wives and eventually the sons and daughters as well. By the early 1980s there were 153 chapters of the Gladiator Sports Enthusiasts, or GSEs, as the group was then called, made up primarily of older teenage boys with some adult branches, and one early effort comprised of a group of women who called themselves the Vestals.

An article in Newsweek claimed that some chapters were

working with weapons that didn't retract but ran a body through. Those accounts went largely unconfirmed, but the GSEs went underground, which meant the organization quickly swelled in numbers.

Then four things happened: Chuck Palahniuk, 9/11, the war in Iraq, and a self-help book selling in the millions called The Mystery. Drawing on the self-actualizing techniques of The Mystery, Caesar's Inc., a holding company located in New York City (not to be mistaken with the Las Vegas group), recognized an opportunity. Caesar's hired a handful of young Ivy League graduates, offering wild salaries capped by travel, BMW, and hedge fund benefits to join a newly formed NoHo think tank called the Senate. Since Byers and Winsome had never incorporated, and held, in fact, no legal or official paper on their organization, Caesar's first move was to incorporate the GSA—the Gladiator Sports Association.

The GSA offered cash prizes to the Neo-Glads who fought in their leagues. The first sixty-thousand-seat amphitheater was targeted for Chicago, beating out Denver, Los Angeles, Seattle, and Atlanta.

America got to know Caesar's spokesperson, a woman with a steely authority who went by the name Sappho. The media focused on her top-model appearance and her Armani suits. She stated that the GSA would "provide a new form of sport slash entertainment slash battle that would capture the American ethos on a scale equal to the NFL." She said Caesar's would deliver one hundred able-bodied fighters for the first event.

A reality television program, The Competitors, was aired to

find those one hundred neo-gladiators. The competitors were required to don original costumes, which would in time set off a fierce battle in a fashion industry grown weary of military wear. And though some said Jean Paul Gaultier's clothes were too flamboyant for actual combat situations, he became the darling of the sport. The Glads, as the competitors came to be known, lived together for eight weeks on an abandoned military base in California, where they attended Ludus Magnus Americus, the first neo-Glad school.

The GSA did not restrict women from competition per se, any more than the NFL does—it was all about meeting certain physical standards. But some said that the sport was hobbled by old-school thinking, the inherent belief that men were by nature more fit to compete, more ready to kill. The women's leagues were small and, in general, poorly funded. And groups across the country battled over the idea of including fighting women. The Gladiator Wives Association didn't help much. And though they received a lot of flak for their traditionalist views, they held to the notion that a Glad wife had a vital role to play in their culture.

In one episode, the men, and some women—the Glads—were taken by bus to visit the amphitheater as it neared completion, which was a pretty sappy show with plenty of shots of the Roman Colosseum and Lake Michigan at sunset. During the course of the filming there were several injuries and one accidental death, and some missed their lovers or families so badly they dropped out. A few people hooked up. One marriage occurred.

Caesar's paid television stations to air Ridley Scott's Gladiator

so they could piggyback their ads around car and beer spots and
Russell Crowe's face. The GSA television ads were Nike-esque,
beautifully muscled in all respects, and print ads ran in popular
fashion and men's magazines. Single images were reproduced on
colossal posters throughout airports and malls. And yes, even Times
Square was lit up with gladiator sport. During that first competition there were no fights to the death, and though lions and other
large cats were added to the excitement, they were declawed,
defanged, desensitized. Fighters were carefully matched. Dwarfs
fought dwarfs, men with nets and tridents fought men with nets
and tridents, light men light, heavy men heavy. Injuries were considered no worse than the aftermath of a rousing hockey game or
a soccer match in Brazil. By all accounts the GSA had pulled off an
elegant feat.

The GSA purchased the copyrights to the official Gladiator Rules
and the 128 Gladiator Bylaws, and Byers and Winsome became
romantic icons, like rotary dial phones. After three years Caesar's
Inc. had a large-scale success on their hands that would soon be
echoed in their gaming division, as well as the licensing of hats,
swords, T-shirts, and toys.

About this time, a man on death row in Texas, Victor
Shroedinger, was scheduled to die in the electric chair but he had
a profound fear of electricity. Hoping to die with dignity for his
family's sake, he petitioned the governor. The governor was an ex-
professional body builder who never missed a GSA game on television. Shroedinger asked to fight any man or beast with nothing
more than a rubber knife. The governor thought the case had

merit. Being a highly persuasive man, he managed to get his own senate to pass a small amendment tacked on (in 6-pt. type) to another bill.

Human rights organizations tried to stop the match. They brought up Corcoran State Prison, where the guards had pitted one gang against another in gladiator-type combat. But the amendment passed by a narrow margin. Shroedinger chose a short knife and a garbage can lid for a shield, and Galliano, who was quite taken by the drama of Shroedinger's story, designed his outfit. Shroedinger managed to stay in the game a full fifteen minutes. He was stabbed directly in the heart and appeared to die a happy man.

Other Texas death row inmates followed in his wake, then other states released their dead men walking to fight—all becoming short-term Glads—pitted nicely against one another. This provoked nonstop media attention, with strident views from academics, parent groups, lawmakers, lobbyists, and essayists. But Glad sport had a way of defying gravity, a way of changing essential rules.

Then there was the man, Wes C., who wrote an op-ed piece in the Times. He pointed to the terrible inequity, that a death row inmate could commit a heinous crime and be granted rights that law-abiding, tax-paying citizens were not. He had Hodgkin's lymphoma and wanted to wrap his life up quickly and to some small glory, to test his mettle once and for all, gladiator style. Several groups supported his efforts, as did a couple of doctors newly released from jail for physician-assisted suicide. There was, of course, strong opposition to letting the op-ed man die in the arena.

*And yet, over time the rules evolved, were challenged, revised, and superseded by new rules. Eventually Glad sport, though not always a fight to the death, certainly offered this possibility.*

*Lyn*
*Daughter of Seven Gladiators*

# CHAPTER

# 1

The clerk asks for my autograph.

—Do it right across my face, he says.

Usually when we're out in public everyone wants Allison's autograph. My mother's as famous as the men she's married. Over the years, she has signed stomachs, tip sheets, shoes, baby carriages, even a sandwich once, and of course thousands of arena souvenir booklets. But until recently, few have asked for my signature.

Before I can stop her, Allison tells the clerk that I'm the daughter of seven gladiators. Allison is on her usual kick. She wants me to open up more.

—*Seven*? The guy laughs. —I bet I've seen you on VH1, right?

—Not really, I say.

—No, no it's ESPN. I know who you are. We're talking *real Glads*, right? Swords, shields, heads flying, arms lopped off? Not that TV show with a bunch of batons and cargo nets, right?

—Mortal combat, Allison confirms with a polite smile, —though not always to the death.

—That's what I mean, he says. —*Mortal combat.*

We're at this store in Cambridge that has an underground operation selling War Tickets. They aren't actual tickets, they're just called that. You place bets on which countries we'll end up going to war with—in other words, which countries we will bomb senseless. The store handles bets on all sorts of standard gambling as well, scratch offs, quick picks. Allison says our chance of winning on War Tickets is a whole lot better than the state lottery and now that I've turned eighteen, I can buy my own.

The glass countertop she leans against is part of a cabinet holding an entire display, a miniature Baghdad scene with U.S. and Iraqi troops, soldiers taking cover, heading out on raids, tiny men and women that look like they've already blown up. My guess is he got that effect by melting them with a lighter.

The clerk hands me a marker now. He holds his hair off his forehead so I have plenty of room to scrawl over his greasy brow. I admit it's really the only space—he's heavily tattooed everywhere else.

I shoot Allison a panicked look, but she continues with her ticket picks. I lift the pen.

—Don't worry if you hit the nose. It's been broken so many times I can't feel a thing.

—This is permanent marker, I say.

—Nothing's permanent, he says.

So I sign Lyn G. quickly and then I buy mine: five Irans, three Afghanistans, two North Koreas. It's easy to feel horrible about this kind of purchase—being a pacifist and all—but if it's going to happen anyway, I just want to make enough money so Allison doesn't have to worry as much about my brother, Thad.

Next time I'll probably spread out, hit more countries, but I'm certain Iran is the place for war, that Afghanistan's a close runner up. Tommy, my seventh father, thinks so. He lives inside the newspaper, and we have a deal—we're going to split the money if either of us wins, so he wouldn't steer me wrong. They say the proceeds go to fighting terrorism here and abroad—well, at least 2 percent. So you could say we're betting on death, or you could say it's the other way around.

When I reach for the change, the clerk says, —You guys aren't screwing with me, right? You're the daughter of *SEVEN* Glads?

I shrug because of course it's true, but when I hear it said aloud like that I think of weirdness, of odd attractions out in the desert where people pay a buck to see a live chicken without a head. It's moments like this I wish I were finished being a daughter. But I know you have to be careful about what you wish for.

—Sick, he says, and winks at Allison.

I wait until we're home, the last of the frozen items put away, which is practically all we buy now, except for razor blades, shampoo, and stuff. Six months ago Allison bought a mega freezer and ever since then she's been down on fresh produce. And maybe there's some consolation in knowing we can preserve everything we want till the end of time.

I watch her load the sink with the breakfast dishes now, the water running hard. She avoids the dishwasher, saying it wears out the plates.

—Can't you just say I'm Tommy's daughter? I ask.

—What are you talking about? she says.

—That guy at the store thought I was some freak of nature. He didn't have to know I'm the daughter of *seven* gladiators.

—You take these things too seriously, Lynie.

—And *you* make me sound like I'm the product of seven types of DNA.

Allison is having a tough time getting the detergent to squirt out into the sink. She's forgotten to remove the cardboard plug inside the cap. I watch her struggle until she gets the bottle open. Then she gives me this look, like all safety devices are my fault.

—I think people get the concept of stepfathers, she says, and looks out at her beloved garden. —I think people like knowing that a widow can remarry.

—And remarry and remarry, I say, raising my voice. —Not everyone is that interested in my lineage, Allison. And not everyone loves Glad culture the way *you* do.

Unwilling to negotiate the bottle another second, she throws it as hard as she can and the blue soap arcs across the kitchen, douses the linoleum, hits the dining room table, spatters the satin chairs, and soaks my legs. She's been through a lot and I love my mother, but she can go off like a Roman candle. Like six months ago when we were driving out in Worcester, going 75 on a 45 mph road, and she kept needling me to talk about my plans for the future, and I finally had to tell her.

—I'm not planning on being a Glad wife.

She practically pulled underneath some guy's rear bumper, as if she were begging him to make a sudden stop. Most of the time she's not like that, and I think whiplash is largely a state of mind. And shortly after the anger subsided Allison went crazy with remorse. Sometimes she has full-blown panic attacks like she did that day and I had to take her to the ER, and pretty soon that whole business—my identity—was about her.

But I know what she's suffered, so I help her clean up, and cleaning up soap is not an easy task because it keeps trying to clean the thing you're trying to clean. I finally suggest that she go lie down and I'll finish up. She stops crying and goes up to the master bedroom and stretches out on the Texas king bed, a moist washcloth over her eyes, her ear plugs in, the way she tries to fuzz out a few days before a match, when what she really wants to do is find a tall bridge, she's so distressed.

It's much worse this time because Tommy's fighting tomorrow—at the American Title fight against a guy named Uber—and she can't accept the idea that she could lose him.

Because that would mean, among other things, losing her seventh husband, the best one she's had, bar none. He's the best in all the leagues really, the one everybody loves. And if you follow the Gladiator Wives Bylaws, which Allison has as long as I can remember, you know a Glad wife can only marry seven times and then she's done. So that's where she's screwed herself. She doesn't want to be done. Allison can't stand being alone.

I know some people see it as a lack of affection, the way I call Allison by her first name. But when you have a mother who spends a lot of time trying to stay young so she can find that next husband—so she can take care of her children, the younger with special needs . . . She kind of messed up in the career department. And she asked me flat out to call her by her first name, so we could be *more like sisters* in a way. I've tried to go along. So it's Allison this and Allison that.

When I go upstairs to check on her, she cautions me to whisper. My brother, Thad, is curled around the mound of her feet under the coverlet, nesting, watching cartoons with no sound on. Even when he's not supposed to be quiet, this is the way Thad likes to watch a show because there's so much noise going on in his head all the time. That's what the doctor told us. The Italian ex-pat pediatrician compared my brother's internal sounds to the rushing, cursing traffic around the Colosseum—Vespas, taxis, micro cars. My eight-year-old brother is a boy of internal cacophony. Allison is patient where Thad's cartoons are concerned, as she is with most things that keep Thad happy.

14

Thad looks up at me. I stroke his hair lightly, and he returns to his state of mesmerization.

Allison tells me how sorry she is.

—I guess I'm pretty keyed up, she says.

—I know, I say. —It's okay.

—How did he seem to you this morning? she asks.

She's talking about Tommy and I say, —Solid. Really solid.

I go into her bathroom and get her *beautiful tranquilizers*, as she calls them, and I bring her a glass of water as well. She kisses me on the cheek.

—I'm going to get completely off these after this competition, she says.

That's her standard line, so I don't know what to say.

—I told you two years ago things would change. Now that you're eighteen, you're free game to the media, and . . .

—*And* I have such an *impressive* list of fathers.

—Well, you do, like it or not.

—Okay, Allison.

—Things will go better than you think once you get used to the added attention, she says. —Why don't you call the girls and see if you can get together with them this afternoon? Do something fun.

This is Allison's other kick: *the girls,* the effort to resuscitate my social life. Although I've always been kind of a loner, except for my best friend Mark, from seventh grade on I had two main girlfriends. Sam: the high-wire act who has her father's broad shoulders, her mother's practically bulging eyes, and a tendency to sometimes talk before her brain kicks in, and Callie: shy and smart and built like a support beam, willing to do anything Sam wants in order to be included. We were the only Glad girls at our high school—and we live in a culture in which most people think it's fun to observe Glads and make jokes about Glads but not mix with them—so we clung fast.

We were all about the things threes produce, sometimes tight and inseparable, sometimes weirdly triangulated and full of drama. We finally broke apart over the asinine junior prom. Sam's boyfriend Dirk had gotten his boy Adam—one of the popular Glads—to ask me to the prom and I had thanked him but said no. Adam was this moron who spent his days and nights watching fistfights on Jerry Springer. He was always taking cheap shots at everybody he could think of with his little BB gun mouth. And there was Sam, acting as if I was supposed to embrace all things Glad.

—I can't believe you said no to Adam, Sam said. —Does anyone around here know how high up Adam's father is in the GSA?

I didn't say that my father Tommy outranked him. She knew that.

I watched her turn to Callie, who swallowed hard, as if she were washing her own little self down her throat.

—I wouldn't have said no, Callie squeaked.

—Exactly. No sane girl would.

Sam couldn't stand it when I just looked at her as I did then, waiting to see if she'd calm down. She had me pressed against a locker room stall. I was still slick from volleyball.

—Go ahead, screw up your life, she said.

—When he comes out of the gym, he smells like a Dumpster on a warm day, I said, hoping to put an end to the conversation.

—That's disgusting, Callie said.

Sam gave her the eyeball and she was about to launch in again when I said, —Besides, the prom is a stupid waste of energy. All those silly little gowns and corsages and stuff.

—What are you, some kind of women's power person? Sam asked.

—Wow, the curse of Cain, I said.

I didn't say I think this whole concept of being a Glad wife is 1950s at best, because she'd tell her mother, who would call my mother. And it's not that Allison doesn't know how I feel, but she tries really hard to keep up appearances, and I have no reason to make things more painful for her. I know that gladiator sport blindsided her and that she stayed for survival's sake.

—You know what my mother says? Sam went on, pointing her French manicure at me.

—I have no idea what Martha says, but I bet it's good.

—She says Allison's crazy and that it's probably hereditary.

Then I lost it and said what I had been thinking for months: that I never had any intention of going to the GWC with her.

The GWC, or Gladiator Wives College, in Modesto, California, is where young women learn in two intensive years to be perfect Glad wives. At one time the three of us had talked about going together and sharing an apartment. Sam's mother, Martha, who's a lot younger than my mother, was one of their first graduates.

Sam shoved my shoulders against the metal stall. That was about the time when I first realized I might be a pacifist, so I kept myself from pushing her face in.

We stopped talking after that. Callie wouldn't answer my calls because she was a hundred percent Sam's now. My friend Mark asked me to prom at the last minute, thinking that's what I secretly wanted. But I told him I just wanted to go paintballing and he was down with that so we suited up and drove over to Somerville. I never told Allison what Sam said, and how things unraveled. When she asks I just say we're all pretty busy.

Allison holds out hope that I'll come to my senses and pack my bags next month for the GWC. She says she's talked to the president of the college, and that they'll take me late because of Tommy's standing.

As I back out of her room now, certain that the tranquilizer is starting to work, I shut the door without latching it so the snap won't make her jump. She has a terrible startle reflex.

I know I have to move out soon, get my own place, my own life. But I stick around as long as I can for my brother Thad. I've been thinking a lot about this lately because they say tomorrow's fight is the toughest one of Tommy's career, and every time I think about that, I feel somehow displaced.

# CHAPTER
# 2

Often, I'm at my fast-food job on Friday nights serving trans fat to the masses. But my boss, Sidney, is very big on Glad sport and Tommy in particular. He gave me a raise of fifty cents an hour the first day on the job when he figured out who I was. And this week he gave me the whole weekend off to be with my family after I gave him two tickets to tomorrow's American Title match.

Once I tuck Allison in, I head for my bedroom and turn on *La Bohème*. While I send Mark an IM, I thumb through *Glad Rag* magazine, look at the crawl on a silent CNN, check the weather, download some tunes, and watch a couple of videos on YouTube. Allison can't stand that I do so many things at once, but that's her burden.

Finally I settle into the window seat, where I try to work on *A History of the Gladiator Sports Association*. But really it's about waiting for Tommy to appear in the backyard so I can see if he looks ready to fight.

For several days leading up to a match Tommy does a series of limbering exercises on the lawn each afternoon. After that he lifts some weights and soaks for a while in the cool, warm, and hot baths we had built in what used to be the garage, so when he isn't working he can feel like he's hanging out at a Roman bath.

On something like cue, Tommy steps from around the side of the house. Allison worked very hard on the garden this spring so everything's in bloom: the forsythia, the pink ladies, and the hollyhocks. And suddenly I'm having this horrible thought that if Tommy dies tomorrow we'll have thousands of flowers for the funeral, because everything she plants has a high yield. And that means her sorrow as well as mine.

I think about going downstairs and talking with him, but I'm afraid I'd just make him nervous. He spent all morning sharpening his swords in the kitchen. While I slathered the toast with preserves and ground the coffee beans, he spun the whetstone, pulling one of his favorite swords across its rough surface. He seemed uneasy. Usually he looks pretty tough before a fight. I wanted to say something then as well, but we both kept grinding.

Tomorrow afternoon he'll take his car in early so he can suit up in the locker rooms of the amphitheater in Boston, Romulus Arena. Allison, Thad, and I will follow an hour later. We'll sit in our usual box and hope to God he makes it, because if he does he'll only have two more matches to fight and then he'll get out of the business for good and maybe we can start to have a normal life the way Allison always promises.

I told Tommy once, when he first dated Allison, that he would make a good trainer. I stopped short of saying he's too smart to fight for the GSA. But Tommy takes his responsibilities seriously, that's the way he is, and it turns out he had already signed his contract.

Now he's pulling the long hose out into the yard and he has to stop to untangle it. He turns on the spigot and starts to water the hydrangeas—a bizarre thing to do the day before a fight. He always spends his time in preparation, even if this means sitting in the swivel chair in the library with his eyes closed, thinking about how he'll take down his opponent. Tommy says it's essential to see exactly what you'll cut, precisely where you'll strike, the way a professional golfer visualizes a ball arcing down the fairway, sailing toward the cup, the effortless hole in one. Tommy has a lot of discipline to see that kind of thing in his head—how he'll sever a man's arm or rip into his face. I couldn't do it. When I'm up in our box and someone gets injured, I typically look away.

Tommy holds his thumb over the end of the nozzle and a fine spray of water hits the flowers. Maybe he's worried they're going to succumb to the heat? I'm trying to imagine when he began to care about Allison's garden. As soon as he's finished, he goes down on his haunches and pulls at a few weeds, inspects the undersides of leaves.

Is he worried about aphids? Is his mind riddled with thoughts of bone meal and mulch? And the way he's doing it—he goes at the whole process delicately, as if he's trying to keep the dirt from his nails. But Tommy's not a delicate man. He's a gladiator. Maybe he has a fragile thought or two, but mostly I think of him as durable goods, tough as any industrial product. He seems to be in some kind of stupor. Maybe he needs some coffee.

I just don't get it. If he thinks he's going to die in the arena tomorrow, if that's what this is about, I can't imagine a dumber way to spend a last afternoon on Earth. Finally, Tommy leaves the flower beds and goes off to the shed.

But now he's bringing out the antique lawn mower! Not the type the gardeners use on Tuesdays when they spring from their red pickup. A whole team of gardeners shaved the grass just three days ago in fact. Caesar's Inc. arranges this service to keep Tommy focused on his game and he always leaves this work to them.

Tommy nudges the old push mower with the double-helix blade into the yard. He pulls his T-shirt off and throws it on a garden chair. Naked to his gym shorts, a bandana round his head, he looks like his own posters. He pulls his long hair into a ponytail. Already he's sweating, and he hasn't even started to mow.

I want to call down to him, to let him know Allison is trying to sleep so that he doesn't make too much noise, but Thad has hidden the window cranks again. If I rap on the glass Allison might leap from her nap, thinking someone's shooting up the house, in that way that one noise becomes another in a dream. I wave my arms over my head to get his attention, but he doesn't look up.

By the time I get downstairs, Tommy has disappeared from the garden. He's put on a fresh T-shirt and jeans, and I find him in the weapons room. I have to say he looks more like his old self now, pushing his wavy hair out of his eyes, his bare feet planted on the Oriental rug. He has an open book in hand. *The Tao of Killing,* one of those slim catchall volumes that says absolutely nothing about the sport or the life, but sells millions of copies. He shrugs, like I've busted him reading a tabloid at the supermarket, and tosses it on a pile of mail.

—What's going on? I ask.

—Just reading some . . . chain mail.

—That's so bad.

—Chain letters?

Sometimes he gets this way with me, as if we've just met and he has to find something clever to say and it comes out awkward. He leans into the sword rack now and offers me a chair. Hoping to let him off the hook, I ask if I can get him something to drink.

—Actually, I was just going to make a smoothie. You want one? How about strawberry mango? he asks.

Then he touches my jaw, cradles it for a moment. I can feel the familiar calluses made by the strap of his shield.

—You all right? I ask.

—Perfect.

While he breezes off to the kitchen, I sink into the easy chair and shut my eyes.

Frank, my first father, I can't remember. He died when I was one. But I don't think any of the others ever made a point of asking me to join them for refreshments the way Tommy does. Though Rolfe, my third father—Rolfe was a mess—once asked me to join him for a highball in the living room. I was eight at the time. I remember hiding out in my bedroom closet till Allison came home. At his funeral some of his family, who had come to pay their respects to Allison, remarked that they didn't mind so much that he had been taken out.

Tommy is the one who's always shown interest. He wants to know if my black eye means someone picked a fight with me at school (I've been ganged up on a few times, sometimes by preps, sometimes by jocks); how many pounds of fries I cook at my hyper-food job in one night (the answer is *plenty*); if my friend Mark's intentions are good; that kind of stuff. Tommy's been around for five years now, though he and Allison didn't get married right away. I never thought their relationship would last.

I hear the whir of a small blade churning up frozen fruit and yogurt in the kitchen, the blender set into the steel sink, the slap of his feet on the parquet floor.

He hands me a straw and we sip quietly.

—This is really good. Did you add a boost? I ask.

—Yes. Dope.

—Wuh?

—Made by Tour de France Ltd.

—You're cracking me up today, I say, rolling my eyes.

—How's *A History of the Gladiator Sports Association* going? he asks.

—I'm still on the American section. I really want to interview Joe Byers, but so far he won't return my e-mails.

Many consider Byers to be the founder of Glad sport, but he's a funny guy, never grants interviews.

—You know, you'd make a pretty good history professor. No, I'm serious, or a biographer.

—Wouldn't Allison love that, I say.

—Not at first.

—I think my head-on-a-platter would express it.

—She wants you to be a Glad wife because that's what she knows. I'll work on her, Tommy assures me.

He rubs the scar that divides the apple of his right cheek into two half spheres, the horizontal line where the pigmentation disappears into an equator. There's a drop of pink on his chin.

—You know, your mother's been kind to me. Good. Kind, he says, as if he has to stumble for the right word.

It sounds like one of those random comments he'll land on. I'm used to letting those declarations hang in the air. Sometimes I wonder if all they have is a marriage of convenience. Nothing would shock. I point to his chin and he wipes it clean.

—We should talk about a couple of things, he says.

His voice hits that low register that makes my intestines bunch up.

—Let's go for a walk. We have time, he says, looking at his watch. —Bring the *History* along.

So I stuff my computer in my backpack and we head out. We live just off Brattle Street in Cambridge, where wealthy people loyal to the crown once lived before the Revolutionary War. There are placards on fences and brickwork, stating who lived in various homes, along with titles, significant activities, that kind of thing. Wood frame, lots of shutters, sweeping lawns, unending shade trees—everything Allison wanted. You hear about occasional vandalism, but I haven't seen a week when the garbage built up around here.

We walk awhile before he opens up.

—Look, I don't want to make too big a deal out of this but Uber's on the fast track and so far he hasn't left any of his opponents standing. If I go down in the arena tomorrow . . .

—You're not going down, I say.

—But if I do, he says.

—You're going to knock Uber's head off in the first two minutes.

You say that kind of knowing stuff when you're the daughter of a gladiator. You grow up saying knowing things the way your mother does. It doesn't matter what you know or don't know. Or if your mother spends her whole existence telling lies and you're just reproducing them.

*Always lend ineffable confidence to the gladiator,* Bylaw 29.

I've read the fifty-seven Gladiator Conduct Regulations to Tommy, more than once, so he could work on his memorization. Gladiators have to be prepared for frequent pop quizzes. The GSA loves that kind of thing. A hearty fine goes to the Glad who fails a pop quiz. You can lose your transportation, your whetstone, everything.

—I guess I just want to make sure someone's going to be there for Thad, he says.

—He's good with us, I say. —Don't worry.

As if I'm worry free.

—I've been watching the tapes of Uber's last six matches, Tommy says. —The fact that he's a lefty doesn't help.

—But if you know that, you'll be prepared.

He doesn't say anything.

Tommy and I have this way of keeping pace when we walk. Though I'm the taller one, his stride is quicker. I have a hard time walking with Allison even though I'm only two inches taller than she is. She likes to start and stop and comment on everything. She's obsessed with each yard and who's planting what. And Thad, well, he takes you on a moonwalk you have to gear up for.

As we near the park, I slide my bracelet off my wrist.

—For good luck, I say, pushing it his way. —Not that you'll need it, of course.

—Your dowry bracelet?

—This girl in San Francisco, they say her dowry bracelet saved her father's life. I read it online last week.

The steel band was made for my first father by a famous sword maker in Japan. It's in the man's style and it's always been large for me. And Tommy's a little guy, only five seven, so even though he has thick hands it slips easily onto his wrist. He says something about wearing it proudly, he's even a little choked up, so I don't get all the words.

He reaches into a pocket in his jeans and holds out a scrap of paper to me.

—I wrote down a name and number for you, he says.

—LeRoy Gastonguay? New York? And he would be?

We head down a short street where we usually turn. In the middle of the block is a park. A single-family lot given to the neighborhood by a wealthy family. There are two benches and a small fountain. The trees offer shade on a hot day. We take a seat.

—He works for Caesar's Incorporated. He's down in the New York headquarters. If you're ever in a bad strait, this is the guy.

—I don't want this, I say, trying to hand it back to him.

—Just hold on to it. And look, the other thing . . . He pushes the nose of one of his shoes into the wood chips packed around the bench. —Don't feel like you have to come tomorrow.

—No, I want to be there, I say.

I don't really, now that he's got me so spooked. And I

told Allison a couple of years ago that I wouldn't be coming as much to the games. But it would be crazy not to go to his match. I know my mother needs me there.

I can tell he's wrestling with things, and maybe my eyes are kind of filling up.

—So let's hear it, he says, indicating my computer. I pull it from the backpack, open the lid, and bring up the file. I hold the screen out to him.

—No, read it aloud, he says.

Tommy stretches his arms along the back of the bench and closes his eyes to listen. He leans his head back. I see the stubble he missed on his neck. And though I don't want to, I think about the fragility of a neck.

Nothing's worse than a Glad going into a fight this way, with a clear lack of confidence. The whole thing scratches at my throat. I have an impulse to tell Tommy that he's the only father I've ever loved, but I don't want to make an idiot of myself. So I let it go.

—Are you awake? I ask.

Tommy cracks one eye open. —Would you start reading already?

—Okay. Okay.

I get to the last sentence.

—Eventually Glad sport, though not always a fight to the death, certainly offered this possibility.

Then I turn off my computer. Tommy nods.

—That's as far as I've gotten, I say.

—You've nailed it, he says.

—You haven't told Allison about it, right?

—You asked me not to.

—She'd just freak again about college and stuff.

—She does have that solid panic reflex, he says.

Then he makes this face, like it's just something we have to go through with Allison, the way we have to put up with metal dust in our soup from his sword sharpening in the kitchen and the fact that I tend to leave the flat iron on in my bathroom and have almost burned the house down six times. But I know her fretfulness digs in, that his patience with her can get as thin as mine.

—Allison said something the other day . . . that you're reading up on nonviolence? he says.

—Which she finds thoroughly humiliating.

—You might want to try Thomas Merton. He's pretty good.

I always stop myself, at moments like this, from asking him how long he'll hang in.

# CHAPTER

# 3

Thad and I have this ritual. We like to go to the Museum of Science on the Friday evenings when I'm not working, after it turns dark. As soon as Tommy and I get back to the house, Allison makes a light dinner for Thad and then I help him find a clean T-shirt and comb his hair for him.

GSA women wear a certain kind of boot made from Italian leather, sometimes sandals with at least fifteen straps—not the pseudogladiator style you see everywhere now—and tunics on occasion. But I wear jeans and T-shirts mostly. Sam and Callie and I used to wear these cutoff *stolas* of our mothers'—the layer that goes over a toga—but that's when you get really annoying comments so I stopped doing that. Of course Sam's the kind of girl to wear barrettes dipped in the blood of gladiators, which she claims they did in Imperial Rome, and this, I think, kind of encapsulates her personality. The most I'll do now is wear a few bloodless beads, a little gold—my beat-in leather jacket always. I really couldn't care beyond that.

And sometimes it's almost easier to be in uniform. At my fast-food nation job, it's really hot and you have to lift heavy boxes of frozen food substance and you get spattered with sizzling grease. But you have this uniform and this cap and you're just one of the underpaid and completely marginalized jerks like everyone else and no one asks if you come from seven types of men—you just fry and salt and squirt and slap and wrap and bag.

I get Thad settled in the backseat and we drive down Cambridge Street to avoid as much rush hour traffic as possible, past the medical facilities, the library, the tattoo parlor, restaurants, the Garment District, the courthouse where Allison has always managed to avoid jury duty, and God-knows-what shops. You can get a freshly killed chicken on Cambridge Street.

Thad's anchored by his seat belt but each time he sees neon lights he ducks. My friend Callie used to go with us, and her presence made for less wear and tear on Thad.

—We're almost there, I assure him.

—We're almost there, he repeats, in his self-soothing way.

Finally we hit the upscale condos, the Cambridgeside Galleria, and the parking ramp to the museum. Inside, we get a locker for our jackets and Thad and I use this machine where we turn a penny into a thin piece of copper with a T. rex imprinted on it. This he will rub for hours between the thumb and index finger of his left hand, because that's what Thad does. He has long eyelashes and soft downy hair that people admire. But he's a big guy, nearly twice the height of his classmates at school, and he has a solid girth, so even though he's only eight sometimes he's mistaken for an older boy and there's a lot of confusion about his behavior.

We head for the cafeteria, where we sit by the big picture windows and look at the lights of Boston reflected on the Charles. A tour boat is anchored at its helm. The stern makes a slow arc across the water as it's pushed back and forth by the current. This always has a calming effect on Thad. We eat french fries in paper cups and watch our reflections in the glass as we become full and satisfied.

Live musicians play jazz and the IMAX lines bulge. After we've slurped up all the Coke we can manage, Thad takes my hand and pulls me through the lobby into the turnstile where we show our passes. The crowds have already thinned out, so pretty soon there's no waiting to punch buttons, lift handles, open drawers, move levers, spin wheels. We ride up the escalator until we're right there in his favorite place: The Playground. Here Ping-Pong balls are sucked up air tubes, people watch their heartbeats on monitors, and try to outrun a sequence of flashing lights. In one room kids leap into the air and if they time it right, they can see flat shadows of themselves frozen on a blank white wall until those impressions start to fade, and then they press the light button again and start over.

The only exhibit Thad likes is the one where he can make a small digital recording of himself on a monitor. He likes to get it to replay and replay and that makes him laugh some and then he says, *I love that.* Though we could certainly make videos at home, I think there's something about the silliness of hamming it up around other people that has a particular draw for Thad.

My brother sees a lot of specialists and physical therapists. He was put on meds when he was four. I call them *elevator* drugs. Without them he seems to flatten out in a way that worries Allison. I know that side effects are part of life, but Thad's biochemistry mixed with the drugs, produce, well, he fires off this steady stream of predictions now like a crawl at the bottom of a screen. You don't want to pay attention to all of it but you do. Beautiful and crazy oracles ride up from the basement of his brain and spill out of his mouth in frequent spurts. He feels compelled to share this stuff with me, as if I'm the local translator or the seer's assistant, and I do my best to take it all in.

Thad looks into the video screen, presses the green button, and the monitor starts to count down from three, signaling that he should get ready for his ten-second personal recording. When it hits zero, he looks into the tiny eye of the camera embedded at the top of the screen and says, in this way that some people would mistake for deadpan, —I'm the most famous person you'll ever meet.

Then he stares, waiting for the tape to stop.

He presses the replay button and there's Thad, his large head and the precise teeth marks in his chapped lower lip. —*I'm the most famous person you'll ever meet.*

Then: the stare.

We both laugh. I tell him how professional he looks.

He says, —I love that.

I count twenty-five additional replays until I say, —I think the show on electricity is about to start. Let's go see the Tesla coil.

When that doesn't work, I recommend the Nancy Drew computer game with the eerie androids, the *Lord of the Rings* exhibit, the new butterfly room.

—If we're really still, the butterflies might come and land on us, I say. —I know you'd love that.

But we are in the ritual and we will be here until he finally looks at me and says, —Can we see Mom now?

This means he's tired and ready to go home. As I take his hand and we walk back toward the escalator, I tell him people will come by and press the replay button and they will see the most famous person they'll ever meet, if they're lucky enough to meet him someday.

Thad likes hearing this and asks me to repeat it a couple of times, which is more like fifteen or sixteen.

Later, when I'm helping him with his seat belt out in the parking garage, I say, —We had fun tonight, didn't we?

And he says, —We had fun tonight.

Thad is not by nature someone who smiles a lot, but I can tell when he's content. We take Memorial Drive back, less lights—or a different kind of light in any case—less neon.

—We're going to go to the stadium tomorrow, I say,

looking at Thad in the rearview as we pass MIT. Because suddenly I realize someone better explain things to him.

He says, —Tommy's fighting.

It's not like him to remember this kind of thing, even if he's told it many times over, so I know he has to be worried. I've noticed Tommy has been spending more time with him lately.

—Tommy's going to lose this, he says.

He points with his right hand but I'm trying to keep my eyes on the road, so I don't get what he's talking about at first.

—What's Tommy going to lose?

—This.

When I tell him I still don't get it, he becomes agitated and then he waves his hand back and forth.

So I wave back at him in the rearview, thinking that's what he wants.

—His hand, he says.

—Tommy's going to lose his hand? I say, and stop waving.

—Tommy's going to lose his hand, he says, letting out a deep breath.

I know the horrible things that happen in the arena, but there's something about this information coming from Thad. Allison shouldn't take him to competitions. We've had endless fights about that. But she says that's what she has to do— it's in the GSA Bylaws—and when she starts talking bylaws, there's no reasoning with her.

We go past Harvard now, Dunster House, and farther up the fat white trees that line the Drive. The traffic slows and we can hear Friday night sounds from the Square. I have to wonder if my friend Mark is there raising hell with his boys before tomorrow's fight.

—We'll be home soon. Maybe you and Tommy can soak in the tubs tonight before Mom tucks you in, I say.

But when I look back, I see Thad has already fallen asleep. Tommy will carry him upstairs when we get home, even though he's so little and Thad is such a big boy. Allison will make sure his night-light is on. She'll put a glass of water on his bedside table in case he wakes up thirsty. Then she'll unfold his green and yellow plaid blanket and tuck this in so he doesn't wake up cold in the middle of the night. She will look in on him a couple of times before she goes to bed to make sure he hasn't had a nightmare or kicked his covers off. He can get pretty scared if he wakes up alone. I think he forgets that we're just down the hall.

# CHAPTER
# 4

I wake up the next day to the sound of the LAWNMOWER. Even though my head is still glued to my dreams, this is way too familiar. I get up and go over to my window seat overlooking the backyard. Tommy's got that antique mower going again. I worry that he's going to snap. It happens to Glads sometimes.

I watch him move from the shade into the sunlight and back again. It's a hot day already and his skin—he's got this kind of shine, like a horse's coat when he's been overworked. I want to rush down there and ask if everything is all right, but he seems oddly content mowing up and back. I decide not to break his concentration. But I'm thinking: this is one much-mowed lawn. When Tommy was out there yesterday, he trimmed the exact same swath.

Tommy skirts the cypress tree now, the mower slowly eating into the bark of the thick exposed roots—could anything test Allison's patience more?—then he stops abruptly.

Dropping the handle, he walks to the middle of the lawn. He looks at the ground and then right up at my windows. He waves. Not his usual burst of pleasure, but an almost regal motion. I raise my hand to wave back, when I realize his face is almost expressionless and his body appears to be shifting in the breeze. How can I say this? It's not that he's swaying from the hips or dancing to something on ear buds. It's more like his whole image is rippling.

Then I get it.

I get the whole damn thing.

Allison is running the Living machine.

All this time I've been looking at a virtual man, a false father.

I sprint down to Allison's bedroom.

She signed us up for Living a few years ago. For the cost of a movie download—equipment sold separately—we are able to invite movie stars, athletes, or even despots, famous dead despots if we want them, and a variety of Glads into our home for a bit of genuine *living*. That's how the Living machine started, as a safe way to train against some of the world's best Glads. And it's definitely a recruitment tool: "Not every young boy has an arena, but if he has a backyard and the Living machine, he can *learn the moves*."

Living is virtual reality without goggles. Caesar's Inc. was in on the launch and has large holdings in the company that produces the equipment as well as the media that the machinery runs. Soon they realized they could add a roster of celebrities. The historical and artistic figures followed.

When Allison lost her fourth husband, Truman, there was a sizable pension, since he had been willing to fight hyenas. Most Glads prefer not to. Allison has never been one to hold on to money. The remarkably expensive equipment arrived in three large boxes with ample warning labels about the use of lasers and what they can do to wall insulation and the cerebral cortex if used improperly.

It took days to put it together and we had a couple of falling-outs over the directions. But once we had it up and running we were able to have dinner with an early Scarlett Johansson, or a projection of Scarlett or a distillation of Scar—we called her Scar—that was very lifelike. I got up from my chair and went over to where Scar was poised, her fork and knife about to dive into her new potatoes. I touched her lips and though they were without real substance, there was a distinct feeling of moisture on my fingertips. She pushed my hand away, or the equipment pushed my hand away, or something in my psyche pushed it away. It's a powerful piece of equipment, though sometimes I wonder if Allison has the settings right.

Scar said, —*I'm still eating.*

That was kind of spooky.

We played Foosball with John Lennon, watched Oliver Stone's *Iraq* with Condoleezza Rice, and painted Christmas gifts with Van Gogh in English translation: placemats, small wooden boxes, and découpage wall plaques.

When it was my turn, I asked for Einstein because I wanted to get a better handle on time. It wasn't about a school assignment and I wasn't, as Allison claimed, trying to be lofty. I had begun to feel that time would always move at an unwanted pace—too fast in good moments, too slow when Allison is in despair. But when I started to press to get Einstein, Allison discovered that her sixth husband, Diesel, had been added to the Living catalog. She moved the bulky equipment into her bedroom and only turned it on late at night when she imagined I was sleeping.

Now I throw open her bedroom door and find her at the window, the Living machine going full blast. She turns as I fly into the room.

—What are you doing? I ask.

—Shh, she says, pointing to Thad.

He's fast asleep, bathed in anime colors streaming from the silenced TV. Thad loves anime. Allison pulls me out into the hallway.

—Where's Tommy? I ask.

—He's already left for the stadium.

—Don't you think he'd be a little upset to learn his double is out there gardening while he's getting ready for the toughest fight of his life?

—What's that supposed to mean?

—It means you should leave some things alone.

—You don't understand, she says, and starts to turn away again.

—Then make me understand.

—If Tommy dies, I become this *thing*, this widow for life. I'm not even supposed to fraternize with men once he's gone.

Tommy is the seventh and seven is the limit, I know. That's it on this earth, according to the bylaws. *No woman is allowed marital congress with more than seven gladiators,* Bylaw 116. And *Gladiator Sport Association Widows, GSAWs, are not permitted to fraternize with common men,* Bylaw 118. Allison knows she could lose her GSAW Financial Remuneration Fund if she goes against the rules. Each year she's been in the GSAW, and with each Glad husband she's married, her share has grown. But the fund can be demolished by flagrant misbehavior, mine as well as hers.

—Tommy's not going to die, I say.

She begins to pace back and forth in front of the photo gallery she's made of our hallway. Most pictures are groupings of Glads, like swarming class pictures, and in each, one of her husbands is to be found.

—Okay, worst case. You petition Caesar's Inc. and you challenge the bylaws, I say.

—You don't get it. I read through the new bylaws again last night. Petitioning isn't allowed. And if I'm out making a living, who's at home with Thad? And God knows *you'll* probably take off.

—I'm not taking off, I say. Because right now, we just have to get through this match. She seems to calm a little and she puts her hands on her hips and looks back toward the bedroom.

*Now.* I'm not taking off *now*, I think.

—I was only testing to see if Tommy's Living version is anything like him. I meant to just turn it on for a minute.

She looks at me with an almost timid expression.

—Did you see? I had him wave at you, she says. —I think he was nice and sharp, don't you? But I'm not so sure about his expression. I think he's missing some quality. I don't know what it is.

—Humanness, perhaps? I hate to tell you, but Living is intended to be a game, something people do for entertainment, for fun. You can't have a virtual husband. That's just not right. And even if that's what you want . . .

—I don't, she says, looking contrite.

—Well, even if you did, you can't tell me that would be good for Thad.

—I could turn the volume down, she says.

I hope she's deadpanning me.

—You want him to have a quiet father who vanishes if we blow a fuse? I ask.

—Someday when you're a mother, you'll get it, she snaps.

—I'm going downstairs, I say.

I get why she's so crazy right now, but I don't have to stand around in the line of fire.

She calls after me. —Virtual reality is very successful in treating trauma victims! Burn patients! Look it up.

I trudge down the blue carpet of Allison's grand staircase.

—You're not a burn patient! I call over my shoulder.

—You shouldn't be so hard on me! Your father was always hard on me! she calls back.

—Which one?

—All of them! All seven! They've all been hard on me like you!

# CHAPTER
# 5

By now Tommy's stepping into his competition gear in the locker room of the amphitheater. But his family is having a later start than planned because my mother kept changing her outfit. Now we take the surface streets, hoping to avoid the afternoon rush hour. The sun is too bright, the heat without letup, and I know just how nervous Allison is because she keeps sliding her fingers off the wheel to dig her nails into her scalp. We're all just nerves and we almost hit a brown Audi that swerves at the last second to avoid us.

The driver, a man with thin gray hair, looks pretty rattled. Allison's hands shake as she lights a Marlboro, trying to calm down. She stays put in the car. The man and I get out of our respective vehicles and look at how close we've come. Our front bumper is less than an inch from the Audi. Like that space between God and Adam. The man looks at the decals on our bumpers and windows.

—Goddamn gladiators, he says.

Then he gets back in his beautiful car, backs up, and speeds away.

It takes Allison a while to calm down from our near miss and she takes a wrong turn and we get lost for a while—which, if you know Boston, is an easy thing to do no matter how long you've lived here.

Normally, we sit in the heirs section, way down in front where cameras are trained on us the whole time, but not so close any blood hits you. But we're nowhere near our box when we arrive, so we just grab the first seats we can find in the stadium because the match is about to start.

Romulus is an open-air arena built to hold sixty thousand fans and it's pretty close to capacity today. I look around at the people who have painted fake wounds and gashes on their bodies. Drinks slop from plastic goblets. Styrofoam truncheons and axes are waved about. Beer is consumed—kegs, buckets, rivers of it. The hot dog buns are in the shape of lances and there are lots of folks with banners made from sheets and flattened boxes: some for *TOMMY*, some for *UBER*. Crazy hats meant to look like helmets and broken skulls. Tattoo concessions, piercing vendors. All of them call out, hawking for business. At home I have one of those giant foam hands with the thumb you can turn up or down or just wave in the air but I've always felt too embarrassed to bring it to the stadium.

This is the American Title fight, so people are watching this one all over the globe. When a gladiator wins the American Title, this is his job: to look large, to be the largest man on Earth really. His name appears in novels, it's shaved into hair art. He might sign a movie contract and he can always get plenty of cameos. Game shows, no sweat. In two weeks his name will be printed down the length and over the breadth of thousands of condoms. His name is packaged and unpackaged and rolls out before us. He grows large and larger. He becomes the sign. He becomes a giant where endorsements are concerned. He helps the population to buy poorly assembled vehicles with tires that will blow out, and small over-wrapped meals, and trillions of bottles of diluted water. His face stops the world. I'd say *she* but no woman has ever won the title, though a couple have gotten close.

We take heat because there's no Glad Husbands Association. But give Caesar's time. They'll find roles for all of us.

We're pretty high up in the stadium here and in many ways I actually prefer this. Because when the American Title is awarded and the victor raises his fists, the fans start pushing against the reinforced steel fencing around the arena. If they knock it over, they flood the arena and hoist the dude up on a carpet of shoulders. But then a lot of fights break out and sometimes people get trampled to death, the tally of bodies appearing in a small box in the upper right-hand corner of the jumbo screens, each one a tiny skull and crossbones.

Uber enters the arena first to thundering applause. I've

read in *Sword and Shield* that he rubs a quart of Glow on his skin before a match. With the black lights that rim the stadium, as soon as he starts to overheat it will look as if that peacock green sweat is pouring out of him like in those sports drink commercials.

Thad tugs at me until I get a Freeway bar from my sack and peel back the wrapper for him. They make my mind too speedy and I think it would be easy to go into road rage even if you weren't driving, but with Thad, they soothe him. His whole sense of time and space has always been jumbled up. Sometimes I think he's living at the speed of light, only I can't see it.

Uber checks his helmet repeatedly and then crosses himself.

When Tommy steps into the arena, all of us stand and flood the air with sound. Everyone loves Tommy.

I see he's chosen the short sword today. But he still looks off to me. There's almost no swagger as he walks into the center of the arena and raises his arms.

—Tommy looks good, I say to Allison.

—Do you think so? Allison shouts above the cheering.

—He's all over this, I say.

—I've heard Uber wasn't *born in* to the Helmet Wearers, she informs me.

Allison likes to make a point of these things. Born Ins are first-generation Glads, their relatives and descendents. Tommy's a Born In. It's a point of pride. I don't know if

Uber's a gladiator born and bred but the blog *Desperate Glad* says: *He lights up the game.* And the *Chicago Tribune* says: *He's money in the treasury.*

Time feels sped up as the cheers build. Tommy and Uber start to circle. I don't know why, but I thought they would take longer to size each other up, that time would stretch out on this one. Competitions often feel slow to me, especially at the beginning.

Tommy slams his shield against Uber's. They deliver several blows in succession, each one striking the other's shield or sword, each sound enlarged by the sound system and the roar of the arena. I want to look away, but today I can't.

Tommy knocks Uber's shield so hard it flies out of his hand. As Uber moves to pick it up, Tommy makes several small slices up Uber's left arm. That's Tommy's signature as he's warming up, to make the small cuts. The crowd loves this. They chant, —*Tommy, Tommy.*

But then in one move, Uber suddenly grabs his shield, turns, and strikes Tommy with his long sword. When I open my eyes I see he's practically taken off Tommy's left kneecap. There's blood everywhere, spurting and soaking into the sand. Before Tommy can right himself, Uber slices him across his stomach. Thank God that one's a shallow cut.

—Why isn't he fighting back? Allison asks.

—He's waiting for the right moment, I say, though I'm wondering the same thing.

Thad's trying to say something now, his mouth full of

thick, sped-up chocolate. Everything about him looks urgent as I glance over. I don't know if he understands what's going on with Tommy, if he understands fully, or if this is about something else, because thoughts are often urgent with Thad. I kiss his forehead. I'm trying not to cry, and I tell him to chew slowly, and to wait, just wait. I tell him everything is going to be okay.

A low rolling chant starts as Uber seems to be giving Tommy time to concede, to pull himself together—I'm not sure what. I'd say this is not the kind of calm you want. If I were a forecaster, I'd say we're in earthquake weather, just before it hits.

When Thad can't take another moment of stillness, he stands in his chair and starts to leap toward Allison, jumping up and down. As I try to restrain Thad, I look at his big eyes, his soft square face, and I imagine how much would die with Tommy. Maybe everything, everything as we know it. Then Thad gets quiet again and slumps back into his seat. I want to take his hand and run away with him but this is one of the first bylaws I was taught; number 96:

*Never leave the stadium when your father is dying.*

So I'm here when Uber raises his sword suddenly and slices off Tommy's right hand cleanly at the wrist joint.

I'm out of my seat, standing in the bleachers as his hand drops to the sandy floor like a chicken wing into flour. Tommy's bludgeon flies and the bracelet I lent him for good luck launches from his arm and rolls to a stop at Uber's black athletic shoes.

Sixty thousand fans rise to their feet shouting:

—UBER! UBER!

For a moment Tommy stands there in his blood-drenched Nikes as if he's thinking over his next move. Of course the point, the whole point, of Glad existence is to die well. And I know Tommy G. is going to die well when it's his time. But I'm looking at Allison now, looking for something in Allison's face to say he'll pull through this one. That the ambulance will scoop him up and get him to the hospital in time.

I stare into Allison's mirrored sunglasses, where I see Tommy suddenly arch back. His chain-mail guard swings out from his hips and lashes his groin. His legs buckle, and his body drops in both halves of her.

Tommy dies right there in Allison's lenses.

*tommy.*

A doctor steps into the arena, checks his vital signs and walks back to the sidelines. Nothing to do.

Just then a couple of ring tones hit the air, like the sound of lone flies trapped between a window and its screen. This is what Glad culture does when a hero dies. They get their phones to ring in unison. After the first few, they all start. We have ringing in our ears now. Massive ringing in our brains, a good way to go deaf and drown out everything.

When the sounds start to quiet, I feel my grief like blood pressure. It pumps in my chest, fills my ears, runs through my hands. It knocks at my temples to get out. I look at the sweat beaded on Allison's forehead. I know her heart is working so fast it could rip through her chest. Mine has already torn in two.

She says, —No. She says no as if someone's offered her potatoes with her dinner. That's the way she does shock.

I say, —Seven.

It's a stupid thing to say even if it's true. But everything has changed for my mother. She will be a GSA Widow till life cuts her from its belly.

*i don't know what to do.*

I whisper this to her, that I don't know what to do. But I know she can't hear me.

*now. now the whole thing hits her.* I can see it. Like a high-rise set off by dynamite charges. I watch the demolition begin in her jaw. Her cheeks go slack, her nose pulls downward, her forehead creases. Her hands fly up as if to hold her brain in place. Her earrings swing back and forth. She's wearing the tiny executioner blades Tommy gave her one Valentine's. Allison drops into the seat next to me. *and i don't know.*

*i don't know anything anymore.* The stadium noise cranks and I realize everyone's looking at the scoreboards. Officials have raised a flag.

—Look. A penalty! I shout, as if this will bring Tommy back to life.

—What? Allison says, clearly disoriented. Her lashes are soaked through and her teeth have cut into her lower lip.

—You have to go down there, I say, pulling at her arm.

She shakes her head. I want her to do something with that bead of blood on her lips. But she's paralyzed.

—Not Tommy, she says.

If I were Allison, I'd be halfway down the stairs by now, trying to breathe life back into him, into his guts, his heart. But Allison sits there like the ambulance on the other side of the gates with its motor running, lights on. Waiting for the officials. Waiting for nothing. What do you wait for after death? Sixty thousand expressions of waiting all around us.

I look at the series of cuts up and down Uber's legs, across his chest, and over his shoulders. The coagulated blood looks like wax dripping down a candle. Each cut made by Tommy, so I know they smart extra hard.

If Uber's weapon is illegally balanced, he'll be dismissed from the league. I've heard that Glads who cheat are sent to live on abandoned ocean platforms, the ones out near the Caymans, where they have no companions or toilet paper— only get limited food drops—and the televisions are primitive and often receptionless. But that could be an urban legend.

The media talk about the ugly relief map of Uber's face as he removes his tight helmet. They became chatty and informational about how to eliminate those marks from the forehead and cheeks. How to get the best fit in a helmet. And one sportscaster talks about which tattoo needles to use if you want to make a permanent tracing on your face: to have that tight-helmet look all the time.

I try again.

—You have to go down there, I say.

But Allison's lost. She'll be better when the cameras are on her and she has to pull herself together. But right now, all she can do is sit in her seat and shake while Thad tries to lean against her. I look for a friend, even Sam or Callie, anyone we know in the crowd who might help out, but I can't spot a soul.

The officials are looking at Uber's helmet now. Tommy once told me that Helmet Wearers spend more time scrounging material for their gear than they do killing. They can't cover all the vulnerable parts of a face—the eyes are left bare by tradition and for visibility's sake—but Tommy believed that real Glads went for exposure, that you shouldn't be anything less than exposed when you fight.

The woman behind us has started to gripe about the penalty flag, shouting, —What the hell are they doing?

She must have taken hours to paint this red gash that starts on her forehead and goes down the length of her nose and splices her lip. She has mock bone and cartilage sticking out.

Thad pulls on my jacket. *TOMMY G.* is stitched in gold letters across the back. He pulls so hard I feel the seams rip. Even though he's on elevator drugs he doesn't have any real control. It's hard to know if he's even registered Tommy's death.

—I have to tell you something, he says.

When he gets going, Thad can have something to tell me every five minutes.

He cups his hands around my ears. —Mom's going to lose the house, he says.

That's the randomness of Thad. And you can't say: *That's nuts, Thad.* You have to play along like you're going to lose the house. Otherwise, he goes into a worse state. And then I feel upset seeing him get upset. And the truth is, now that Tommy's dead, we can live in our house forever, well, at least until Allison dies, because Tommy always fought a clean fight. And that's in the rules. *Fight clean and a gladiator's family enjoys ongoing and generous subsidies.*

—Things will be okay. There are other houses, I say to comfort him.

I straighten his hair so it's out of his eyes. Then I sit down next to Allison and put an arm around her shoulders.

Suddenly I realize that Uber might think my bracelet is actually Tommy's because it's a wide, flat band made in the man's style. I feel sick knowing he could reach down and pluck it off the arena floor. It just sits there by his feet, like an eight ball ready to drop into a pocket and end my game. Because the thing is: *No man is allowed to hold your dowry bracelet, except your father. If a man holds your dowry bracelet he's required, according to GSA law, to marry you,* Bylaw 87.

I watch Allison pull her small yellow coat around herself, as if this will wrap her tight enough to get through the worst day of her life. She says, —He shouldn't even be in the league. They're going to nail this guy, she says, looking at the penalty flag again. —You watch. They'll boot him right out.

Uber unclips his mic from his black and gold breastplate.

—Wait!! he shouts, slamming his voice into the sound system.

It's eerie the way people go quiet in waves.

Here is this giant who will be able to sell anything to anyone, and he's standing in the middle of the arena, Tommy cut to pieces in front of him, the penalty flag up, and then—and this is something I can only record and not explain—Uber hangs his head. He touches his chest. I swear I see him mouth the word: *tommy.* Even if no one else does, I see it. My skull freezes. This is like being in some kind of sick fairy tale. He has no right to look like he cares or that he's pledging allegiance or something.

In the still, I hear the soft drink machines recharging, the sprinkler tanks filling, the cotton candy spinning in the dead quiet, in the rising heat as Uber looks dumbly at the ground. Everyone in the stadium stands up now, if they haven't already, and they touch their hearts and they hang their heads to honor Tommy. And then, after what seems like minutes, though it must be seconds, Uber breaks his stance. He looks up at the crowds and he reaches down. His long black braid swings forward.

And he picks up the bracelet.

# CHAPTER

# 6

Uber angles my silver band this way and that, catching and bending stadium light. When the close-up comes on the screens Allison gasps and a winnowing sound erupts from her throat.

—That's your bracelet, she says.

*A gladiator has the right to handle, pick up, and generally plunder any object his opponent abandons to the arena floor,* Rule 44.

I can't feel my spine anymore. My knees are air.

—Why was Tommy wearing your bracelet? she asks.

I can barely get the words out, but I tell her the truth, that I lent it to him for good luck. If this were about a matter we didn't agree on, she might say something with a sharp edge to it, something unfortunate about luck. But at this moment in time, about this issue, we are allies.

—We have to get it back, she says.

Now the lucid images arrive on the jumbo screens. I'm aware that you can see Tommy's corpse just about anywhere on the planet with only a slight delay. And if it weren't so terrible, I'd say there's something mystical about this, this ability to be everywhere at once, as if his ashes were strewn about the globe.

Uber slips my bracelet onto his right wrist and begins to walk across the arena toward the staging area. Officials trot after him, one of them calling him back. Thad starts pushing at me, and Allison . . . I don't know how to stanch her emotions. The officials are arguing.

Thad cups his hands over one of my ears and shouts, —THE HAND IS POINTING AT YOU, LYNIE!

I turn his head and cup my hands around one of his spongy ears, and shout back, —That's Tommy's hand! Tommy's dead, Thad! His hand isn't pointing at anything!

It's hard to forgive yourself for being that harsh, that wrong with someone you love, even if it settles him down. The thing is, Thad doesn't have an unkind bone in his body. And I think I'm pretty patient with him most of the time, probably more patient with him than anyone except Allison. Really patient. Because he's one of my favorite people. But sometimes he's a lot to deal with. Before I can tell him how sorry I am, a bank of cameras light Allison's head and bust. The media has found us.

Allison blinks into the lights and her image sputters onto the giant screens. I watch her *there* as she stands next to me, wiping her tears away. She is suddenly luminous, almost together in an instantaneous way, the cracks of her psyche temporarily mended. She mirrors her new role as a GSAW. I think of portraits of Roman noblewomen. Right now that's Allison.

I am the sliver by her side: the braid of long hair, part of an eyebrow, half an eye. It's easy to be out of the picture. I can't move fully into the frame or shift completely out of it, we're pinned so tight by the crush of people, everyone wanting to get into the shot now, waving to friends, pulling up their T-shirts to show their abdomens, sometimes their breasts.

It's what we do. We want to be there: on screen.

The sound system issues this alert: *Remain seated. Free water will be distributed shortly. Remain seated.*

The sprinkler system goes on. Thousands of free bottles of water are handed out.

Like Tommy's corpse, you can see Allison's face from any geographic point on the globe now. Even in Katmandu you have only to find an Internet user and see Allison's splendor. She floats in the Earth's atmosphere in millions of copies. Allison here and Allison everywhere. She is, for all intents and purposes now, a god.

She grabs my hand. She's trembling slightly. Turning from the cameras she says, close to my head, —Why are they holding up the blessed ambulance?

Three officials in green-and-white-striped shirts are talking with Uber. They go over and look at Tommy, they get within inches of his body. They point to his wounds with their pens.

They measure his body parts with skinny measuring tape that snaps back into their palms.

—I'm surprised they haven't offered free parking yet, Allison confides in me.

She does a beautiful job with bitter when she's up for it. Ever since the GSA went through its major restructuring they have frequently offered free parking for anyone who makes it out of the stadium within twenty minutes. They've been accused of doing this because it ups the trampling numbers. Caesar's likes to boast a good trample the way NASCAR likes to have their flameouts. I know how quickly we could get separated and crushed by adulation. She knows this too so she's keeping Thad as close as possible.

Thad begins to say in a singsong voice, —Lynie's getting mar-ried! Lynie's getting mar-ried!

His words volley against my tight eardrums, against my grief. Then Thad is calm and maybe a little embarrassed. He sits down in his chair and looks out toward the spectacle of moistened people.

—Lyn's not getting married, dear, Allison says softly.

Thad whispers back, —Uber has her bracelet!

I didn't even think he knew this rule. How can he know some things so precisely and miss other things entirely? In the confusion, I don't know how much the media has picked up—if Thad's pronouncements were detectable. Does the world listen to *every* word? My brain is a racecourse of thought.

The red PENALTY sign starts to flash. The word blinks on and off like a cursor. *PENALTY. TOMMY G.*

One of the refs turns on the mic at his hip, makes a gesture with his right hand as if he's cutting his left arm into sections from his shoulder to his wrist, and says, —Unnecessary small cuts. Provision 187. Loss of rank. Dishonored.

The booing starts.

The crowd throws their plastic water bottles into the arena. Bottles rain down on the officials. The air turns to cylindrical hail. The officials do not look happy, one guy takes a full water bottle right on the nose. They look like ants in a downpour.

I realize this sounds impossible, but the plastic containers form a nearly perfect ring around Tommy, and glisten in the lights.

Allison clutches me hard now. I don't think she realizes that her fingernails are digging into me, rib by rib. I am practically lifted onto my toes from her pain. Suddenly she backs off and shouts, —Provision 187? What the hell is that?

—I don't know. I can't hear anything! I shout back.

But we know what this means: Caesar's Inc. will, in essence, eliminate his death, his benefits, his place of honor.

—Tommy's retirement funds, she says, realizing she'll lose this money now.

I know the whole thing was rigged. It's always rigged. They never like to pay out to the family. They must have come up with Provision 187 just this morning.

I had often thought when Tommy G. died, I'd cry in a pure way. I'd tear my hair out by the roots. I'd pull out my eyelashes so the tears could run unimpeded. But nothing can express this.

Now the sirens go off, and the horns. And the cars whiz into the center ring, and the tall clowns—the ones dressed like Mercury, a full team of eight—lift Tommy G.'s blood-soaked corpse into the air. His long wavy hair sweeps the ground, touches some of the bottles, as they hoist him into the ambulance.

*i can't think.*

Down in the stadium, several sections below us, chairs are being uprooted from their rivets. I can't see Uber anywhere. A fence comes down and is thrown into the arena. A manic-looking clown with high-arching eyebrows and a tulip in his hat—he's crushed. Officials, a couple of them go. People rip the wings off the Mercuries. Off their heels, as if they're insects. The weapon carrier who gave Uber his drink just minutes ago appears to be dead. People cry out, yell, scream. Everyone screams.

I get my jacket off and push Thad's arms into the sleeves, zip the zipper.

—I'll meet you at the house! I tell Allison.

Something hits me in the back of the head then, something heavy and dull. When I touch my head, I feel blood.

She wants to fuss with me, but I tell her there's no time. I tell her I'm getting the bracelet back before anyone knows it's mine.

—You'll never get to him, she says.

But she fishes some cash out of her wallet and I throw this in my bag. I give Thad's meds and Freeway bars to Allison. She gives me a small hairbrush. I almost laugh but I see her need and simply take it. She sees I have one of those Tibetan Buddhist tracts in my bag—something she would normally toss out if she found it in my bedroom—but she doesn't say anything. I have one of Tommy's short knives I use for cutting through plastic packaging, cleaning my nails, and stuff. Allison has one of her own, so there's nothing to exchange there. We work without conversation, trading things back and forth. Her weariness covers me like a hot wool blanket and I feel like I'm going to pass out if I don't move. Then I see the light on my phone.

—God, my battery's almost dead. Don't call me. I'll reach you as soon as I can, I say.

For years I've thrown millions of pixels together in my head, trying to see what it would be like to leave them. It was never this way.

Thad shouts, —Your hands are going to turn red with blood, Lynie!

—I'll find water, Thad. I'll wash my hands. Stay with Mom.

I turn back once, to see the way Allison holds his giant, weak head against her breast as they head toward an exit.

*chaos.*

# CHAPTER

# 7

Tommy showed me how to get into this hidden place underneath the stadium. It's a long corridor without windows or electricity—where I'm trying to get to Uber. It's the only entryway free of paparazzi.

Tommy always had a cigarette lighter with him. Somehow I've lost mine in the exchange with Allison. So I'm moving four inches at a time, hoping I don't smack into anything. I realize the beta-blocker I take for the matches has started to wear off, which means my heart is ratcheting up.

This is where they used to cage wild animals when they needed extra holding pens. So it smells blessed rank down here. I didn't mind it when I was with Tommy because he thought there was something cool about this place, something kind of anthropological.

One time I stood in the dark with him and watched him as he smoked a cigarette. When he took a drag, we both lit up. He laughed at my skittishness and I pulled the lighter

from his hand and held down the button for a while. Sometimes memory rips you and that moment, that experience of
light, keeps going through my brain like burning fuel. It's
hard to imagine that Tommy is gone, even though I saw him
cut out of this world.

The walls are damp, every surface tagged, drawings from
people who were here before us.

He said, —I guess everyone wants to go back to the womb.

It was a dumb joke, this place is not where I'd imagine
anyone coming from, but I laughed anyway. I loved his voice,
especially when I let my thumb off the lighter and it turned
dark again and he was nothing but voice and I could imagine he was six-foot-six and fifteen years older and finally
right for Allison.

—I don't, I said.

And I didn't. I never wanted to return to the crawl space
of Allison or the belly of the cosmos or wherever we hail
from. Not because there's something wrong with her, entirely,
or wrong with the universe, entirely. I mean, I love Allison
and feel sorry for her, for it. But you don't want to travel
backward.

—Yeah, well, that's what makes you smart, he said.

He didn't say it sarcastically. Tommy meant things like
that. I looked down at the crown of his head, the smoke
swirling around it. I took a drag from his cigarette and then
he took my hand and showed me the way to the locker
rooms.

*Remind him constantly of his victories. Keep his heart warm even if you have to set the house on fire,* Bylaw 32.

I don't know if Allison did that enough. She was kind of burned out by the time she married Tommy. Or she was just too taxed with Thad. I think they hooked up because of her position, the influence she could offer. I don't know. I think she loved him. Probably more than I understood.

I open my phone now and use it as a flashlight, weak as it is, because Tommy told me you can run into false doors down here, that it's easy to get lost, that you never know who or what you'll find. And that thought has my skull pounding. I can feel a patch of sticky blood where I got hit in the back of the head. I remove my T-shirt, wad it up, and hold it there with my free hand.

I want to call Allison but the reception is worthless down here. I begin to take pictures with my phone. Not for the images but for the small pulses of light the phone throws off. I'm draining my batteries for light.

Water is coming off the pipes now, it's drumming on my shoulders and head, dead water running down my back and chest and arms. That happens when they turn the fire hoses on the crowd in the stadium, so I know what's going on up there. And I'm feeling sick wondering what they've done with Tommy. That's something I've never wanted to know before—what they do with the people who die in the ring. Because we always left right away and the organization took care of all of the arrangements, and all we had to do was make it to the funeral in one piece. Allison has never talked about what happened to them and it's possible she doesn't know. But I suddenly feel guilty for not knowing if the caskets of her husbands, my fathers, were sometimes empty or missing parts. Thinking back on the succession of men Allison married, I'm convinced this was true: that there was a lightness to some of their caskets.

What I'm really worried about is that someone will steal Tommy's hand and try to sell it on eBay, though I don't know what it will be worth now that Caesar's Inc. has begun the process of downgrading him.

The noise of the stadium crushes overhead, the vibration drills into my bones. I find a doorknob.

I've been in this room before.

A few pieces of stalled-out equipment. Old signs. I take a dozen phone shots, just as things start to settle down overhead.

I know what it's like in the arena now. My fifth father, Larry, used to watch old news clips of the war in Vietnam. Guys in the jungle, blown to hell, yelling, *Oh my God, I've lost my leg!* I had to ask him to turn the sound down all the time. I couldn't take it. *Help me, somebody help me!* Maybe he thought if he had us as crazy and grief-stricken as he was some score would even up. Larry knew a lot about chemical compounds. Napalm. He was always trying to figure out some legal way to hide explosives in his Glad weapons but he was taken out before he realized that dream. Tommy was different. He liked a clean weapon, a pure fight, no gimmicks. Maybe Tommy was the only one who made any sense.

Now I know where I am.

I crack the door open and peer into the locker room. There are two lines of benches and the floor is soaked, empty champagne bottles strewn about and the sound of a shower going. The cameras are gone and the paparazzi have disappeared. I remember to turn my phone off. My head still hammers but I'm not bleeding anymore, so I put my bloody shirt back on. If he's anything like Tommy was after a match, Uber will be in the shower for hours.

It's weird that no one's around; typically there are handlers of some sort. I guess it's possible Uber dresses his own wounds. Some guys do, but not many. Allison did all of Tommy's until they had a big fight and he asked me to take over, which I didn't want to do because I knew it would hurt Allison's feelings. She's the one who taught me how to stitch, how to wrap, which tinctures to use. Sometimes I feel all I do is hurt her.

I'm about to slip into the main room when two men come into view and I slide back just in time. I recognize the short one in the T-shirt and jogging pants, the thin buzz cut—one of the better trainers in town. —You need a rubdown! he calls into the shower area.

—I have someone coming over to the apartment. That woman who does Thai massage, Uber calls.

—You know I'm happy to stick around, the guy in the suit yells as he adjusts his shades.

—Just make sure the bodyguards stay put for a while! Uber says.

His voice is deep and resonant and full of shower room echo.

—We should be celebrating, the suit says.

I feel nothing but rage, yet I just have to keep my mouth shut.

—Yeah, well, that's what you guys are for. We'll talk tomorrow, Uber says.

—I've never seen him like that, the suit says in a low voice to his friend.

—It's tough when you take out your hero, you know? the trainer says just before he opens the main door at the far end of the room. As it widens I hear the paparazzi flame up, so many flashes going, I can't really see anything except bright and dark shapes. The bodyguards push the crowd back. Slowly, the men make their way into the throng.

And before long, the room is almost quiet again, except for that lone shower thundering the concrete floor. I enter the stale air of the men's locker room, where I met my fathers a hundred times after their matches.

Uber's clothes are slopped over a bench. I go through his pockets. There's an inhaler, a St. Christopher medal, and a small comb. Maybe this is the weakness of the Helmet Wearer? This anxiety that his hair is continually being crushed and deformed so he feels he needs a comb in the arena? The sign of an endlessly vain man?

The shower stops. I hear a loud sigh as if he's decompressing. Then the sound of metal curtain rings whip along a steel rod. Wet feet slap against the painted floor. He looks awkward as he stoops to walk under an archway, a towel tied at his waist, his hair soaked. Finally he looks up and sees me standing there.

He's wearing the bracelet.

Most of the Glow has washed off. None of my hatred. He studies me, cinches his towel tighter.

—Yeah? he says.

I'm surprised he doesn't recognize me. It's not that I'm famous or anything, but Tommy, at least, always knew about his opponents' families. Some pictures of me circulate too, a lot more lately.

But Uber does look worn out. Tommy got that look at home sometimes, but then he suffered from bouts of melancholy and I always tried to take that into account and not feel like I had done something wrong. Maybe Allison's right, that Uber doesn't have the true gladiator look to his jaw. Maybe he's just an ordinary guy who pumps a lot of iron, someone who always feels a little down on his luck no matter how things go, his hair thinning in front, which could be the constant grating of the helmet. In any case, not the way Tommy used to look after a match, certainly after winning a title match. Tommy had a playfulness after he won a fight that drove Allison insane. He took us out to big dinners afterward, insisted everyone eat steak.

—You're not allowed in here, Uber says, like he cares but doesn't care.

I'm a little short on words for my father's murderer. There should be something I could say to make him realize he's the most pathetic man on Earth, but I can't find it just now.

—What do you want me to sign? he asks, softening a little, as if I've been waiting for his autograph.

His autograph, his blood, his baby, his life—Uber doesn't know what I want, and I'm not saying. I know what I want, but it's like my whole body is iced. My mouth filled with cold.

His sex, his money, his interview, his aura—he doesn't know.

The cuts on his arms and legs have started to bleed again on his still-damp skin. His wet hair drips down his shoulders, down his chest. Tommy used to look almost weightless after a fight, luminous.

Maybe Uber's raking his fingers through his hair now to tame it, maybe it's a nervous thing. Uber isn't a bad-looking guy, but out of the arena he doesn't seem very self-possessed.

—Look, I . . . , he starts to say.

And then it seems like, well, like the way to get this weary soldier is by surprise.

*Caging* happens when a woman rushes into a locker room and throws herself at a gladiator, slamming him for an imprint of his blood. She has to get him when he's just come out of the arena all pumped and cut up, before his wounds are dressed. Some women imprint the blood on their clothes—that's called *shrouding*. One woman got Tommy like that. He had taken a blow to his brow so the blood had poured freely that day. She got a clear impression of his face in the middle of her T-shirt.

Other cagers hit the locker room with nothing on above their waists and if they succeed, if they get enough blood on their bare skin, that's called *contracting*. A woman who contracts will go back up to the stadium and get swarmed by cameras. Some women get married in that state, with the blood on their skin, in their hair. Others, if they're beautiful enough, get modeling contracts, invitations to appear on TV shows. Or they contract some kind of blood disease and die eventually.

But I have all of my clothes on, my T-shirt back in place, and I just FLY at the man. I push through the air like I'm not moving at all. Suspended, really. Then I smack hard against his body, against his chest, his stomach so he'll think I'm just there to cage him. I guess I hit him twice. Hitting, bouncing off, hitting again. Cars do that in accidents sometimes. They can hit the bumper and then the trunk.

Somehow I get my legs around his waist, one arm around his neck. Twisting around, I try to wedge the bracelet off with my free hand but he makes a fist so I can't get it off. We stick together because he's so damp, my skin burns as I try to pull away. My hand around the bracelet, I feel the design etched into the metal. He won't give it up. He thinks he has some of Tommy's power now, but what he's got is my fetish—my worry, my memory, loss—everything you can pour into metal.

His free hand circles my back. Now he's holding me as much as I'm holding him. Like a ride at a carnival, I'm trying to find the safety release because I'd rather sail into the air than stay on. I start pounding on Uber, pounding against the dumb muscles that won't unlock. And then I do the stupidest thing. And not because I want to—it's the last thing I want. But I'm crying.

*tommy.*

Tears sheet my face. My insides sting as if there are thin slices cut across my lungs, over my heart, a million small cuts. There are rules against a gladiator's daughter crying: how, when, where. I'm breaking eleven of those rules. My head could be shaved for this, my tattoos erased—certainly the one with Tommy's name—I could be exiled to some lowland that floods constantly, a place where the Red Cross never lands. And I just don't care.

Uber's body slackens. And then, like he needs to be some kind of rescue man and pull a building off me, he guides me to a seat on one of the benches. I'm hyperventilating. As soon as my breath slows, I push him away.

He goes to his locker and gets out a pair of glasses. His lenses are thick like jar bottoms. His eyes trapped in jars.

—Jesus. You're Tommy's girl, he says, seeing me for the first time.

Tommy always said you have to get curious about your opponent if you plan to beat him. So I study the way Uber moves. He brings me a wad of toilet paper to blow my nose. I notice the way he favors his left side when he walks. And when he holds out a cup of water, I see the big thing, that his right arm doesn't extend fully. Probably a surgery that fell short.

The way his hand shakes holding that cup of water, maybe he thinks I'm fragile or delicate. And that thought makes me laugh. I laugh so hard I drop the cup. It hits the lip of the bench and the water soaks his legs.

—Don't worry about it, he says, and sits down on the opposite bench about three feet away. He leans in toward me. And I wonder if that's tenderness to a guy like him. He looks like he doesn't know what else to do with himself. There's something almost clumsy about him, really. He's busy trying to keep his towel in place, adjusting it carefully. I see his ears redden. He has earlobes like Tommy has—like Tommy had—the unattached kind. But one of them is split in two. I guess someone yanked an earring out once.

We both consider the blood on my T-shirt. He gets up and walks around behind me to see the back of my head, though I don't make it easy the way I keep turning to make sure he doesn't do anything crazy.

—I could do something with that if you'd let me, he says, indicating the gash.

—I'm okay.

I notice that his second toes are longer than his big toes, and my grandmother, my mother's mother, told me that's a sign of stupidity. He has young feet, not callused or corned, but I finally take another look at the thing I've been trying to avoid, my bracelet. I point as if I've forgotten how to speak. His wrist is pretty raw from my work.

He says, —Listen, I know this won't help to hear, but . . .

I cover my ears.

He stops.

I take my hands down.

—It's just that Tommy, I worshipped . . .

I cover my ears again.

He stops.

Sometimes I think I've inherited the silence of gladiators because I can do silence for hours if I have to, though there are people I could talk with all night—it was like that with Tommy sometimes.

I finally say, —I don't care what you thought about Tommy. But the bracelet, that's . . . my family's.

—I'm sorry. I should never have . . .

He slides the bracelet off and holds it up to the fluorescent lights for a moment, like he's got possession of something otherworldly and he's trying to memorize all of its features before it shape-shifts. He starts to turn it around, to read the inscription.

—*I change, but I cannot die*, he says, repeating the words.

He puts it back on.

—They said—the officials said—since it belonged to my opponent, I'm required to keep it on, at least through my next title match. It has to do with some new rule. The thing is, if I don't, one guy said, they might add another year to my contract. As soon as I can take it off, I'll be relieved to give it back to your family.

—You're the most pathetic man in the world.

It doesn't take much to wound the guy, from the look on his face. I ask if he has a lighter and he actually comes up with one, after he shuffles through his locker.

I don't look around, I just go back into the dark passageway. I'll wait for a while, until the photographers clear out. Then I'll make it up into the stadium again.

—Wait! I hear him call after me, but I don't wait.

# CHAPTER

# 8

As I look around the stadium, the post-traumatic sky is almost navy blue now and the bodies are gone. Tommy always said Mass General is the best hospital in the country for stampede victims, so I imagine a lot of them are over there, crowding the halls on gurneys, some in surgery. There's even a specialist for clown injuries. Tommy was pretty loyal to the clowns and made large donations to the hospital.

The cleanup crew will come in the morning. All the power in the stadium is off for the night. The jumbo screens are down and the only light from the moon is caught in the nearly perfect ring of water bottles that surrounded Tommy. But his body's gone. Maybe he's risen from the dead. He'd do something like that—rise from the dead. It's eerie that the bottles are still in place that way. Like one of those roadside memorials with family photos, stuffed animals, things no one wants to disturb.

*tommy.*

I slump down on a damp bench, kick some trash aside.

I have to get home and take care of Allison and Thad but I'm seven ways to tired and need to lie down for a few minutes. Uber will leave by the GSA door, especially if he hopes to avoid the throng that can build at the gates, and no one hangs out in the stadium at night. I know because I've done that a couple times with my friend Mark. So I'm not too worried, but I get my knife out of my bag anyway and tuck it under my body, just in case, and then I let my thoughts drift.

Some people think violence is nothing when you're raised in Glad culture. They say we have no feelings, that we don't value life. There was a comedian who said we collect death like fast-food toys—something we enjoy with a quick meal. Or something like that.

What they don't get is this: a Glad has an incredibly strong sense of reality. Dreaming is not, strictly speaking, what we hope for, what we encourage or need. And if you stop dreaming and get real, you have to accept the fact that violence is a part of life, part of nature. Ask any biologist. To a true Glad, the arena is the only fair fight.

Two people sign up to test their skills and bravely take their consequences. We don't consign slaves, we don't shackle or bind anyone to fight unless he happens to be on death row when he arrives at the stadium, and even then, this guy has petitioned hard to fight, gone through several screenings. He's free to drop out and return to prison up to the last minute. And though there was an idea floated by one congressman to have illegal aliens thrown into the arena, that guy is strictly a monster and was eventually knocked out of the club for molesting his young aides.

I have my bones to pick with Caesar's Inc., but no one has to sign their stupid contracts, especially not the multiple-year ones. But the deals are more than lucrative, or at least they seem more than lucrative, so people sign.

Tommy always said it was our country's stealth activities he couldn't stand, the forces neatly stacked against a person where the concept of fair fight just doesn't exist: the military game, corporate culture, divorce courts, insurance companies, the IRS, government wire taps.

—*You take a boy, eighteen, throw him into a war he doesn't understand, in a country he's never even read a book about, because some president has some good old friends and family members heavily invested in certain companies that have to move some products like aircraft or oil or hospital beds, now that's nuts,* Tommy would say.

The thing is, I have been thinking about the loose chinks in the basic pro-Glad argument for some time now, which may have something to do with my being a bit of a dreamer, something Allison likes to harp on me about. And now that Tommy's dead, the chinks are more like gaping holes. And though this is all that I've known—this culture—my mind stabs away at it until it just can't stand.

The first time Allison took me to a gladiator match I was five. Mouse, my second father, was on temporary disability from the arena then, so we made a day of it, stopping for a picnic at Walden Pond before heading over to the stadium. Mouse liked the deep water in the middle of the pond and the way people crowd near the shore to avoid it. He had a broad laugh, and was once a suspect in a big art heist but never served any time. This was, of course, before he found the Glad life.

Allison reminded him several times that day to watch his ribs. She had him taped in white adhesive from his armpits to his swim trunks to help mend the broken ribs. There was no Thad then. Allison stretched out in the sand, bits of mica clinging to her legs, lighting up her skin. Mouse was the first one who taught me there's only minimal gain in talking. I saw the way he studied Allison's glow in a mute way. Then we packed up and headed over to the Romulus.

I have a clear picture of the newly painted blue benches in the stadium that day, and how beautiful Allison looked with one of those thin magician's scarves she likes to tie in her hair. She had me sit in our reserved box, where she crouched down in front of me and took my hands. Her straight skirt stretched tightly over her lap. Her nylons held her knees so they looked like small pale balloons.

—Kitten, we're going to see some funny things today. Men being . . . a little silly.

She rubbed my knuckles with her thumbs as she spoke.

—If we see anything that makes us a little sad or upset, we just have to make a game of it.

I said I wanted to play a game. And she started over.

—The men are going to look like they're having a big fight.

Your father is a famous fighter, so this is something we're proud of.

—He's a gladiator, I said.

—Yes, exactly, and we know that gladiators have weapons. Like . . . axes and knives and . . .

—And clubs.

Mouse had given me a boy's plastic club and a matching sword and shield with spikes like small nipples. I had my own bludgeon made of balsa wood. Allison didn't approve of this kind of thing for *young ladies* but there weren't many women's leagues then—an idea she would never take to. She had been newly widowed when she met Mouse, and she was eager to make a go of things with him, so certain standards were overlooked for a time to please him.

—Yes, clubs too. Good girl. So nothing to be concerned about. And I brought your coloring book and crayons. And look, she said, reaching into her bag and pulling out my favorite stuffed animal. —I brought your dog and her pajamas if she gets tired.

Even then, I knew it was important to get to work dressing my dog Lucy, that if I didn't Allison would keep talking and rubbing my knuckles and making me nervous. I sensed her fragility the way I knew her scent in a room she had vacated hours earlier. Allison straightened up and sat next to me on the bench and said, —If one of them loses an arm or a leg, we just say *too bad* or *poor man*.

—Poor man, I said.

—Sometimes I look at the big screens and it makes it a

little less . . . real. And you know, when I cut up poultry for dinner . . . , she said, starting on a new tack.

And that's how Allison began her lesson about making associations, about ways to detach and get through rotten experience. A man loses a hand in the arena. It hits the sand and that's a chicken wing dropped into flour.

I don't have any memory of seeing the fight that day. In fact, I don't remember what it was like to see the fights before the age of nine or ten, and by that point matches were something we attended regularly, like church.

My family was heavily filmed. So Allison taught me how to look and what my face should and shouldn't give away to the cameras, as if she were designing a will and the public was one of her beneficiaries. And sometimes we experienced a personal loss and those were the dark times when Allison seemed to disappear entirely, as if she had only been an overlay on a screen. Someone would go to the grocery store and buy us canned goods to last a month, or they'd arrive with casseroles and other soggy dishes, and we wouldn't leave the house for anything.

If I have a girl someday, Allison has often told me, I will be expected to bring her to the amphitheater for the first time when she's five. It's four for a boy. A couple of weeks ago, I stopped hedging and just said, —That's never going to happen.

Watching her face fall, I might as well have said: *Thad's run away* or *The house is on fire.*

I wake with a start. Allison says I'm such a sound sleeper I'll make it all the way through Armageddon in a deep slumber. But some random brain synapse lets me know I'm about to roll off the bench in the amphitheater. It's the middle of the night and there's a stadium blanket covering me, and a towel under my sore head. I can feel the official GSA embroidery at one corner of the blanket, so I figure this has to be Uber's.

I'm relieved to see he's not around, though it's a little creepy being alone in the stadium this late. When I sit up, I feel like I've been in a hard fight. The arm I was sleeping on is basically dead, my hips numb.

Sucking the last juice out of the phone, I call Allison.

—Are you all right? she asks, her voice raspy and urgent and I know she's been crying and chain smoking all night. I explain about falling asleep but not about caging—she'd go insane if she knew I had shrouded Uber. I'd go insane if I let myself. She wants me to crash at Mark's so I'm not out in the middle of the night any more than I have to be.

—How's Thad? I ask.

—He ate a big dinner.

—Did he say anything on the way home?

—I don't know. Probably, yes. He said something. It doesn't matter right now, does it? she asks.

That's how I know Thad has made a new prediction that Allison is worried about.

—Tell him I'll be home in the morning and that I miss him.

I explain that Uber wouldn't give me the bracelet back, that there's this new rule and as far as he knows, it's our family's bracelet. Of course she and I know, but neither of us wants to say, that technically I'm supposed to be his fiancée now—if he wants to pursue it or if Caesar's Inc. finds out.

I tell her to go back to sleep.

—I can't sleep.

—Drink some of that tea.

—If it worked I would.

I tell her she's going to be all right, that we're all going to be all right. The way Tommy would have said it.

The phone goes dead. I hoist myself up and grab the knife I tucked away and slip it back into my bag. Then I make my way down the stairs, and go past the covered concessions and locked vendor booths. I wind my way out of the turnstile.

The streets are jammed, the lights blue, and some people double take when they see me but they don't ask for autographs. I pull the blanket tight around my shoulders and up around my head and make my way toward the subway. This used to be a neo-Glad neighborhood, so there are plenty of leftover gladiator sports bars. Then all the rich folks moved in because they thought that was a cool thing to do and now a lot of the Glads can't afford to live in the area. So it's strictly pseudo culture and I can't wait to get out of here.

Replays of the American Title match are on all the giant screens as I move down the street. One bar called Steamers projects the fight onto a thick wall of mist. Steam jets embedded in the sidewalk shoot straight up into the air, another series of jets come off copper piping above. The replay action appears to be taking place on the sidewalk—a regular Disneyland effect. And then I'm walking right through their weapons, through Uber's legs and Tommy's chest and life being one second and death being the next. And when I'm on the other side, and I look back down the sidewalk, it's just so much steam and colored lights, and I feel hollow as a tree that's been gutted by lightning.

And suddenly I want someone to come up to me and say, *I loved your father. Tommy was the man.*

Because then I could say, *He should have won.* Or, *His fans meant everything to him.* But when I play these conversations all the way out, they're full of self-pity and I really have to get off the street and take care of my head.

Even if I could look away from the pictures of him fighting in every bar—in slo-mo, in flashplay, psychedelic patterns and Warhol color grids—the audio is cranked so loud I hear every last sound that comes out of his chest as if my head is leaning against it. I hear his effort to turn things around and win, at least to stay alive—I know he wanted that.

Then the way the crowd calls, —*UBER, UBER!*

And just before I duck into the subway, I see that Visigoth reach down and pick up my bracelet again.

# CHAPTER
# 9

Mark's family lives less than a block from the subway, on a high first floor, directly across from a lighting shop that's always ablaze. His family saves a lot on electricity. They have no shades or curtains on their windows. It's just light pouring in at all hours, the feeling of wattage—and I've never been happier to be anywhere.

I let myself in with the key above the door frame and go past his parents' bedroom. Lloyd, his father, or maybe his mother, Julie, snores within. Julie's a total Glad wife and the best stitcher in the city—a veritable surgeon. She met Allison when they were both freshly widowed from their first husbands and Mark and I were toddlers. Mark doesn't remember his first father, but his second father, Lloyd, is one of those Glads who managed to run his contract out. He got through a whole year of competition with only a small dent in his forehead. Then Julie had a dream one night that he would lose his nose and both his ears if he signed up for a second year. Since Lloyd refused to wear a helmet with face gear, like Tommy, she found herself investigating face graft-ing online. Pretty soon she couldn't sleep at night, thinking about loving one man with another man's face. And the day she woke up from a dream about Lloyd having some dead man's face, she convinced him to become a trainer.

Sometimes she teases him that he's too quiet to be a good trainer, and that he really should be more upbeat. But that's Lloyd. He's Head of Instruction at the Boston Ludus Magnus Americus and he'll see a pension one day and maybe keep more than a few guys from losing their extremities, because he really cares about his boys.

Mark opens the door before I knock, like he knows I'm there. We do that kind of thing. The second I see him I lay my head against his chest, my face pressed into his pajama buttons. Mark is a good six inches taller than I am and he has large, nicked-up hands and smells of cigarette smoke and gel pens. When he runs a hand down the back of my head I flinch. He turns me around the way his mother does if she's looking for a confession about something. He's the kind of guy who will confess to almost anything if it makes her happy. Of course, we're all like that with Julie.

Mark makes me sit on his unmade bed now with its stale sheets, and he disappears into the hallway. A minute later he's back with Julie. She's wearing her monkey slippers and robe. On another occasion I might crack a primate joke, but I really have to lie down.

—Tell me what hurts, Julie says.

—My heart?

I can feel my chin quiver. She holds it for a moment, kisses my cheek, and says, —I know. All of us love . . . we all loved Tommy.

Then she starts in, asking me to follow her pen, shining a flashlight in my eyes, asking me to squeeze her fingers. She tells Mark to boil some water. While I lie down she quickly braids her hair so it will be out of the way. In Mark's bathroom she scrubs up to her elbows, keeping an eye on me in the medicine cabinet mirror. Then Julie dries her hands and examines the back of my head, shifting the clumps of matted hair about as gently as she can though each movement makes it throb more.

When I loosen the blanket and let it fall to the bed, she stops and studies the pattern of blood on my T-shirt and gives me this look. A lot of women caged Lloyd when he was active Glad.

—I was trying to get the bracelet back, I say.

—I knew it was yours, she says.

I had forgotten about their new wall-mounted television— the kind with overkill magnification, 3-D icemaker, foot massager . . . I'll stop.

Mark returns with a clean set of sheets and bandages, and his mother's medical bag. We can hear the sound of the TV at the other end of the apartment.

—Dad's up, Mark says.

—Now, let me understand this, Julie says. —You *shrouded* Uber to get your bracelet back?

—I was trying to distract him.

—You *shrouded* Uber? Mark asks.

He makes a low whistle and gets out his phone. He starts to scroll down the screen. When Julie gives him a look, he goes off to retrieve the boiling water.

—I told Uber the bracelet was the family's.

—Ah, Julie says, setting out her syringes, her slim little saw, and plenty of clamps.

I explain the new rule and why I can't get it back yet.

—He actually tried to tell me how much he loved Tommy, I say.

—That's despicable, Julie says.

Mark brings the pot of water and sets it on a hot plate on the floor beside the bed. Returning to his phone, he says, —Are you shitting me?

He pushes the image in front of my face. On the *New York Times* web page there's a photo of Uber in the arena. His arms upraised, his skin oiled, helmet off, hair in place, sunset cresting the stadium. *The bloody red light,* some call it. In a side-by-side photo, I'm seen entering the stadium last year, my head down like I'm being dragged off to jail.

The caption reads: 14 minutes ago. *WHEN MUST A DAUGHTER MARRY HER FATHER'S MURDERER?*

—Allison's going to drop dead, I say.

I am. I'm going to drop dead right here, right now.

When Mark's fingers fly to the next screen of the article, there's a picture of Allison and me when I was five or six. I'm wearing a flared skirt, waist-high jacket, and hard black shoes with buckles. Allison's in a slender teal dress nicely belted, her hair swept up in back. We're standing in front of the GSA amphitheater in Chicago and she's holding my hand. I don't even remember this picture. Not that I'm suspicious of its authenticity. There were just so many pictures taken every time we went to a stadium.

Mark reads aloud. The story spells out the Glad law that has me strung up—the solid fact that in Glad culture, I'm required to marry Uber because he looted my dowry bracelet.

I take the phone and skim over the journalist's historical references to brainwashing. They always think Glads are brainwashed. There's some analogy about the heiress named Patricia Hearst and the Symbionese Liberation Army. And there's the business of how a group or sect can impair their children. The Mormons—they always parade the Mormons out—the Christian Scientists, the rabid polygamists. At least there's some discussion about the film Sofia Coppola's making on Glad girls in New York City. They say it's beautiful, but maybe too beautiful. Sounds like envy to me. But now my head pounds so badly I have to stop reading and hand the phone back to Mark.

—It says the reporter went through a thousand photos of bracelets until he matched it with the one on your wrist. I'd say the guy's a little slow, Mark says.

—We'd better call Allison, Julie says.

I look at Mark, his large sad face. There's something about the way his jaw is formed or the way his goatee is trimmed around it, the quiet eyes, the stain of blue gel pen on his lower lip. Sometimes he makes me think of a buffalo or a bearded centaur, a quick Picasso sketch. And sometimes I know he has more than a brotherly affection for me, but we prefer to ride on the rim and avoid conversations on this topic.

—Allison might be asleep, I say.

Just then Lloyd sticks his head in the door, his hair pushing up every which way with that sleep-bent expression. When he sees Julie cleaning my wound, he exchanges looks with her.

—She's on every major news program, Lloyd says, nodding in my direction.

—We know, Lloyd. Be a dear and get the chloroform off the top shelf in the pantry, Julie says. —Then call Allison and let her know Lynie is in safe hands.

Julie begins to make a tear in the bottom hem of my T-shirt so I won't have to pull it over my head, telling Mark and Lloyd to turn the other way.

—But . . . but you can sell that! Mark gasps, meaning the T-shirt. —All right, I'll shut up, he says.

He turns around as Julie rips it up to my neck and snips the collar and sleeves. It feels like every last thing I have is being cut away from me.

—We're going for total bravery tonight, Lynie girl. After I

get you washed up, I'm afraid I have to shave part of your head.

—Just shave it all, I say.

—They come not single spies, Mark says.

—Get your father's electric razor, Shakespeare. And hurry, love.

# CHAPTER
# 10

I feel as if I've slept a thousand years since I heard the low hum of Lloyd's electric shaver against my skull. My head feels breezy, exposed. Mark brings a glass of water up to my chin, angles the straw into my mouth, and tells me, —You missed some stuff.

—My hair?

—She did a really clean job. And this you'll like. The stitches form the letter *T*. She said when the hair grows back, you'll still be able to feel the place where the knots were. An homage—to Tommy.

I try not to tear up.

—I listened in when she was on the phone with your mom last night. Allison and Thad are staying put for now. The press are ten deep around your house.

—She probably likes that.

—Actually, she sounded pretty unhinged.

—I better get home.

Then Julie swoops in to check on me while I'm brushing my teeth with the new brush she unwrapped for me. She and I are close enough in size. Through the foamy toothpaste, I ask to borrow a T-shirt and jeans—she's thrown mine in the wash and they're still soaked, she tells me.

—Dress for the cameras today, dear.

—I'm not entirely Allison's daughter.

—People will be watching, and whether you like it or not, you represent Tommy today. That's what will be foremost in their minds.

I would argue the point, but I know it's useless with Julie. And the only thing she'll loan me is this blue silk dress with a bodice and a skirt so long it trains. To make it worse, she fishes around until she finds the nearly sapphire necklace she wore when she married Lloyd, and fastens this around my neck. I look like a dark blue bride. I get some makeup on my face, which is kind of weird because once your hair is gone, where does your face begin or end?

When she pads down the hall to make breakfast, Mark asks if he can draw a skull and crossbones on my head. This has something to do with the new semi-erasable tattoo kit he's purchased.

—I don't think so.

—I could do a sword and shield above your brow.

—Maybe later?

—The Colosseum?

—You're insane, I say.

He's sweet to try and make me laugh. He settles for putting his arms around me. His beard tickles my head and his T-shirt smells of burgers. I slip out of his arms and go over and look behind his closet door at the full-length mirror.

—You're as beautiful as Portman in *V for Vendetta*, he says.

I know better.

—Allison and Julie don't *really* want me to marry Uber, do they?

—They think you should consider it . . . under the circumstances. And I think you should run away with me to Saskatchewan.

—I don't think the Canadians are wild about Glads.

—We could bring our ultralite lances to impress them. Mexico? I don't care. The happiest place on Earth? There has to be one small hiding place the infrared cameras can't penetrate.

—I have to see how Thad's holding up.

—Bahrain? New Orleans? I don't want you to marry this jerk!

Lloyd drives me home in his mercenary van. Mark volunteers to sit in the seatless back, rolling around with the loose nunchucks and brass knuckles. I sit shotgun. I'd feel better if we had a gray New England sky, but the day is so much sunlight and full-blown trees and rasping insects and heat. I fish a pair of sunglasses out of the glove compartment that sort of fit if I push them up and tilt them to one side. The lenses are pretty scratched.

—Check this out, Mark says. He gets up and lunges forward, so I'm just able to grab his phone before he pitches into the back again.

—What am I looking at?

—*The List.*

So I pull that little window up and stretch it and squeeze it and scroll forward and back, looking at The List, his new Web site. It begins with: *The Last 24 Hours,* today's date near the top. He has a tally going of ruthless events: bombs—car, suicide, and pipe; triggered land mines; people who starved or went hungry because a dictator or junta wouldn't let humanitarian aid into their country or because the stateside lunch programs were cut; those who succumbed to AIDS; wars, insurgencies, takeovers, and crackdowns; rapes, incest; road rage incidents; collisions; the number of elderly beaten for their social security checks—they even went after a 101-year-old woman for thirty-three dollars.

And pretty soon I find my thoughts are adding to the types and methods of violence and cruelty. He hasn't covered half the TV shows, the stabbings over in England, and you know, we're all just savages. But I have to shake this mood off.

I hand the phone back to him.

—You have a sick mind, I say.

Lloyd gives me a sideways glance and nods in agreement. Our house, the house we're about to lose, if you put your faith in Caesar's and my oracular brother, looks like a crime scene. The media are thickly settled over the lawn and deep into the flower beds that Allison spent three years bringing to full zeal. Some of the reporters stand about with coffees or microphones held like limp appendages. Many are on their haunches or spread out picnic style. There are TV vans and camerapeople in droves. As Lloyd pulls close to the house, the swell reminds me of an inflatable toy suddenly getting air pressure.

—Drive around the block, Dad! Mark insists.

But it's too late, the van is swarmed. And though Lloyd is a fierce driver and could probably run a large crowd over with ease, he's not really like that and we're solidly wedged in. The press shouts my name while Mark pushes in between our bucket seats. Reaching over, he cracks my window.

—Let her get out of the van!

Lloyd slides around me now and gives my door a solid shove. Then he pushes his way into the throng. He's wearing one of his shrunken T-shirts that conveys his work on both his major and minor muscle groups. Everyone pulls back just enough and Lloyd opens the door for me. I step out, my glasses sloping off my face, and I catch my foot on the hem of my dress. Camera lights blind me as I straighten out the material. I lean over and whisper in Mark's ear, —I just want to stroke out.

I've never understood why anyone wants to be famous.

Mark gives me this look that tells me that at least one

other person on the planet Earth gets what's going on. Voices fly at me again and Lloyd puts a hand up and says, —One at a time. One at a time.

—Do you plan to honor the Gladiator Sport Bylaws and marry Uber? a short leathery reporter asks.

Every bit of GSA information I've ever read or considered, loved or hated, pools in the bottom of my skull like spent motor oil. As other questions fly my way, I'm trying to wrap my mind around this one idea: *Do I plan to marry my father's murderer?* I cling to the image of Allison in one of her cocktail dresses and five-inch heels, talking to the media. She rarely gives anything away she'd rather not and she's very good at weaving in the things she intends to convey. She is the embodiment of spin, though she'd hate to hear me say this.

—I've just lost my father, I say, feeling the words travel out of my mouth in that same slow register at which everything around me continues to move. —I plan to see how my mother and brother are doing, and then take things from there.

I stare off at the living room windows. I wonder if Allison is peeking through the curtains or watching me on TV, or attempting to do both at once.

—Will it be your mother's decision? Will you marry Uber if your mother agrees to the marriage?

—Allison has always encouraged me to make my own decisions.

—Did you shave your head in protest—are you hoping to get out of this wedding to Uber? a reporter in a boxy jumpsuit asks.

—I took a blow to the back of my head and received . . .

I have a quick whispered consultation with Mark.

—Twenty-two stitches, I say.

—Why have you hired bodyguards? another photographer asks, nodding to Mark and Lloyd.

Lloyd pushes his way toward the mic. —We're family friends and we're only too happy to lend our support.

—Lloyd, you've fought in the GSA, you've trained some of America's finest. Has Lyn asked your advice about Uber?

—I'm afraid I'm better at discussing swords and tridents.

—Lyn, how did you get injured?

This from a tall male reporter with chopped blond hair.

—People were cheering wildly for Tommy at the stadium, I say. —I think a bottle flew out of someone's hands in the excitement.

—Do you think it's possible that someone aimed it at your head intentionally?

I look up at the house again. Thad is pacing back and forth in front of his bedroom window now. He waves. I wave back. He motions frantically for me to come into the house.

—Glad fans everywhere have shown enormous respect for my family and thought Tommy G. fought heroically. Their loyalty is helping my family through this loss. It is, however, a rough sport. People do get killed. Though I should add that Caesar's Inc. works very hard to ensure maximum safety to those who attend the competitions.

Mark whispers in my ear, —You're good.

—Have you met with Uber? another reporter asks.

—No. Not yet.

—So you plan to?

—There are no plans at this time, I say.

—Do you dream of becoming a Glad wife?

Up in the house, Thad pleads with me to come inside. Cameramen and photographers push their equipment as close as possible now, closer. The soggy summer air presses in. And I realize that I'm right there, at the end of a perfect media moment. All I have to do is come up with something that rings with warmth, something that conveys hope to a million girls about the life of the GSA wife. Then I'll be out of here, released into our home, into Allison's mind, my brother's predictions. But there's something about this particular question. I think of the number of times Allison has been asked about any plans to become a Glad wife again. And suddenly my mind is thrown into reverse and I just toss off an answer, the first thing that comes to mind.

—Sometimes I dream of becoming a gladiator.

Questions fly now, boy. Lloyd whips into action, his arm around my waist, and with Mark at my other side, they draw me toward the house. CAMERA LIGHTS SHINE through my eyeballs all the way to the back of my head, and I bet the *T* formed by the stitches lights up. Reporters push in tighter and Lloyd and Mark elbow toward the front door. I let the questions dissolve into the air like so much insect repellent.

When we finally get into the foyer with its buckets and buckets of condolence flowers, I look at Allison and try to get some air. I have seen her through the loss of six husbands (I'd include my biological father but I have no memories there) and both of her parents' deaths, but I have never seen her look this bereft. She presses me to her bosom and kisses my cheek and asks me to turn around so she can see the stitches. She reminds me that hair grows back. She tells me she's sorry.

Exchanging kisses with Lloyd and Mark, Allison invites them into the kitchen to eat the sandwiches mounded on silver platters, the casseroles and salads, all from the neighbors. The plasma screens are on in the living room so she can see three news stations at once. There's no doubt that she knows what I've said to the press. But she won't take this up with me, not yet, not in front of them.

# CHAPTER
# 11

I enter Thad's room slowly because sometimes he stands inches from the door, eager to catch your energy before you get in the room, and a couple of times he's been bruised across the forehead or nose this way until we figured out his patterns. But this time he's crowded under his train table, the Lionel system in full roar, tiny milk cans loading onto a platform, people trying to get to Pasadena or Toronto or someplace in a great hurry. The boy who typically likes a low gradient of noise finds something comforting in the train table and that particular thundering.

I know turning the train set off without warning will create a crash in his mind so I call out to the conductor. —Bridge out! I'm hitting the brakes!

I ease the power knob to off and the trains come to a rest. Maneuvering my dress, I get down on the floor and lie close to Thad, who remains coiled beneath the table waiting for the repair crew. I tell him not to worry if he sees some bandaging on the back of my head.

Then, because he insists, I show him, moving this way and that until he's satisfied.

—Did someone crack your head open?

—Just enough to let some pressure out. I'm okay, really. Julie put a few stitches in the back. I'll show you when I change the bandages later.

—Do you have a Freeway bar?

I try to always have a Freeway bar for Thad but all I have left is a Bullet. I fish this out of my bag and peel back the silver wrapper. The lines in his forehead relax as he sucks the candy like a giant thumb. Thad is big on anime so there are posters everywhere around his cowboy bed and over the turtle tank. Sometimes he'll take one of the posters off the wall and spend hours tracing a big-eyed girl with pink flowers in her hair, fighting a demon.

—I'm sorry about all the people in the yard, I say. —They'll get tired of being here eventually and go home.

—You better watch out for Allison's bed, he cautions.

I wonder if Thad's on the prediction track again.

—I fell from the clothes tower, he says.

—You okay?

—I'm the most famous person you'll ever meet, he says.

I run my hand over his hair.

—I remember that. But did you hurt yourself?

—I want a bandage like yours.

—Then we can match, I say.

—I want that.

—Me too. I'll find one in a little while. You know, Mom's

feeling a little nervous right now, so she's probably trying on too many outfits and they just kind of pile up on the bed. She wants to look good for the media. If you climb on the clothes, she gets worried.

—Something's wrong with Tommy, Thad says, as if he's just remembered he turned a pot on to boil three hours ago.

—We're all feeling sad because we lost Tommy in the arena last night. Do you remember seeing him fight?

—He needs a safe job.

—I know, I say, thinking I'll wait for a better time to explain. He tends to fuzz out on the worst aspects of reality until he's ready to grapple with them. I reach out and take his hand.

—Tommy's going to miss us as much as we'll miss him, I say.

—You love Tommy, Thad says.

—We all do.

—But you're going to lose your head.

Thad is more than still now, looking circumspect.

—Ah. I see. Did you let Mom know this? I say, and touch my throat.

—I said Lynie's going to lose her head.

—Okay. That's okay. So look, I'm going downstairs to talk with Mom for a while. I think your favorite show's on soon. Will you come down and watch it with me?

—You're my favorite show, he says, looking at the rough wood of the train table, touching my name in blue marker there. Sometimes he likes to write my name on surfaces. I hug Thad lightly because I don't want him arresting suddenly and bashing his head on the table.

—I love you, Thad.

—I love you, Lynie.

I'm headed to my room to change when Allison calls me to come downstairs for a minute. I stop and get a scarf out of her top dresser drawer and tie this around my neck, feeling the Marie Antoinette chill in the air. The thing is, Thad's not always right about his predictions and even if it is true, it might not happen for another fifty or sixty years, and by then maybe I'll be grateful to lose it.

Allison calls a second time from the library. We have, thanks to my first father, Frank, one the best collections of books on gladiators and ancient Rome in the United States. Some in English, some in Italian, French, and so forth. Many are illustrated. I spend a lot of time hauling volumes up to my room, poring over them, and as much as Allison hates it, taking them into the tub with me.

There's a Living experience that Allison loves, based on an old television production of Jackie Kennedy's tour of the White House. And when Allison invites Jackie into our home, so to speak, she complains bitterly that the press has never done a program on our house, on our remarkable library.

—They could shoot it in a similar style to your tour, Allison likes to tell her. —I could wear my large sunglasses. I know our home isn't as big as the White House, but it is impressive.

—You'd want to give them the history behind the collection, Jackie always says, turning her teacup so the lipstick print faces away from Allison. —How the first book was purchased, what it means to you personally, how each husband enlarged upon or codified the collection. Why don't you visit us at Hyannisport this summer and we'll discuss this at length?

In many ways, I think it has been Allison's most simpatico Living experience—sitting with the president's femme like that—because Jackie was frozen in a particular slice of time with Jack, and Allison could relate. Sometimes Allison mimics Jackie's honey-on-melon voice. Coming home from school, I've walked in on her giving the tour to the walls. If Allison could be frozen in time, I don't know which husband she would have about. I suspect Mouse. I imagine she still retained a hopefulness about things then.

Now I drop into an overstuffed library chair across from hers and she hands me one of the bottles of water with Tommy G.'s name printed on the label. It has an illustration of Tommy pouring water over his head, fresh from competition, streams of diluted blood finding his abdominal muscles—the deeply quenched look. We have about three thousand bottles in the basement up on shelves in case it floods.

*we know not what we do.*

—Mark and Lloyd left, she says, and runs her hands along the arms of her chair, up to the edge and back again.

—Thad told me he took a fall.

—Barely a scratch. But he was pretty startled. Have you had lunch? she asks.

She looks into her glass, clinks the ice cubes together.

—I'm fine.

—You're always fine, but have you eaten? she asks.

—Yes.

Though now that I think about it, I guess I haven't.

—Do you think Thad's predictions are getting a little worse? I ask.

—It's possible he needs his meds rebalanced.

—Maybe he needs to get off his meds.

God, she's even dressed like Jackie today, in one of those straight, trim suits, belted at the waist, a smart little jacket. Black, of course, for mourning. She looks as weary as I am.

—Don't start, she says.

—Okay, well . . . I wanted to tell you I've decided to get a full-time job. To help out, I say.

—I spoke with the president of Wives College again. Their doors are wide open and she's assured me they could offer you a full scholarship. You and Uber could have a long, protracted engagement. That would give you time to think things through.

—I already know how to dress a wound. I know the bylaws, how to *comport* myself in public.

She unpins her pillbox hat and puts it down on the table next to her.

—How to comport yourself in public? Like making insane statements about wanting to be a gladiator?

—I got tongue-tied. Can we just let it go?

She rubs her fingers into her face as if the deep musculature is in pain.

—I meant to say wife, gladiator's wife.

—No you didn't, she says.

—How do you know what I meant to say? All I can think about right now is Tommy.

—I just do, and yes, that's all any of us are thinking about.

—Okay, well, maybe if it's a choice, I'd rather fight for something than have it carved out for me.

I ache when she picks up the hat and spears the stiff fabric with the pin. I know she's at the outer limits of frayed, but she insists on talking.

—You make my entire life sound ridiculous, she says.

—You chose your life. And that's a whole lot different than someone assigning a husband to you because of some obscene rule. And by the way, it was your husbands who taught me how to use a sword.

—What are you talking about?

—You don't remember the plastic sword and shield Mouse gave me, with the vinyl belt and greaves? I was six, Allison.

—That doesn't sound like Mouse.

—I don't think my being a girl, or a gladiator's daughter,

even occurred to him. If he had played ice hockey, he would have slapped blades on my feet and pushed me onto a rink.

—He was just having a little fun with you. Mouse could be a great kidder, dear.

But my memory is vivid here. While we trained in the backyard Allison stood by the kitchen window, her hair thinning and dropping to the linoleum like needles off a Christmas tree. She did her best to go along with Mouse, however, to hold on to her second husband as long as she could. I explained that he padded my sword arm with a *manicae*, that he told me repeatedly that I was to stab, not slice, if I planned to take out my opponents' organs, if I intended to win.

—He used to shout, *Don't decorate your opponent! ELIMI-NATE her!*

—He got a little carried away sometimes, I know.

But at that age, with nothing more than the pole of the basketball hoop to strike, the sound clanging in my head, it didn't feel like he was just getting carried away. Right now, all I can do is look at her.

—Now I remember. I gave that set away to one of the boys down the street after Mouse died. Funny, the things you forget. I know you were spending a lot of time in the library then.

It's true that I became more content to study weapons than play with them, to learn about Caesars and slaves, the meaning of bread and circus, the Forum . . .

—And then Truman . . . , I say, referencing her fourth husband.

—What on Earth did Truman do?

So I began to tell her that one day in fourth grade, I was pig piled in the girls' locker room.

—You aren't serious, she says.

—Um, that's what they do to Glad girls.

—Then I must have gone in and talked to the principal, she says, looking nervous.

I explain that the girls were careful and hit my torso and upper thighs only. So you couldn't tell there were bruises under my school clothes.

—God, who would do that to you?

—Monica and her friends.

—But Tommy got Monica's parents a discount on season tickets to the amphitheater, what, three or four years running? I'm going to call them right now.

—This was in fourth grade.

She starts to rise and I motion for her to keep her seat.

—Truman took me over to the Ludus Magnus Americus and he had this woman train me so I could stand up for myself.

Allison tilts her head to one side and I look to see if her brains will spill out, because there doesn't appear to be much holding them in place now.

—Go on.

—Truman gave me this safety-orange tunic, and a fiber-glass shield about half my height. Then he matched me up with a wooden sword and shield from the equipment racks. There was a young trainer named Leona who worked there.

—You're scaring me.

I didn't say that Leona had a tattoo of Nero on one arm.

—Leona set up a dummy for me.

In its first incarnation, early in the sport, the Glad dummy was a scarecrow to the slaughter. Just a couple of crossed wooden poles held together by leather straps, a shirt, and sometimes a hat stuck on top, to indicate the approximate location of the head. Later it looked more like a seamstress's form with chest armor and helmet. But I had the current generation, like a padded crash test model with all the gear. It had mechanical arms that flailed about to mimic some kind of crazed in-battle motion. Once Leona had set it up, she and Truman gave me a few basic instructions.

Then a bell sounded.

This particular dummy needed work. It sounded like a cat in heat each time it raised its left arm. And maybe eliminating this sound was on my mind more than anything when I went after it. And maybe, I mean it's even possible, I saw myself doing battle with the girls at school who had signed me up for this whole business. But mainly I wanted to try and do a quick, neat job and avoid embarrassing myself in front of the attendants who had all pretty much stopped their work to watch the gladiator's daughter. *Stab, don't slice, and get out,* I thought. I knew about joints, I knew about weak spots. I brought my sword down hard enough to knock the right arm out of its socket. I watched it fly a good fifteen feet as the crew cheered. I delivered a second blow and the left arm flew.

Leona slapped her six-pack abs, and told me to go for the gut—the one area that's never protected. Then she reattached the dummy's arms and repadded the chest. She turned the speed up a little, adjusting several controls. I wasn't a pacifist then as I am now, and I meant that innocent dummy no harm, but when the bell rang again, I suddenly had the whole crazy life up on the register, all the things kids had said to me about being the daughter of savages. I don't tell any of this to my mother, of course.

—The weird thing is, I turned out to be really good at it, I say.

—Good at fighting a dummy?

—Yes, I was.

With the short sword, I peeled back the dummy's shield and went up under the ribs and into the heart, which popped out of its chest like a biscuit flying off a Teflon pan. The trainees who watched joked around, some gave me kudos. I felt a heat gather in my bones. A bead of sweat ran down the outside corner of one eye. Taking over, Truman said I should try the net and trident this time. Something Mouse hadn't taught me, and I thought: Good, I'll make a complete clown out of myself. Then Truman will be happy to head for the car, and we'll be done.

But once I took a stance, I felt the weight of the chain in

my hands, the balance of the trident. I whipped the net out, like snapping a dishtowel, and in one shot I detached the chest armor. Then I plunged the trident into the guts.

Of course I don't burden Allison with these details either.

—There is such a thing as beginner's luck, she says.

That's what Truman claimed all the way home in the car. He had the kind of bruise that settles into the ego.

—But what if it's hardwired in my circuits? I've actually thought about that sometimes, I say.

—Are you thinking of becoming a *regular* gladiator or a *nonviolent* gladiator?

—I'm thinking I didn't ask for any of this.

# CHAPTER

## 12

She smooths out the wrinkles in her skirt and goes over to the large aching desk. We have lived in this house for ten years, and I have never seen her use this desk, not once.

She sits in the swivel chair. —I probably shouldn't tell you this so soon, but we've pretty much lost everything.

Now she shows me the face I'm helpless to defend against. Oftentimes that face cycles through and the enormity of her situation hits and then I see the trapped person, the woman who is starting to go mad from anxiety for herself and her kids. For all the stuff we go through, Allison and I have always been tight and quick to anticipate each other's moves. At one point we did everything together. The distance between us was like a one-second filmstrip, so brief you couldn't replay it or the machine might jam. And though I could rail on her for all of her stupid choices—and God knows I've done that more than once—I heard the master-bedroom arguments when each one of the fathers, except Tommy, accused her of putting Thad and me first.

So I want to say, okay, well, go a little mad. Just don't go too mad.

A couple of times she's had what you could call *faux deaths*. They're faux because she always makes sure she's rescued in time. She has checked herself into a hotel or used a friend's house to get into this ritual kind of death. I didn't know most of this until Tommy filled me in about a year ago. And he didn't realize I didn't know and then he felt horrible for bringing it up. Allison often puts such a good face on things. I had no idea she had thought about leaving this world.

—We've got the books—we can sell them as a collection, I say, looking around the library shelves. —And we don't really need all this furniture.

She starts as if I'd said she didn't need her children.

—The helmets alone would bring in enough to support us for a year, and I'm going to be working . . .

—Take a breath, dear, she says, which is her way of saying *STOP*. Looking me straight in the eyes now she pulls a hand-delivered letter out of the top desk drawer. She hands me the sheet of official Caesar's Inc. letterhead.

—Read it aloud, she says.

—"In celebration of your new life." What does *that* mean?

—Go on, she says.

—"In celebration of your new life, we're lighting all the candles and making plenty of wishes." Someone seriously wrote this?

—It gets better.

—"You, Allison G., noble widow of seven gladiators, six fully meritorious, are the first woman in recorded GSA history to achieve the status of *Uxor Totus*"?

—*Uxor*, wife. *Totus*, complete. Finished. A finished wife, she says.

—"We hope you will seize the many opportunities ahead to support Caesar's Inc. and our mission of offering assistance to GSA Wives and Widows worldwide." Blah, blah, blah. A donation envelope? They want a *donation*? These are their condolences?

We are both aware that Caesar's Inc. has gone through dramatic changes over the last couple of years. It began with a hostile takeover, then two hundred administrators and thirteen hundred arena workers lost their jobs. There were times when Tommy lost heart over some of the new requirements—they suddenly had him fighting three extra fights than originally agreed to—otherwise he would have been out six months ago. I know he felt superstitious about the whole thing, and even called it a bad omen. He said they were acting like the military in wartime, only he wasn't a soldier. He talked about going underground, and considered the idea of fleeing the country. Allison was the one who kept faith, who convinced him to hang in, to work out his contract and be done. One thing they shared in common was the dream of what life would be like when he had wrapped things up with Caesar's. *Viva la vida*. They would have the house, the yard, there were trips to plan, possibly a full-time assistant for Thad. They talked of building an apartment for me over the garage.

I'm about to express my rage at Caesar's when she hands me a second letter.

We've lost the house.

She has been hit with a new bylaw. A lobotomy of a bylaw.

*low, low these bylaws.*

It has to do with Allison being a GSAW landowner. Caesar's handled the loan and now they're saying her down payment has been revoked and she's defaulted on her loan. *Out of their generosity and compassion,* Caesar's Inc. is granting us a full *90 days* to find shelter. *AND* they encourage her to get a small tattoo in a discreet portion of her body—which probably means just above her C-section scar—with the words *Uxor Totus* in bold colors.

On top of this, we have lost all of the furnishings—something about their being purchased with the intention of enhancing the value of the house; the china and silver—this to offset certain auditor expenses; the entire collection of gladiator books, which will aid in establishing a staff to manage the distribution of the contents of the home, including her ceremonial gowns, and yes, all the helmets and weapons, the heavy and light trophies, the new and antique shields. Even Thad's anime collection and the tiny milk cans that are loaded and unloaded on the Lionel system. No mention is made of her jewelry—a glaring oversight—though she only has the one necklace of any value: the emerald. In this same letter is a notice of increase to her insurance rates, including but not limited to: health, life, disability, and something unique to Glad culture: divorce insurance. And then this, in bold, at the bottom of the letter: *You have our every assurance, that once Lyn G. agrees to marry Uber, as stipulated in the GSA Bylaws, we would be able to restore said properties . . .*

If ever there were a moment to neatly and cleanly lose one's head this would be it. I have to say something to her and I don't know where to start. But the front doorbell rings suddenly and Allison touches my face and seems to brighten.

—Hold on a minute, Kitten.

She walks into the foyer, her heels clicking purposefully on the wood floor. I decide I'd better follow her.

—You're letting the reporters in? I call.

When she turns round I already know what she's going to say.

—I expect you to be dignified for Tommy's sake.

Then she pulls the front door open.

*UBER* has come to call.

# CHAPTER
# 13

I glare at Allison.

*UBER* stands on the other side of the threshold with the media at his heels. They hurl questions. Camera lights pelt me, soak my skin.

I'm reminded of just how tall Uber is, and wide as a freezer unit through the chest and shoulders, the man I hate. He smiles dumbly at me. In the crook of his right arm he cradles two dozen black and blue roses and a new Lionel car for Thad. Laced in his fingers are the handles of a Virgin Records bag.

Though he is standing just three feet away, Allison calls, —Come in, Uber. You are welcome.

Allison's pretty good at doing an Imperial Rome impression. She has a way of throwing her voice so the last meager reporter on the sidewalk can hear. But at the moment they're all in a crush, pushing toward the door, shouting questions.

—*How do you feel about Lyn marrying Uber?*

—*Will they live here with you?*

All Allison will give them is a pale smile until she's ready for the full interview. She looks at Uber and asks him to help with the door. He hands Allison his Virgin bag.

—*Lyn, Lyn, what do you think of Uber?*

—*Any honeymoon plans yet?*

—*Allison! What would Tommy say about this alliance?*

There's some kind of commotion in the crowd, though I can't really see what's going on from my angle, and the media rush the door hard now. Uber draws a switchblade from his pocket. The roses still tucked under his arm appear to bloom from his chest though not as perfectly as they did with that actress in *American Beauty*. When he touches the button his blade telescopes into a sword—you can buy these knives everywhere in Tokyo now—and the paparazzi love this gesture. They try harder to blind him with their flash equipment as Uber pushes against the door to shut it. He has it nearly closed only to realize a man's hand is pinned between the door and the jamb. The guy screams, —*I LOVE YOU, LYN!* and Uber, putting his sword up, opens the door wide enough to push the guy in the chest, sending him back against the photographers. A roar of laughter rises as Uber bolts the door.

—They're pretty bold today, Allison says. —Come the back way next time.

—Next time? I ask.

They turn to look at me but no one says anything. Allison

coughs politely. Uber weaves around the buckets of hyacinths and gladiolas, the vases overcrowded with bird of paradise and mums, in order to stand near me.

—We've been a little overwhelmed with tributes, Allison says.

—Of course, Uber says.

—Of course? I say.

—I spoke out of turn, he says, looking toward the rug.

He begins to hand the roses to me, perhaps to put things on better footing. But seeing my reaction, he looks confused or guilty or both, and lays them in Allison's arms. She rocks back on one heel from this small attention and thanks him.

Uber is wearing traditional courting clothes, which look like a tuxedo with vertical razor cuts down the length of the jacket and matching tunic, and sandals that lace up to his knees. I guess he always has a slight imprint of his helmet on his face. Either that or he got up early to work out in full gear. I look at the slices Tommy made in his legs, each one about an inch apart. Like ladders they travel up Uber's calves and thighs, and I hope the sandal straps are rubbing the man raw.

I realize he and I look like members of a wedding. I unwind the train of my dress from around my ankles where it's bunched again, and take the flowers from Allison's arms and arrange them in a vase. It's a lot easier than making small talk or eye contact. She asks Uber to head into the living room, and she says she'll be right there. Then Allison leans into me and says, —Nothing to worry about, if you were thinking he might be married. He's not. And he only just turned twenty.

—Look at my face. Do you see any worry here about Uber's marital status?

—We're going to get on the other side of this, she says vaguely.

Seeming to think this over, she adds, —I think less cynicism would help to get us there faster.

I tell her, —*My bad*.

But she has already headed back into the living room and I'm not sure if she even heard me. Much as I want to go upstairs and crawl into bed, I know Allison would get too upset. When the flowers are in place, I stand by the entry and watch the show. The front blinds are drawn but the soft couches and chairs catch the light from the backyard garden. Allison appears to be engaged in a quiet domestic scene. The video camera is on a tripod by the piano. I can't believe she's decided to record this meeting. So we are here in the living room and we are there, on the fifty-seven-inch plasma TV, each moment absurdly captured. Allison looks keyed up, hyper.

Uber takes the pair of glasses with those thick lenses out of his pocket and his eyes shrink. He seems to recognize us anew.

—It was kind of you to let me come, Uber begins.

He actually seems happy to be here. I hope he knows I'm not.

I see a signal slip between Uber and Allison now that floats in luminous code across the living room. Though I can't decipher all of it, I know today's meeting was arranged while I concussed at Julie's house. Whether she abhors the man or not, Allison has arrived at a new plateau of survival where all might be forgiven, not just in time but quickly if this will shore us up.

When Allison catches me loitering just outside the living room, she motions for me to come and join them.

—I asked to fight someone else. I don't know if they told you, Uber is saying.

I watch as she guides him to a chair, where he sinks lower than I remember Tommy sinking. Of course Tommy knew that chair and mostly avoided it. Allison has returned the Virgin bag to Uber and now he sets it on the coffee table with particular care. He looks at me, perhaps waiting for something. A reaction? Should I have one? My fourth father, Truman, used to play a game where he'd place an object like a watch or a toy rolling pin in a plain paper bag and ask me to guess the contents by feeling the outside of the bag. It drove him crazy that I would stare at him blankly, unwilling to play. Now I have this dreadful feeling that Tommy's hand could be inside the bag.

I look at my bracelet sitting on Uber's wrist.

—Because you were afraid? I ask.

—I don't think that Uber . . . , Allison starts but I interrupt.

—You didn't want to fight Tommy because you were afraid? I ask again.

—We certainly understand the requirements of the GSA, Allison tells Uber, hoping to put an end to my bad behavior. —Though this doesn't quell our loss, she concludes.

Uber looks a little uncertain about where to go from here, as if he's forgotten if his brain is right- or left-footed. Maybe he doesn't know the word *quell*.

—Tommy was the reason I got started in Glad sport, he says earnestly.

—I wouldn't tell the paparazzi that. They already think you're stupid enough, I say.

Allison jumps to her feet. —Lyn!

—It's okay, he says. —Really, it's okay.

Allison takes her seat again, slowly, giving me a solid warning look.

When I first learned that Tommy was fighting Uber, I made a point of *not* reading up on him. It's easier to be detached that way. But this morning Mark and I sat for an hour or more poring over everything we could get on the guy. Words that came up frequently: *idealistic, gullible, ardent.* One reviewer said: *perhaps a little stupid around the edges.* There's always some romanticism in the way that gladiators are written about.

He looks up now and sees himself on our TV screen. I'm aware of the intense effort this man puts into building his physique. He's changed little since I saw him in the locker room, though maybe his expression has softened some. I wonder how much this is about living up to Caesar's expectations, now that they're interfering in everyone's personal lives. He looks at me there on the screen. I never get why people think they can stare at you on a monitor when they quickly break their gaze if they're looking directly at you.

Last time Allison recorded me like this I had blue streaks in my hair that she couldn't stand. God help her if she ever sees me on Second Life. I have wings there, a short lace-up top, leggings, something like a gladiator skirt, bunny slippers, and a spear through my chest. I know she would question me about the spear ad nauseum, thinking it means something. I have makeup streaming down my face. But the wings, I spent a lot of time on those. The delicate work made me think of building a cathedral. I could feel kind of silly but everyone does stuff like that in virtual reality.

—The new GSA rules are making things pretty tough, he says, trying to shift the conversation.

—There are ways around rules, I say. —Are you sure you want the camera on? I ask my mother.

—We can erase it later, Allison says.

—Isn't that what Nixon said? I ask.

Uber looks like he doesn't know whether it's okay to laugh or not, and coughs into his hand in a choking kind of way. At least he's aware of history. Allison excuses us and guides me into the foyer, one hand tight around my arm.

—Lyn, please. Tommy . . .

—Tommy wouldn't have let him in the house.

—You're wrong. Tommy would have done whatever was required.

—Whatever *you* required, I mumble but I guess it's loud enough for her to hear.

—You're wearing me thin. Just get to know him a little.

—I'm supposed to sit here and listen to him talk about how much he loved Tommy?

—As soon as he's gone I'll take Thad to the park so you can rest.

—You get that there's no way I'm marrying this guy, right?

Then I follow Allison back to the living room and take a seat on the piano bench, at the opposite end of the room from Uber, so I'm just past the point where the camera can record me. Allison has popped the piano lid for dramatic effect today. I often wonder why we have a grand piano when no one plays it, though sometimes Thad sits on the bench and goes into a state some might call improvisation. I begin to think Uber is an improvisation of Allison's.

—I'll get some refreshments, Allison says, looking terrifically awkward as she heads toward the kitchen.

When I get up, Uber says, —I brought something for you. He reaches for the bag.

—No thanks, I say.

Uber swallows that large nut in his throat. We sit without talking for what seems like five minutes.

—A friend of mine deals in antiquities, he says, and holds the bag out to me.

—Roman, probably, I say.

—Yes. Your mother told me . . .

Allison pops her head around the entrance with a tray full of ice cream treats in small dishes.

—Uber? I have vanilla and chocolate.

—Actually, nothing for me right now, he says. —Maybe later?

She looks pleased with this response. I guess because it implies he'll be around for a while.

—Lyn?

I shake my head.

—I'm going up to check on your brother, she says.

Uber remembers the train car and jumps up and hands it to Allison, who says, —Thad will be delighted.

I watch her ascend the staircase with the tray, the train car rolling back and forth between the dishes.

Uber removes a leather case from the bag. Unlatching the clasp, he lifts the lid. There's a crown of thorns cushioned in velvet. I don't want to show too much interest but I do move a few feet in his direction. Most of the thorns have been broken off on the outside, and wire has been laced through to hold it together. As I get closer, I see that there are marks that might be insect damage, certainly moisture has taken its toll. It's quite beautiful, though I doubt anything like this could hold up that long. Tommy would have liked it. He collected birds' nests as a boy.

—I can't accept it.

—You don't have to decide now, he says, looking a little fragile at the corners of his mouth.

—I've decided, I say, returning to my seat. —That's the way I am. When there's a decision to be made.

We both sit quietly for a few more awkward minutes. I don't check to see if he's looking at me on the monitor. I'm not. I'm not doing that.

—I was thinking of going skeet shooting tomorrow, he says.

I'd laugh but I don't know if he's saying this straight up, and honestly, I don't care.

—Maybe you'd like to come?

Allison must have told him I used to shoot with my sixth father, Diesel.

—You just don't get it, do you? I say, poised to leave.

—This morning, Uber starts to say, —there were pictures of you and me on all the news stations, a close-up of the bracelet, the text of the bylaw.

I have the feeling he's worked this speech into a familiar groove in his head.

—The press was saying our situation would become a cause for debate around the globe, he says. —I can only imagine what you're going through.

—You're serious, aren't you? Unbelievable.

—I'm sorry. About everything. But not about meeting you.

—Jesus Christ.

Now he's off on sap rap.

—What?

—Words can't express it, I say.

He looks wounded. He'd make a lousy poker player.

But enough about Uber. Because I'm suddenly aware of this series of familiar sounds coming from the kitchen—the sounds Tommy typically made when he came home from work, when he put his sword and shield up and threw his keys and lunch box on the kitchen table.

—The Science Museum has offered to open the museum up one weeknight so we can visit. You know, so we can look around and people won't be there to gawk at us, Uber presses.

Allison must have coached him on this one as well, hoping I'd say, *Gee, Thad would love that!*

—Gawk. Right. Excuse me, I say. —I'll be back in a few minutes.

I push through the swinging door and find Tommy standing at the long kitchen counter in his jeans and a fresh tee, making up a plate of food for himself. He has both of his hands, all of his stomach, and I assume that bulge is his kneecap. Seeing him there, I slump to the linoleum floor, grazing my head on the mega freezer on the way down.

—You okay? he asks, his mouth stuffed with pineapple cubes.

Looking at the spread, he says, —What's the occasion?

Tommy always did love to eat. I don't know what to say as he heaps his plate with finger sandwiches and fruit salad, pull-apart rolls and smoked salmon, cheeses and rhubarb crumble, those neighborly foods that start at one end of the kitchen counter and go all the way to the other—the spillover on the kitchen island and table—lined up to make a thousand meals for the afterlife.

# CHAPTER
# 14

—She must have left the Living machine on, I say aloud.

—Thad bumped into the on switch, Tommy says, taking a bite of cheese and cracker.

Sitting on the kitchen floor, I feel around at the back of my head. No sign of fresh blood, just a dull ache from hitting the freezer. The pain coils around my temples and slowly settles behind my eyes.

—Did he see you? I ask.

—I don't think so. I was programmed to appear in the yard.

—Allison? She must have seen you.

—Nope. I've been out taking a tub in the bathhouse. You all right?

I feel truly dumb talking to him this way.

—You should try the Brie, it's really good, he says.

There's something about sitting here, watching him move about the kitchen with his *I'm So Glad* T-shirt, the slap of his bare feet on the linoleum. When he bites into the crackers, the crumbs that break free seem to drift down to the floor in slow motion. Like a rain that makes you aware of each individual drop and no rush to the pavement. He's very filmic, this *Tommy*. More motion picture than video.

—I've lost my appetite, I say.

—What's wrong?

He finds an open spot around the casserole dishes, sets his plate down, comes over and crouches in front of me the way he would sometimes, to console, to talk earnestly. Tommy could be in the middle of any number of things and he'd stop and pay attention to what I had to say or what I couldn't say at all.

—*You're* wrong, I tell him.

If it's crazy to talk like this, the craziness is in finding something nearly comforting here. He reaches over as if he's going to adjust the scarf at my neck, I'm certain he wants to, but then he seems to change his mind. And that's the way Tommy often was with me, reaching out and then slipping back a notch, because he understood natural boundaries and respected them. I think we all did, the family.

—I guess you'd know. You are Lyn, aren't you?

He tilts his head, scans my features. Maybe he's concerned that his recognition system is on the fritz. Well . . . not that comforting.

—You look like Lyn.

—That's me.

—The one who loves me the most, he says matter-of-factly.

That particular smile, that's pure Tommy.

—God, I hope you didn't tell Allison that.

He appears to think this over.

—It's not as if she doesn't know.

—Who programs you? I ask.

—We welcome all inquiries.

—Okay, okay.

It's easy to get caught up, I guess, thinking something, someone is other than it, than they appear. And when I stop to think about it, I have no idea about his inner workings. How he swallows that food and where it goes. In all the Living visitations, I've never seen any of them use the bathroom or get sick to their stomachs, nor have I seen the food enter the mouth only to drop through them like an object down a transparent elevator shaft. I know that having a solid take on physics would probably be an aid to understanding this particular form of virtual reality, and I admit my limitations on that subject. I've always been better at history.

I get to my feet, the headache worse at the higher altitude. Again he starts to reach out, as if he might offer me assistance, but he pulls back. I see that the designers have executed all of his external features perfectly, down to the way he slouches. He even has that slightly turned front tooth.

—I can provide you with an interactive brochure, he says.

—Just assure me that Allison hasn't seen you since you died and became a salesman.

—What do you mean I died? I died?

—Yes.

—It's possible my obituary pages are down. Funny, I don't know what I'm supposed to do if I'm dead. Usually the equipment corrects once I'm reinstalled.

I straighten out my train yet again, trying not to trip.

—Did I get in a car accident? One of those big pileups?

Tommy never enjoyed driving. I feel an impulse to place a palm against his chest, to check for a rapid heartbeat, to calm him down. But I know, despite recognizing the familiar mannerisms, the diction, the chapped lips, my hand would go all the way through him and touch the baseboards of the sink.

—I'll tell you another time. Until I can turn the Living machine off, we should find a place for you.

—But I'm starving.

—Okay, well, take your plate out to the baths.

—If you have any knives that need sharpening, you could put me to good use. I can handle any size blade, any thickness.

—Go around the hedge so no one sees you.

—Sure thing. And Lyn?

I stop and look at that face again, the eyes, the scar dividing one cheek, and I'm aware that this will probably be our last meeting, and that it really shouldn't hurt like this.

—I've missed you, he says.

—Don't say things like that.

Once he's on his way, chocolate-covered strawberries roll off the edge of his paper plate and drop onto the flagstones. I take a deep breath and go back through the swinging door.

# CHAPTER

# 15

I pause for a moment to look at myself in the hall mirror. It's funny how you can forget just how bald you really are, how vulnerable. I need to go upstairs and lie down. I need to drift away from the episodic life. But first, I have to get Uber straightened out. As I approach the living room, I call out,

—I'll go up and tell Allison we're done.

But Uber is no longer sitting in the easy chair. He's moved over to the piano, his face obscured by the lid. He's turned off the camera and the monitor.

—I was just saying, I'll let Allison know we've concluded our visit.

Uber stands to his full height, walks over to the box with my gift, takes the crown and places it squarely on his head. Then he pulls this down, maybe in an effort to make it fit snugly. The few remaining thorns snap off, a ring of them spill onto the white carpet. A trickle of blood runs down his forehead from the sharp wire holding the crown together. It trails just past the corner of one eye, and down his cheek.

In the quiet, I notice the sounds of the paparazzi outside.

—I'll never be able to forgive myself, he says.

—I'll get the first-aid kit, I say.

And I can't help but think that if he isn't flat-out crazy, maybe he really did have some attachment to Tommy.

—Wait! he says.

Uber lunges in an effort to grab my arm. Tripping over my dress, I sail forward and land stomach first.

I begin to think our relationship is purely physical.

—Are you okay? he asks.

I sit up quickly and avoid his outstretched hand. Uber crouches down in front of me. Lousy déjà vu splits my brain—there's too much Tommy in this gesture— but Uber's approach is a strictly clumsy imitation.

All I want in this moment is my bed. Knock the whole house down to the foundation, just let me sleep. I can't take on this guy's worries. In order to ditch him, I ask if he wouldn't mind getting me some water.

I tell him there are paper cups in the downstairs bathroom, so he doesn't go into the kitchen and spot *Tommy*. I've got to turn the Living machine off.

—I'll be right back, he says.

I'm halfway up the stairs when Uber bounds after me like a young dog, water slopping out of a Dixie cup.

—I'll try to keep this short, he says. —It's kind of urgent. Well, not urgent. You'll probably understand. Or maybe not. I just have to say it.

The guy's in a complete knot, and though I don't want to,

there's a part of me that can't help feel sorry for him. I down the water and let the cup parachute to the foyer that's no longer really ours. Then I continue to climb the stairs, Uber and his intentions in tow, until we reach the second floor.

—I'm not here out of convenience, he says.

—Out of inconvenience?

—You have Tommy's sense of humor.

—He had mine.

He closes in now.

—Your mother told me they're taking your house.

—We'll be fine, I say.

—I haven't told anyone this. I'm thinking of leaving the country . . . for good, he says, his voice quaking.

—I have no idea why you're telling me this. But the media would hound you to death. You're still under contract, right?

As soon as the question slips out I start beating myself up for caring.

—I'll figure something out, he says.

—I hope you keep your tetanus shots up.

—What?

—The wire. That's a pretty deep cut.

He looks embarrassed as he remembers the crown. He tries to pull it from his head, but it's tangled in his hair. He looks frustrated, like he wants to punch someone out, himself maybe. As I help him unravel the thing, he tells me that sometimes his melancholy Irish side gets the better of him.

—But I always spring back quickly, he says.

I really don't know how to answer Uber. I prefer to have a solid enemy, nothing dilute. This is starting to feel dilute.

I hand him what's left of the crown and I'm aware of the sound of the trains coming from Thad's room now. My brother starts to shriek in a happy way. I see that the ice cream dishes have been put out in the hall, as if Allison is staying in a hotel and housekeeping will be by to pick up. We are in a state of decline.

—Come with me, he says when we get to the top of the steps.

—Come with you?

—Abroad, Canada. I don't care.

It seems everyone wants me to go ex-pat suddenly. I feel like I've been called up for a draft.

—There have to be other ways to get a headline, I say.

—I don't care about headlines. It's just, and I know this sounds corny, I've tried to think of other ways to say it. When . . .

—It's not necessary. You don't have to say a thing. Please don't say anything.

—When I met you, I had the sense that I knew you, that I'd known you for a long time.

I lean against the wall and try to imagine how, in a handful of days, I've leapt out of my old life to find myself in a place of pratfalls and awkward declarations. And the funny thing is, I know this guy's being straight with me, that his heart is suddenly on the line, and who knows, it's possible

I might even like the guy for being such a big dope if circumstances were different. But they're not.

—You're irrepressible, aren't you? I say.

—At least come with me tomorrow, he says, smiling a little.—Your mother tells me you're a good shot.

—I'm all out of skeet.

—I have skeet.

I wonder if I actually need to remind him.

—I can't be with a man standing on my father's grave.

I watch him wince and hang his head, about to say something.

Thad's door opens just then and Allison slips out, looking back as she typically does, to make sure Thad will be okay without her for a few minutes. When she sees us, she comes over to examine the blood on Uber's face, her eyes moving back and forth between us, no doubt looking for signs of marital optimism.

—I was just showing Lyn how a crown of thorns is worn. I guess I got a little carried away.

—I'll get the first-aid kit, she says.

—I have one in the car. I was coming to say good-bye, to thank you.

—We're very glad you came. Lyn? she says, expecting me to agree. —You look tired, dear.

Bewildered is more like it.

—I think she should rest for a while, Allison tells Uber.

—Call you in the morning? Uber says to me.

I want to ask what kind of show we're in. It feels like a comedy.

—I'll probably be asleep, I say.

—Lyn is exhausted, poor thing. Time for a good long rest. We look forward to hearing from you in the late morning.

I decide not to correct her *WE*, happy to let Allison be the one to see Uber out. Once they're downstairs, I dash into her room and turn the Living machine off, the lights on the panel shutting down one by one. I already feel an odd pang about sending *Tommy* back even though, from my vantage point, I can't see him dissolve.

I grab one of Allison's sleeping pills from her bathroom and go to my bedroom, get the dress off, and take a few pictures of my bald self in the mirror for posterity. I send Mark a quick text to update him, climb into my pj's and fall asleep, and keep jerking awake and finally fall like lumber dropped into a mill, ready to be stripped of my bark and drawn down to the size of a toothpick, until I'm nothing but sleep.

# CHAPTER
# 16

—Wake up. Wake up, dear.

I'm aware of my mother and Thad crowded on the edge of my bed, Allison rocking me from side to side. Usually I wake to the radio alarm, to reports of suicide bombers, new strains of illness, hackers playing on my cranial nerves. Allison gave up on wake-up calls years ago.

—God, what time is it?

I crack one eye to look at the clock. I have been asleep all of fifteen minutes. I pull a pillow over my head.

—I know you won't wake up until tomorrow afternoon, she says, removing the pillow. —So we should talk about Uber.

—We should sleep. I took one of your pills. Or did I take two?

—I'm tired, Thad says. —Can I sleep on your trundle bed, Lynie?

Normally I would remind him that he's eight now and

that he's too old to sleep in his sister's room. But I sense this is about grieving, so I say it's okay.

—You need to get your own pillow.

—I'm going to get my own pillow, Thad says.

When he goes off to find it, Allison springs on me.

—He asked for your hand in marriage, did you know that?

She looks like someone who has gone through an extreme medical procedure and lost many unwanted pounds too quickly.

—He already has Tommy's hand.

—You didn't say that.

—I didn't suggest that I . . . suggest that I . . . I'm so tired.

—Sometimes life asks us . . . we'll talk tomorrow. Everything will be all right. Is your head okay? she asks.

—Hurts.

—Do you want me to call the doctor?

—Sleep.

—He said you won't marry him.

—The doctor? I ask.

When I finally open my eyes, my mother appears to be split in two, her two selves wavering about.

—Uber, dear.

—Can I shut my eyes now? Unless they're already shut.

—Absolutely. But I want you to think about this, so you feel you have a safety hatch: you really wouldn't have to put in more than a couple of years with him.

She begins to rub my arm.

—And we'd make sure you were heavily insured. It's not such a bad thing being a divorcée of a famous Glad. Remember that woman we met in Chicago last summer, the one who divorced the Brazilian champ? Men fell all over themselves just to get her a bottle of water. And sweetheart, you have no idea—the endorsements you and Uber will be offered. In a couple of years everything will be straightened out. You'll see.

—I know you're scared, I say.

Thad is back with his pillow. I'm aware that Allison wants to say more. Instead, she makes sure that Thad takes his shoes off. He never likes to slip into the covers as I do. He likes to rest on top, ready to launch, so it will take a while for Allison to coax him.

She gets up and pulls the trundle out now. When Thad slides down onto the little bed, he has those big eyes going and I know he might be in this expressive state—staring at me—for hours. She kisses him several times in that gentle way he likes, and she says good night.

When Allison's heels recede down the hall, I tune in to the sounds of the media outside. They call my name in the thick summer air like a pack of cicadas, asking me questions, asking me what I'm going to do.

When I think about what I'm going to do, it's hard not to think about the way she did things. Of course Allison had no idea what she was getting into when she met my first father,

Frank. That was before the GSA existed. Frank was a podiatrist who had the respect of his community and a strong desire to find a second wife, as his first had died young of a malignant tumor. And Allison was a new patient with a deeply embedded ingrown toenail. He was, it turned out, the head of his local GSE chapter, something Allison found out several months after they married, when I was well on my way. There was a large collection of booties and onesies stacked in my nursery, waiting, when he sprung this on her. I think her fear of being a single parent allowed her to accept the news of his secret life with anguished calm.

Frank went out on a Thursday night to Glad—that loose transitive verb that never adequately describes those first bloody competitions—and his body was found that Friday morning outside the local cemetery, as if his spirit had walked for some distance and had waited for the morning guard to come along for a proper burial. Someone must have dumped him there the way people will take a dog and throw it out of their cars by the side of the road, expecting whoever lives nearby to take it in.

A week later a man and woman showed up at my mother's door. No doubt I was clutched in her arms, pulling hard at her hair. She thought they were missionaries and intended to send them away, then FBI agents when they showed her Frank's photograph. But they were official GSE comforters. The woman had lost her own spouse to the competitions, and she explained that the other families had put money into a helmet for Allison.

Reluctantly, Allison let the man and woman in and fed them cherry coffee cake—one of Frank's favorite boxed recipes—and listened to what they had to say. They showed her a short soundless film of her husband dressed in a homemade outfit, which made him look like a field-hockey gladiator. Then they presented her with an envelope full of cash. Mouse, the male half of the comforters, had only been in the sport six months. He had a compassionate disposition, spoke to her tenderly, and before he left he asked if he might stop by again, unofficially. He always arrived with armloads of groceries, bags of disposable diapers, hammer and nails to make any household repairs Allison could use, and a level of tenderness she had a hard time resisting.

When Allison married Mouse, of course, there was no secret about his activities. Shortly after their honeymoon in Atlanta, he was sent to the Boston area to start a new branch, and Allison, not one to tolerate being alone for more than a few hours, accepted his love and a copy of the gladiator laws and bylaws. The organization was changing, and she was asked to sign a paper saying she understood her commitment to her second husband and his society, which she confessed to me she never even read. Then she settled into a life, taking me to see the Swan Boats on Sunday afternoons, the Freedom Trail, the Charles River, in every way attempting to express normalcy and optimism.

# CHAPTER
# 17

Thad's snoring cracks the air, and I give him a little nudge and he rolls over and quiets. Then his legs push against the covers of the trundle as if he's running down the street. He never leaves the house without one of us so I'm curious to know where he's headed. I think about that often, where I'd go if I were Thad and had my freedom.

My guess is he'll become a professional psychic one day. I don't mean the kind that keeps a crystal ball in the front window of a shop or burns your credit card with generalized sympathy over the phone, but the real thing, an oracle. That's what I picture every time Thad tells me about being this famous person he imagines himself to be—that he'll have his own following. His hedge-fund clients will make great killings off his predictions, and God knows how many romantic liaisons and births and deaths he'll spawn by opening his mouth.

Of course the thing that kept me up all night was trying

to figure out how *I'm* going to make a killing now without losing my head.

It's five a.m. and I place one of my old stuffed animals next to Thad in case he wakes early. Putting on my robe, I move around the ladders of light along the floor from the half-tilted blinds, then I wash up in the bathroom. I tiptoe past Allison's room and head downstairs to make coffee and grab a couple of donuts from the freezer. Allison likes to place last bits of food in freezer containers, marking each item with its contents and freeze date. Last night she marked them with little more than: *funeral food*. Even though the light is burned out, by the look of things we'll be eating funeral food for a few years. I can barely get the freezer lid closed. Then I realize the lid is no longer ours and other people will plunder our larder, so no worries.

While I gently nuke a couple of donuts, there's a tapping at the front door. At first I ignore it, thinking it's just the paparazzi, but then an envelope appears under the door. I recognize Caesar's logo in the return address box and peek through the curtains to see a courier heading back to his truck. I put the envelope in my robe pocket and carry the tray out to the yard. Standing in the cool shade, I survey the garden, amazed at Allison's ability to provide abundant life when she wants to. I look at the number and variety of pansies and violets, and I almost expect to hear them singing like the flowers in the animated *Alice in Wonderland*.

I feel that distinct vibration in my feet and that low sound and realize: the pump is running. The pump that keeps the hot tub hot and the warm tub warm. I freak, thinking *Tommy* is loose again. But when I enter the bathhouse, I find Mark soaking inside. His chin rests on his crossed arms spread out on the rim, his face glowing, eyes closed, legs stretched out behind him.

—What are you doing? I ask.

—Wow, I must have nodded off.

—You came over to soak?

—My dad thought we should be over here in shifts for a while to keep an eye on things. I got the first shift, of course.

—And you're already falling asleep on the job?

He pushes away from the side. I see the tiger tattoo on his chest and then I realize he's trunkless and look away.

—Get in, he teases.

—Maybe later.

—Donuts. Look at that. Just what I was dreaming about.

I put the tray down on a bench and I take a seat. It's low enough, and the rim of the tub high enough, so all I can see are his head and arms now. This is completely unlike him, this getting up early. I can imagine the scene: Lloyd rousting him for duty, pulling him out of his bed by his feet until he lands squarely on the floor. The pan full of cold water thrown at his face when that doesn't work. He's even worse than I am about mornings.

—You okay? he asks.

Ever since Tommy's death Mark has been trying to convey something that he can't exactly express to me. Mostly it comes out in this kind of vague question.

—I'm fine, I say and sip my hot coffee.

—You know, I come with complete mood recognition. I read body language, speech patterns, facial expressions. I can read the heat patterns in your skin, your moisture levels. Your tongue is particularly dry right now. So maybe not entirely fine? I suggest rehydration.

—Stop, I say, and toss him a donut. —So Allison definitely wants me to marry Uber.

Mark sticks the donut in his mouth so it's out of the way, cups his hands together and pushes at the water, causing a small wave to rise over the lip of the tub and spill to the floor, running toward the drain.

Taking the donut out, he answers, —Like I said, you can't marry Uber.

—I know. But I'm not sure what to do yet.

—You'll think of something.

—I just got a letter from Caesar's. Shall we see what they're up to now?

I take the envelope out of my robe pocket and tear the end off, pulling the letter out.

—Ah. They want to know how many bridesmaids I want. They recommend eight.

—Eight is a very *harmonizing* number.

—Right. They *encourage* the color lilac for the bridesmaids' dresses.

—Encourage black.

—There's an address in Boston where fittings will be held

once I send them my list. Blah, blah, blah. They SAY the entire wedding will be shown by satellite television. Oh, you'll love this. They're going to cover the *prewedding* activities, including but not limited to, my *dressing* for the *BIG EVENT* with my closest girlfriends present.

—There's no way you're doing this.

—They suggest I buff up a little for the lingerie shots.

—Discreet cameras tucked artfully in your wedding suite? What the hell has happened to Caesar's? Even Lloyd— loyal Lloyd, company man—complains about them all the time now.

—They say, once I launch my wedding plans, I will need a *solid base of operations*, so . . . so they're prepared to help with that.

—And that would be what?

—Aka: our home. They can, once I *sign on* to marry Uber, restore our Brattle Street residence to our full and ongoing use with . . . six pages of stipulations.

—They're trying to turn you into Lady Diana.

—Pre- or post-crash?

—Definitely post. Wow, helicopters, he says, and looks up to the skylights.

Two TV station choppers are visible in the panes of glass now, the noise crowding us. Suddenly Mark stands to his complete height, water streaming off his naked body. He has a beautiful body but I'm not looking until he gets a towel on. I can't help wonder if they get a clear shot through the skylights. Mark comes over in his towel and sits down on the bench, radiating heat, steam rising off his arms and shoulders.

—Okay, so maybe I do have an idea. Are you ready for this? I'm thinking I might just petition Caesar's so I can fight Uber.

—Are you crazy? he says, his mouth full of chocolate glaze.

—Look, they're out for blood one way or another, I say.

—Try money and publicity.

—Exactly. Blood, money, and lots of publicity. And what better way to supply all three than to send the daughter of seven gladiators into the arena to win her freedom?

—So you're suggesting you die in the arena because . . . ? he asks.

It's not often I see Mark this rattled. He tends to go along, to find paths of least resistance. Maybe he gets that from working on computers. He likes to do twisted things with graphics and programming and that takes a lot of patience, as far as I'm concerned.

—Not *die*. I don't want to *die*. Uber would go easy on me—he doesn't want to fight me.

—I wouldn't count on that.

—But I'm Tommy's daughter and he revered Tommy—I told you that.

—All that reverence didn't keep Tommy alive.

—He was under contract. If Lloyd was still fighting and they asked him to fight his mother, he'd do that.

—Well . . . Grandma's dead. And that's exactly what you'd

be doing with Uber, fighting under contract. But this isn't . . . oh, man, you like this guy, don't you?

I can feel my skin warm. But I don't think I should have to explain. The truth is, I feel kind of sorry for Uber. And Mark gets jealous sometimes, I know that. So I decide it's best to circumnavigate.

—Maybe all I'd have to do is maim him enough to end the match, I say. —Or ask for one of those timed matches. Ten minutes, no more . . .

—Jesus, Lyn. I'll marry you, I told you that.

—Thanks for the huge favor.

—I don't mean it that way, he says, nudging closer to me, the glaze shining on his lips, his goatee still wet from the bath.

—I could lose something small. Like a toe. That might be enough for them. We're just talking toes here. Not major commitments. Not death and dismemberment. No one sacrificing herself on the altar of marriage.

—Technically, that's dismemberment.

—Okay, so he could collect on that. I've got ten. I can give one up. And then this whole thing would be over. He only has a fight or two left before retirement.

—So there's nothing you want from me? Mark asks.

I can see he's stopped joking. His straight hair goes halfway down his neck and it's dripping water on his shoulders now, like dark icicles melting. Mark's always been there for me.

But he's making me nervous now and I stand up and pace a little. He jumps the moment and stands as well. He grips my upper arms, squeezes a little, like he's about to kiss me or make some kind of declaration. He's making overwrought eye contact now—those long lashes of his. I'm straining my neck to watch his face change. I begin to feel like I'm in some weird romance vehicle where all the men wear towels and drip with emotion. I love Mark. I really do. And I do have certain thoughts about him sometimes, but I'd never risk losing him as a friend. You can't lose everyone. I'm looking at his feet now, water tapping onto his feet. A million hours of friendship shifting into weird silence. Usually, I can talk with Mark about anything. He's the only one who knows what happened in Rome last year. But I can't have a conversation about *us*, not now. He finally lets me go like he's read everything.

—I want you and Lloyd to train me on the sly, I say. —To see if I could pull this off. There's a gutted storefront in Davis Square. It was a dance studio once. Still has mirrors and a bar. Windows taped with newspapers—entry onto the alley. All we'd have to do is get some lights in there.

—You know Lloyd, he laughs. —He's always up for shit.

—So you're in?

—As long as you don't take my nose off. I love my nose.

—I've always said that: you have a great nose. Let's go inside. I'll make you a real breakfast.

# CHAPTER
# 18

Last year I went to Rome with my family. Goddamn Rome.

Tommy's GSA ranking got us into the Colosseum at night, after the public had moved past the vomitorium and left by the gates. The horrible Victor Emmanuel monument lit up in the distance, the ruins, sitting in a café late at night, the airflow against your skin from the Vespas—you had to love Rome.

They even let us walk around the lowest level of the Colosseum. Flashlights in hand, we entered the grassy walkways of the underground rooms where the exotic animals had once been housed and carefully underfed. I watched Tommy as he moved past the dark cages.

I began to think about my legion of fathers—the ones before Tommy. I don't mean I saw their specters. No spirits stepped from behind broken walls to try and set some record straight with me, to confess or apologize about anything, to claim love—it was, after all, their love of the sport that fueled them. These were not, strictly speaking, family men.

My thoughts moved one and then another around the arena. They had all been in Rome at different times and I gather they had left thirsty and dry eyed from taking it in. I don't think any of them thought much about being fathers, and probably not a lot about romantic love, except for Mouse—he was crazy about Allison. But most of it was about being neo-Glad in the world's top league, the constant effort to stay in the game. And Allison was the high-water mark in the world of Glad wives. These guys were strategists, survivalists for as long as they could be. Some people say that's the way to go: young and strong. But that's fascism. I don't want anyone stamping me out early.

There was one moment, when we were in the uppermost tier of the stadium. Tommy had stopped climbing and surveying and he just leaned against the warm stone and went into something like a trance. We had walked miles that day, but I don't think it was fatigue. I looked at his jaws as they tensed and relaxed, his gaze far away, and I felt certain he knew what it had been like to be in the arena in ancient culture. I felt I did. When we finally broke from our mental flight we looked over at each other and smiled, as if to say something. And maybe he looked a little embarrassed after that because he had shown me too much, peeled the tough skin all the way back.

Of course no one knew what to expect from Thad in Rome. On the plane I heard Allison tell Tommy she thought it was a bad idea to bring him. But Tommy had insisted he come. He was the one who had the most optimism about Thad's future. Not that he wanted him to be a gladiator—Tommy wasn't that crazy—but there are GSA jobs that require little training and almost no attention to detail. Waterkeepers turn on the sprinklers and sometimes they give the crowd a jolt with the fire hose. Junior Camera Operators have monitoring equipment embedded in their baseball caps and move around the stadium so we get constant chaotic views of the arenas on various Web sites. Lockers lock and unlock the gates and train increasingly in the concept of the lockdown. But a bunch of those solid citizen jobs have been downsized, and there's no way Thad could handle any of those tasks for even five minutes. I loved Tommy's faith though, and how he took to Thad from the first.

We were surprised to find that Thad was quieter, more settled than normal while in Rome. Tommy and Allison bought him a full gladiatorial outfit—and not the plastic and polyester kind, but a beautiful thing in leather. The helmet and sword and shield were of balsa wood and he loved that. Sometimes he said his feet were on fire and he asked for water to cool them off, though we were in Italy in late April, and his feet felt only mildly warm to the touch when I'd help him pull his shoes off. In the outdoor cafés, he would reach underneath the table and pour glasses full of *flat water* or *water with gas* (sparkling water) on his sandaled feet.

For two weeks we didn't hear a word from Thad about the future until I took him to the Piazza del Popolo, where we found a spot on some steps one afternoon. There he sputtered out predictions to anyone who passed by. A large American woman solidly lodged in a *Roma Roma* T-shirt cornered him and asked about a variety of friends and relatives of hers and I just didn't have the heart to pull him away, he seemed so pleased to talk with her. Although there was some variety in his oracular responses—mostly about her family members who worked together in a recycling plant—he kept saying that this friend or that would die at sea. Finally she stopped him, held on to his arm tighter than I know he liked, and said, *—We're taking a cruise ship back to the States and you've just . . . named all of my friends on the ship.*

Then she got up with this drowning expression on her face, saying she was going to convince her friends to change their reservations to air travel at once. How they would avoid the ocean, if they were on their way back to New Jersey, I had no idea. But in either case, it's hard to put much faith in floatation cushions.

I thought about checking the news that week to see if a party of friends went down over or in the Atlantic, but I didn't. Even though I know he can be off at times, it's easy to get spooked by his oracles. This aside, I had good times in Rome with Thad, telling him stories to make the animals come to life in the Colosseum, expressing how beautiful it once was with the velarium fluttering overhead. We toured the baths and he liked this because he and Tommy often took baths together out in our converted garage, though he did keep asking where the water was. Of course Allison was all about Palatine Hill and talked a lot about the tile work and reincarnation, trying to decide which empress she must have been.

—It's possible I was more than one, she said.

I sent a message to Mark about my favorite temple in the Forum built by the Emperor Antoninus for his wife, Faustina. In the eleventh century AD workers found it impossible to pull the columns of the temple down in order to put a church on the site, so they built the church around the columns. I thought this said something about love. Mark said I should watch my romantic backside. I said, —Okay, okay.

But you really have to surrender that entirely when you enter the Pantheon.

Allison was off shopping for a handbag that afternoon. Standing outside the Pantheon, the great doors wide open, I collapsed my umbrella and saw that it had begun to rain inside. I would have to lie down and die to describe the quality of rain as it drifted down from the Oculus, that perfect round hole in the ceiling. Typically, Thad's a little distressed by rain. But Tommy took his hand and slowly pulled him toward the centermost point of the room, whispering gently to him the whole time. I have been in buildings with leaky roofs, lived in a couple of those when Allison was between husbands, but I had never been in a building designed to invite the rain in, and if it isn't overreaching I'd say it was miraculous standing there like that. I took Thad's other hand and we let the rain pour down.

Looking up toward the Oculus Tommy said, —Isn't this the best thing that's ever happened to you?

It's not often that Thad looks directly into your eyes. So you know that something's coming when he does. He stared for a long time into Tommy's wet face and finally said, —You have a year left.

Unlike the hard liquor of his predictions that get no mixes or sodas to soften them, Thad said with unusual generosity, —I'll miss you, Tommy.

And in that rarest of rare moments, Thad began to cry.

I swear it wasn't just the rain. And Tommy had a look, as if he were trying to read his own obituary in four-point type. He made an effort to smile, to comfort his stepson. Then Thad hiccupped loudly. Funny how I'd forgotten most of this until now. Of course I'd never taken to writing down all the predictions, though maybe I should have. And sometimes forgetting can be the best way to keep from getting depressed. Although some people take this concept too far and then they think the Holocaust should disappear before their sick little eyes. If you try to forget too much, those buried memories work like worms in your brain, eating up your psyche.

Tommy kissed Thad on the top of his head and said, —So let's have a hell of a good time while we can.

When Thad's hiccups came in quick openmouthed

bursts we had to leave the Pantheon. We were just cracking ourselves up, and quickly found Thad a large *limonade,* which cured everything. Neither Tommy nor I talked about what Thad had said and then we were swept up in a crowd and pretty soon Tommy was signing autographs and I snapped pictures with a lot of other people's cameras and phones so they could all get into shots with Tommy. He got stopped a lot on the streets of Rome and recognized in museums, and asked to sign gelato cups and backs of knees and straw wrappers. He was pretty popular over there because they knew him as the real thing and not some guy in America waving a plastic sword around, rapping about the glory of Rome. It didn't hurt of course that his mother was half Italian. And there were, among the little crowds that gathered, many women.

We had a beautiful hotel near the Spanish Steps. I shared a room with Thad, and Tommy and Allison were by themselves in another, of course. There was one morning when Tommy was feeling under the weather and the rest of us had gone off to Palazzo Borghese, where we were scheduled to take a tour. We had gone early to enjoy the park and hoped to wind Thad down a bit before entering the museum. When we realized Allison had left the tickets in the room, I volunteered to take a taxi back to the hotel so we could make the tour on time.

I figured Tommy was asleep when I arrived at the hotel because I had to knock three times. Finally he came to the door, but opened it only a crack. The smell of drugs wafted my way.

—We forgot the tickets, I said.

His eyes were bloodshot and he looked apologetic and half-witted. Busted for doing one of those things he kept telling me never to do.

—It's all right, I shrugged. —I don't care.

—All right? he said, looking confused.

—People at school smoke.

Then the sound of running water started up. The kind of pounding water that fills a tub in a hurry.

—How did you do that? I said, but I was already starting to get it.

—Do what?

—Oh, I don't know. Start the water in your tub while you're standing here not letting me into your room?

Tommy was used to me saying exactly what I had to say. He made an act of contrition out of his face.

—I better get those tickets, he said.

That's when I noticed a skirt and blouse draped over the desk chair. A blouse Allison wouldn't be caught dead in. As soon as he realized I was looking over at the clothes, he said, —Hold on, and closed the door on me.

I wanted to take off but I had to tough it out, for the tickets. A minute later, Tommy opened the door again and handed them to me. The water had stopped. The clothes had been removed. I could tell he was trying to figure out what to say.

—Allison might have come back to the room for these, you know. You get that, don't you? I said.

He made a fist with his right hand and rubbed it into the palm of his left. All the cuts. The man was a walking scar.

—Not a very heroic moment, is it, Kitten?

—She calls me that and I don't really like it from either of you, I said.

I turned and started down the hall, heard the door click shut. That's the way I've always been when there's nothing left to say. I walk. I drive off. I part the sea and run, as far and fast as possible. But this time I turned around, strode back down the hall, and knocked hard. Again I waited for him to open up.

—You have no idea what we've been through! I shouted at his dumbstruck expression. —NO IDEA! Allison drives me crazy, but she's always been there for me and she hangs in with Thad while everyone else goes off to work or dies or goes to school or the club or gets lost.

Someone had to defend her. I hoped the people down at the front desk would hear me, the women bent over cleaning the rooms on the floor below, the waitstaff in the small café.

—Allison knows, he said quietly. —This woman is no one. But it was wrong to bring her here. It will never happen again.

—Screw you, I said.

Then I realized I had to run and find a taxi or get into a

whole thing with Allison. That was Rome. Messed up Rome. If you ever wanted to spear love through the chest, this was it. I don't mean I had romantic feelings for him, but Allison did. And anyway, I'm talking about the whole idea, the whole rotten business of love.

After we got through the museum and had some lunch and saturated our cork brains on ART until they could no longer float, Allison said it was time to take Thad back to the room. I told her I wanted to do some shopping, so maybe she could drop me off. I was seventeen then, had my phone. She wasn't keen on the idea, but she had her hands full and said yes.

I went to the nearest American Express, converted some travelers' checks to Euros and asked this man at the desk to help me look up the location of the GSA training school in Rome. I don't think anyone recognized me there, and no one seemed to think twice when I signed up for a training session. I didn't do it to be something—I had no thought of being a gladiator—I just wanted to get back at Tommy, and maybe at Allison for always going along. I knew it would mess with their heads if they found out.

The place was pretty well cleared out. I didn't know they don't practice on Saturdays in Rome. But there was one guy hanging out. A lean Italian man named Giancarlo, maybe six or seven years older than I, and he offered to put me through some paces. We were the exact same height, and he was all about the eyes. He showed me some moves, and talked about how to psyche an opponent, how to manipulate a shield. In some ways, I felt happier than I had in a long time that afternoon. Because I began to get why people do marathons, triathlons, kick boxing, I don't know. It's this thing of finding a quiet zone, and then breaking out from that place in bursts of concentrated energy—that's how Giancarlo described it. He told me I was a natural, and that made me fight harder.

We used blunt wooden swords, yet my body bruised up and even bled a little. When I got back to the hotel room, I went straight for a bucket of ice, and made sure Thad didn't see me fresh from the shower. If anyone called Tommy to let him know I was over at the school, I never heard.

Giancarlo called the next day to see if I was coming back for my next training session. I told him I had a pretty busy schedule. He begged me to do Rome at night on his Vespa, to join him in his garret. After a few calls, I found some excuse to slip away. We kissed. We walked through the Jewish district back toward my hotel. We walked around more ruins and embraced. I told him someday I might come back and find him at the school. He coaxed and coaxed and we had lunch together and he explained many things: about ancient brickwork, columns, coffering, loggias. Giancarlo had wanted to be an architect, but his father died when he was a boy and he had taken on the role of provider from an early age.

Just before it was time to meet up with Allison, I would quickly dash into a store and buy something to show that I had been shopping. Insisting she see my purchases one day,

Allison said I should be more discriminating. And rather than make a thing of it, I asked her if she thought I should return anything. She was so pleased that I was asking her advice. So then I had to return things, retracing my steps—which would take some time, of course—which was about tucking the items back into my suitcase or tossing them out. That's how I bought more time in the tiny arena of the training school, and enjoyed Giancarlo's company. I thought I never wanted to leave.

My parents would have died if they had found out, but everyone had their secrets, it seemed. And after that, I began to reconsider Allison's husbands, gathering up events and gestures I had pretty much thrown away, explained away, and I thought of them differently.

It took me some time to lose my anger with Tommy. But it was hard not to soften after a while, living in the same house like that. I know Allison was confused, since he and I had always gotten along so easily and he kept apologizing in different ways, though we never talked about it directly again. Sometimes I wish we had and other times I know it was their business, not mine, and I just didn't want to know.

Then I realized that Tommy had begun to treat me like someone old enough to look behind the curtain. He told me about Allison's faux deaths. He told me what we should watch out for—which included her being too manic, too low, too detached, too doting. He told me to hang in with her, no matter what. He said he always would.

I'm not religious at all. But I took a class in high school on world religions. And my teacher explained the story of Job this way: it was the point at which Job got truly pissed at God that his relationship with God matured and his faith deepened. I don't mean Tommy was a god, though some people thought so. He was just some guy Allison met when she needed to figure out her next move, her way of keeping faith with survival. He was a gladiator born and bred, a high-paid neo-Glad who had a soft spot for Thad.

When we returned home, Giancarlo and I Skyped and e-mailed constantly and I had a hard time showing up for family meals because I didn't want to pull away from the computer. He said he was going to come visit me in America. He said I was the only girl he could ever love. But then, after a few weeks, I think he met someone else. His e-mails slowed and then stopped. It really kind of screwed me up for a while.

# CHAPTER

# 19

—Uber called, Allison says. —I couldn't find you.

I watch her apply her lipstick and then throw the tube back into her purse. Thad and I are tucked in close in the backseat watching the fans waiting on the other side of the gate. I can see they're making Thad nervous.

—Okay, I say.

Before we go anywhere Allison rides up and down for a while, adjusting her seat. She's waiting for me to show a little interest. She looks at me in the rearview mirror. Up and down while I look at a text.

Sam wants to see if I can get together with her and Callie. I guess she's feeling remorse at losing a suddenly high-profile friend. I keep writing back: *Return to Sender*. She pretends it's a joke and chats away.

—Is Thaddy's seat belt right? It looks twisted around. By the way, Uber asked me to tell you he's sending the crown off to a restorer. He'll bring it back as soon as it's ready.

Then he apologized of all things. I think this really says something about his integrity, don't you?

—Hold on, I say.

I've shut Sam off and I'm trying to help Thad. I tell him we're going to wear sleep masks today, and put one of Allison's blue silk ones on him. I worry that once we pull out of the drive all the flashes going off will send him into convulsions. It's a steady stream of blinding wattage now as Allison backs up. I'm reminded that when you see a picture of a celebrity on TV or in a magazine, grinning to their gums, they aren't smiling *at* anyone, because they can't *see* anyone. They're smiling into a wall of painful light.

Allison hits the switch, the gates open, and the car inches forward. The photographers push against our car doors now. They angle across the windshield and throw themselves at our rear window. I won't let Thad take the mask off until we're headed into Boston.

—Please drown them out, I say.

Allison reaches over and blasts a morning show on the radio. *The weather will be fair, not too hot, not too cool.*

—Not too hot, not too cool, Thad says.

A few dirty jokes, money giveaways, the traffic blocked up at the Lever Connector, talk and laughter, and we've finally pulled away. I get out of my seat belt for a moment, stretch into the front seat, and push the CD button. Mozart's *Così fan tutte* fills the car.

Although she and my succession of fathers have drawn

varying degrees of attention from the media, this level of interest is different. Every time they shout their questions at me, about whether or not I'm going to marry my father's murderer, I feel like someone who's been shot up in a mall or wedged into a well unable to move, without a rescue crew—somewhere between dead and stuck. I can't tell exactly how Allison feels about the fact that the focus has shifted to me because she has her personality face on, that expression that lets the media know she's self-possessed and plans to stay that way. In either case, she's dropped the topic of Uber for now.

I never know how she does it, but Allison is pretty good at sloughing off the paparazzi when she's determined to get her car through physical space—though I'm certain she rolled over a photographer's foot getting out—and eventually we're moving toward downtown, with only a few cars and motorcycles tailing us. As we enter Storrow Drive, one of them pulls up alongside the car. Questions are screamed at me, mouthed, pantomimed. My name is called. My name, my name, my name. Tommy's name. Uber's blessed name.

I wait for Allison to go into that tenuous place where she could be one way but she could just as quickly be another. She might suddenly realize, as we slip over the BU Bridge, that there's money to be made in writing her autobiography. And this could trigger an anxiety that she'll get a contract but that writer's block will set in. And then she'll start to think that if she suicides, someone will write a biography instead and screw it up, screw her up, her children. Ever since Tommy told me about her faux deaths, I've chronically looked for the warning signs.

I wait to see if Allison will crash us just to get the pressure off. But maybe she's okay.

She turns off Mozart and the soft voice of the GPS kicks on. I take the sleeping mask off Thad, who loves that voice and sometimes repeats everything she says. For several miles this dial-up woman tells us how to steer around bridges, neighborhoods, derailed trains. Tommy bought it a few months ago for Allison's birthday and mounted it in the dashboard to make it look factory built. It has kept us from dead-ending or taking the wrong road I don't know how many times.

—Where are we going? I ask.

—You'll see, she says.

I whisper to Thad, telling him we're playing a guessing game today—It's called: *What's Our Destination?*

I make up random bits to the game as we go because I have to do something.

I tell him, —Where we're going there will be a long beach with sparkling clean water, big soft lounge chairs with lots and lots of pillows to curl up in, and plenty of fresh fruit, and we can just listen to the waves and relax all day.

I have no idea what I'm talking about, maybe I just want a vacation. Thad seems to take this in and give it serious consideration. He tilts his head and his eyes get huge as if he's finally understood something.

Then he cups his hands around my ear and whispers, —We're going to the end of Mom's rope.

Just then, a photographer on a motorcycle inches past us on the left like the witch peddling past Dorothy's house, holding her camera out with one hand, shooting rapid fire as Allison moves us across the city.

Allison is looking a little trapped, definitely wobbly.

—I should have put my hair up, she says, popping open the mirror embedded in the visor and spreading out the wisps of her bangs along her forehead as she drives.

—Allison! I say to snap her attention back to the road.

Just then a Hummer—the model they make in case you have to take out three family cars at once instead of the usual one or two—slowly pulls up on our right. Inside, a gang of photographers lean from the windows, whistling and calling to us. Allison gets distracted by their snarking.

—I can't believe how many are keeping up! she says over her shoulder in an almost buoyant voice. —Look at them. This is all about you, Lynie.

And I'm certain I hear a sense of loss under the elation, a regret that this isn't all about her. Then I see where we're headed.

—THE WALL! I scream.

She swings away, narrowly missing the underpass and almost hits the Hummer.

—Woo! Did you see that? she laughs, her manic side in full bloom.

I'd offer to take the wheel, I'd insist, but there's no place to pull over. Besides, I don't think she'd let me, she seems so empowered. She cuts the Hummer off when she shifts lanes suddenly. The horn on that thing has the power of a paint stripper.

When it gets blocked in by a slow-moving taxi, Allison pulls ahead and things get quiet for a little while and we listen to the sound of the tires bumping over the steel bands in the road, the rhythm working like a prayer on my scattered thoughts.

Emerging from the tunnel suddenly, we bear a quick left and then U-turn in traffic—completely ignoring the recalculations of the GPS—and I realize we're driving to Tommy's athletic club. We're in the palm of the city, as she calls it. That place where gold freely changes hands. Allison loves Newbury Street. She pulls into the parking structure and swipes Tommy's card. The gate goes up and we pull in without the paparazzi. We drive up a couple of levels, circling, circling, and she drops us at the entry on the third level.

—I'll get a parking spot. You take Thad inside, she says.

I've only been to the club a couple of times. It has that postmodern suffocating-to-death-in-affluence-and-status feel to it. Lots of blue glass and steel, and in the women's room the faucet handles are embedded in the mirror and the sinks look like delicate bowls ready to shatter if you drop a bottle of makeup the wrong way.

Caesar's likes its top players to join this kind of club, invitation only, of course. So Tommy went along, though he was more comfortable in a Quonset hut with a bunch of iron pumpers—nothing but free weights—no music, no towels, water fountain busted, just a steady flow of sweat, the occasional grunt or life-affirming *oof*. But the good thing was he brought Thad down here a couple of times a week to build a little strength with a personal trainer, have a light massage and some lunch. Thad is crazy for all the televisions—the way they're lined up, the images dancing together.

It seems our mother intends to carry on the tradition, at least until Caesar's yanks the plug. I'm relieved when she walks through the entry. Not that I actually thought she'd drive away and leave us exactly. As she approaches, she wipes her fingers under her eyes to remove her melted eyeliner but she's not quite getting it. I never know if I point this kind of thing out, if she'll be grateful. So I let her go ahead and check in at the desk. She comes back to where I'm thumbing through *W Magazine*, cracking up over the way they keep adding gladiator items to their fall collections.

—Thad does his routine with a guy named Ira. He's very nice. Young, sweet. You'll see, she says.

The tension in her face is still there from the drive, the way Silly Putty holds a comic-strip image as long as it can.

Thad can't sit still, he's so happy to be here. I can tell because he paces by one of the ceiling-to-floor windows, looking down at the paparazzi—back and forth like a boy looking at lions in an arena. Then Ira comes out, shiny black hair, clear brown eyes, a small yin/yang tattoo placed on one shoulder. I think it's a fake but no one's perfect.

Ira greets us and starts talking about all the fun things he has planned for the afternoon. They're going to hang upside down like monkeys and play on the balance beam and lift some two-pound weights, and pretty soon Thad has taken his hand and they've passed through the swinging doors of the men's locker rooms. Of course no one has to convince me: exercise is sanity. It always calms Thad down, certainly does me, I wish Allison could find more time for it, though sometimes she gets on the elliptical trainer in our basement in long, intense spurts like she's drunk for exercise and then I worry that she'll never get off.

We take the back stairway, slip down an alley, and head out onto Newbury Street to shop. I really want to tell her about the dark smudges under her eyes, but now she'll be really annoyed that I didn't tell her right away, so I have to let it go. She puts her sunglasses on and lights up a cigarette. It's very humid out and the smoke clings to us in low clouds before it dissipates.

—I've talked with our accountant and Al—you remember Al, our family attorney? I've read through all the correspondence, the stuff Caesar's has sent out since Tommy's death.

—You're scaring me, I say, as I try to catch up. She loves to cross on the red lights.

There's something about the tone of her voice. She looks steadily at the shops now, devising her plan.

—There's a semiprivate home we might be able to get

Thad into, just until we get settled in a new place. It's state funded but I'm told it's cheery. There would be other kids his age.

The words catch like fish bones in her throat, which she tries to clear by taking another drag of her cigarette.

—We could visit him every day and he'd be with other kids. I guess I said that. You and I should be able to afford a studio apartment in our neighborhood for a year, maybe a little longer, after I sell anything we have left to sell. Which means you'll be able to go to a regular university if you get scholarship money. We just have to get through this rough patch. You know what they say, no pain, no . . .

Her voice sounds like so much helium and I'm choking down tears and I'm trying to think of some way to dissuade her as we dodge and weave in the foot traffic.

—I'll talk to Uber, she says. —I was the one to encourage things. I must have been out of my mind. Shock makes us . . . irrational. You understand that, don't you? But if you think it would be better coming from you, I'd be happy to suggest some tactful ways to put things to him. I have the feeling he's a rather sensitive young man. So we don't want him to feel rejected.

—I intend to follow all of Caesar's guidelines, she continues. —It is, after all, the life we've chosen, well . . . I've chosen for us. I know, maybe not the best decision in hindsight. If I tell you this in strict confidence, you can never tell anyone I've said this.

She lowers her voice. —I think what they're asking of you

is insane. I'm sorry I was in such a crazy place that I couldn't see things clearly. I told myself Tommy could die, a million times over. But then when it happened . . . But I've talked with our accountant and our attorney—you remember Al. Did I already say that?

I grab her arm so she'll stop walking.

—We can't put Thad away.

—Of course not, she says. —Not away. They said it would be nothing like putting him away. You have to know how painful this is for me, Lynie. Thad's my baby. But while he's in a temporary living situation, just for a few months, I'll be able to put our financial life together. I was thinking, and don't trash this idea until you've heard the whole thing out, but I was thinking that I could start a consulting business. You know, for young Glad wives—how to dress, how to hold an interview, how to negotiate with non-Glads in the trades. I mean if there's one thing I know . . .

I don't say that if I reject Uber she will be shunned by those bright young GSA wives for all intents and purposes, because she knows this already. She just doesn't want to accept the idea that the body she looks at in the plate glass windows is the one she inhabits. And I don't remind her that her course list is right out of the curriculum of the ridiculous college she wanted me to go to in the fall, because she knows that as well.

—You wouldn't be able to cope an hour if you institutionalized Thad—and you and I would never speak again. I hope you get that.

I see how small the corner is—the one she's backed herself into. Her nose turns red and I'm afraid she's started to cry under her Jackie O sunglasses. I know the next thing she'll do is sit down on the steps to some fancy shop and tell me how sorry she is again. And then I'll be up for nights worried about her. I want to tell her how much I love her even though I have to keep pulling away, but lately everything is jammed up inside me. So I say the only thing I can say at this point.

—I guess I didn't tell you yet. I'm going to go on a date with Uber. To see.

# CHAPTER
# 20

—To see? Allison asks cautiously, taking some tissue from her purse and blotting the lower rims of her glasses.

—If it would make any sense to spend some time with Uber. I'm not saying it would. It probably won't. But I've decided to consider it. You know, objectively, I say.

Later I'll make a call to Uber, of course, to see when he's free, so she'll never find out there wasn't actually a date in the works.

—I guess it couldn't hurt to give it a little objective thought, she says. —We could get Thad on a waiting list and hold off on actually placing him there until we see. But I'm still going to sketch out my business plans, get some input from Al. I really think I might be on to something.

I'm hoping her system won't wind tighter until she springs into a real mood.

—You really need something new if you're going out. And there's a suit I was looking at. Right over there, she says, pointing to a boutique in an old brownstone across the way.

—Look, I don't want you to feel any pressure here, she says as she holds her hand up in an effort to stop the traffic.

*ah, no pressure.*

—You're just going out with him once maybe, she says as she bullies a limousine into stopping.

—You don't have to see him again after that if you don't want. You can even leave the date early if it's insufferable. I'll give you taxi money. This is your time, Lyn. It shouldn't be about anyone else. That's what I've been trying to say. I'll do anything to put things right. How's your head today?

—It still hurts, but not too bad.

She digs a bottle of Brain Freeze out of her purse and hands me two tablets.

—This morning I was looking at that TV station, she says. —And they had a feature article about how young girls are suddenly shaving their heads and having initials tattooed into the backs of their skulls. You've started your first trend, she says, starting up the stairs to the shop. —Did I say I'm thinking about going on a diet? I don't want to look wan, just lose five pounds. More than that would ruin my face. I was like you for years, you know. Always svelte. You're such a beautiful girl. I hope you know that. I really do think I can get things right this time. For us. So I don't want you to worry, if Uber . . . if you decide you don't want to pursue this, she says, pausing at the landing.

Allison's mind won't stop running. She's always been like that. Down the street, into the car, back up the stairs to see if Thad's all right, out the door again to hand her husband the sword he left on the front hall table. If she could run after me all day to see what I get up to, she would.

—Are you going out to dinner? she asks.

—Too much conversation. Maybe the movies.

—The photographers might use their infrared cameras to track you. Remember Mabel Wong, Glaucous's wife?

—I'm not sure.

—Glaucous wears blue chain mail. Anyway, the media planted a tiny camera in his wife's popcorn when she went to the movies with a *questionable* male friend. They got a whole stream of intimate moments on film. But what they didn't count on was her swallowing the camera. They had her on film down to her alimentary canal.

—You're making that up.

—Well . . .

—You're so bad.

At least manic brings out her sense of humor.

—You know he's fighting a match in a couple of days.

—Uber? I thought his next match wasn't until September.

—It's a benefit for Children's Hospital. I think you should go. You can raise some money for a good cause and it would give the media just enough, without giving them anything at all. Afterward, you could go out for a bite to eat with him.

Allison suggests I would make the more striking and photo-heavy statement if I arrived at the benefit match in simple black. So I let her tug me along, feeling like something fixed to the rear bumper of a car. Inside the shop, she goes to work.

—It should convey the right message, she says.

The message being that a woman can express grieving in good label stock.

I keep telling her I don't care what I wear but she goes out of her mind about this stuff. I think she's always found a way to contain the things she can't talk about by fastening zippers, collars, cuffs, hooks and eyes, and belts.

I have to tell her several times that she doesn't need to sit inside the dressing room with me to remove the dresses from the hangers. But she wants to be there, like I'm picking out my wedding dress or something. I'm going the limit to restrain myself and ride the mood.

In the eighth store, I lose it. The space is so small we knock knees when I pull my T-shirt over my head. Before she hands me the same dress I'm sure I've tried on in three different stores already—just like one she wore when she was twenty and turned heads—she checks the price tag. Allison makes a small but perceptible click with her tongue, which is, I know, her way of expressing weariness over the cost of a well-made outfit. And with this cost, the cost of everything else, because that's the way it is with Allison. Things build exponentially and drop quickly. And though I understand, I understand, I understand, I can't understand another minute.

—You have to stop! I yell. —You just have to stop! I don't need your help. With anything!

As I try to take the dress off in that wedged space, all we can hear is the camera that's mounted on the ceiling, moving back and forth, watching me undress. And when I finally get it over my head, I see that Allison looks as if she's losing oxygen. She makes that face, like women in the other dressing rooms must be whispering about her. She stops removing dresses from hangers. She just lets the black fabric sit in her lap like a pet she doesn't know what to do with.

Then she gets up and excuses herself, waiting outside the door until I finish dressing. Her mood shifts entirely. Like a funeral procession, we go back to the store where we had placed something on hold. When I think we finally have things sorted out, a dress bag in hand, she suggests we browse the makeup selection before heading back to the club— which is her way of normalizing, I guess.

—You really shouldn't go alone, she says. —To Uber's match.

I can hear it in her voice. A new panic has set in about my personal safety. We hit on this one frequently. I rim my eyes in sample eyeliner, tilting the counter mirror. She begins to work that theme about things being a whole lot different than they were when she was my age—how we can't just go about freely anymore. Maybe she wants me to take her on my date with Uber? I don't ask.

The lines around my eyes thicken.

—I'll be fine, I say.

She almost laughs and then she quickly speeds through a catalog of people who could harm me in this world.

—Rapists, arsonists, hackers—don't laugh, I'm serious— identity thieves, murderers, for Christ's sake, Ponzi artists, biographers.

—You have to calm down, I say. —No one's writing my biography. And I can always take Mark along.

The clerk, who has been waiting for an opportunity to interrupt, steps over to us with an ingenuous smile and asks if she can show us anything.

—Cotton balls, I say, indicating my botched effort with the eye pencil.

All of my fingertips are blue with color. From a drawer this woman puts three cotton balls into a tiny plastic bag and says that will be a dollar. I give her a look but Allison pays out before I can stop her.

—You're not the parent, she tells me when the woman has gone. —Don't tell me to calm down like that in front of other people.

The lines around my eyes smear badly as I work away. But I catch something of Allison's expression in my peripheral vision and know I better look at her.

It's obvious that she's doing her best to keep it together.

—This rule, that you can't marry anyone else, it's obscene, I say.

Not that I want another father, certainly not another gladiator.

—*Uxor Totus,* she says, almost in tears again.

—Do they just sit around someone's back office down in New York and make this shit up by the hour? It's probably botched Latin at best.

—It's been harder lately, she says. —It's been hard to

believe I've made any good decisions at all. About any-thing.

—You're fine, Allison.

—Look what I've done to you—this whole situation.

I hand her a clean cotton ball. She wipes her eyes. Threads of cotton stick in her wet lashes. I tell her to be still as I gently pull the bits of white out.

—I'll take Mark with me to the match, and I've got the dress. Everything's cool.

Sometimes it's a toss-up as to who takes more energy, Allison or Thad.

—I've been trying to figure it out, how it happened, you know? I don't mean the sequence of events but my complete lack of thinking. You know I always wanted to have a family. That was the important thing. That's the one thing I can say I did right.

—I know that.

—And I didn't go out and pick a Glad for a husband. You know that too, don't you?

—Tommy kind of explained that.

—Tommy did?

She looks away, considers this, and continues.

—Things will work out, I say. —You're just tired.

Maybe I say this to get away from the counter, from the store, the hunt.

I've started to have that feeling I get about Thad. I've called Julie three times already to check on him. But I just want to get home, make his favorite dinner, and watch something idiotic with him on TV.

I'm aware of my mother's voice again as if she's calling me from the far end of a hallway.

—You think you'll ever be able to forgive me? she asks.

I've thought about what it would be like if she told me one day that she had screwed this whole business up. But I assumed she'd be eighty or something. Allison looking back. Allison's work of creative nonfiction. And when I anticipated her atonement I thought I'd be relieved, that I'd have a sense of clarity or peace. I imagined saying I understood because in many ways I do and I feel nothing but sad for her. But now that she wants me to say this, my throat feels dry and I start coughing.

So we stand there with our eyes completely messed up in this stupid store on Newbury Street. I'm hacking away and she's sealing and unsealing the bag that holds the last cotton ball. After a while I stop coughing and I can see she's given up waiting for me to say something. Her arms kind of go slack and she hoists her purse up on her shoulder again.

And if I were to ask Allison to forgive me for something? Maybe it would be about cracking my head open and letting the monster out of my skull—the one that doesn't want to be her. I don't even want to pretend I do anymore. And that's shearing right through the cord that binds us.

—We better pick up Thad, she says.

# CHAPTER
# 21

We train in secret every night at five unless it's just impossible to shake the media. Today I put on a pair of tight pink jeans, white wig, lime green blouse, and red sunglasses in order to leave work, hoping to pass for Avon, the girl who mans the register. I take off at a clip in five-inch tiger skin heels—the way she does—running down to the subway with my other clothes in a couple of value meal bags, just as the paparazzi careen into the drive-through looking for me.

Most of the time I tell Allison I'm still salting fries when I'm already in gear—building strength, not burgers. She mentions the change in my physique, and I tell her I'm doing more weights and less cardio when I work out, because I read something about osteoporosis and don't want to get it. She gives me a funny look and then goes off to find Thad.

I had to tell Lloyd what I'm up to—that I'm trying to see if I could compete—so he'd agree to train me. Always one to promote the women's leagues, Lloyd loves the whole concept.

He dug up this beautiful silver and copper breastplate for me to train in and promised not to tell Julie. On the first evening, Lloyd tears up, saying he wants to see that moment when the daughter of seven gladiators steps into the arena. Later, Mark said it was like watching DeNiro's La Motta in *Raging Bull*, to see his father carry on like that.

I wanted to say, *This is about survival, Lloyd, that's it, nothing more.* But after a while, standing there watching him choke up, I felt pretty awkward and said maybe we should start and he said, *Yeah, okay sure.* And I went straight for the dummy's small intestines, not because I was angry at Lloyd, just at a lot of stuff that Lloyd wouldn't understand.

When I get down to the subway platform, I stop being Avon. I pull off the wig and sunglasses, get my Glad boots on, and throw my leather jacket around my shoulders. The minute I get on the Red Line, people begin to stare. Some people always stare, a lot of them at my boots because they have as many straps as the sandals, and are therefore undeniably Glad.

The air rushes hard now where I sit and there's a Ring Bearer at the far end of the car working away with his blowtorch—one of those people who practices complete nonviolence, except to subway cars, I guess, and has 108 piercings on their bodies that they fill with tiny rings.

A couple of years ago when the city got sick of all the graffiti, they got really efficient at stopping taggers. But then it became a fiscally unsound policy as we entered our current epoch, to spend all that money on sandpaper and baking soda and labor to keep the graffiti off. So the cleanup slowed and they pulled back to study the problem, and the bogus report that came out—I believe it was as streamlined as *The Life and Opinions of Tristram Shandy, Gentleman*—stated that Ring Bearers do most of the tagging. So the next guy who was hauled in for tagging around the city—who just happened to be a Ring Bearer—was actually ordered by a judge to remove all of his rings for one year. No one could quite match the punishment with the crime, and I remember Allison saying how crazy that was, paying a probation officer to check a guy's empty piercings. —They should be checking for empty stomachs, she said.

Allison has a legitimate thing about hunger. She was really poor when she was growing up—I mean barely-any-food poor—which explains a lot of things.

Right after his probation ended, the rings that guy removed, all 108, were found in a glass display case in the judge's house. The way a museum might exhibit amulets wrapped up with a mummy, he had this mannequin laid out in a case, complete with every piercing in just the right place. It was like showing off a collection of Third Reich glassware or Saddam Hussein's pistol. And I think this made some people take a step back from any vague respect they might have held for the court system, while the rest of us had already backed up so far we had long since dropped off the edge.

But you can't put a good virus down. So the Ring Bearers

who used to tag, ride the trains now with mini-torches, cutting extra windows in the subway cars—in the shape of peace signs, of course. And that's how panel art got started—sculptors taking the metal panels the Ring Bearers cut out and using them in their work. There's a famous artist in SoHo who's made his whole career on the stuff. And why not, if you're going to imprison someone for draining a can of spray paint or wearing too many rings, you might as well go crazy and cut the place up and make something of beauty out of it.

The district attorney filed a lawsuit against the SoHo guy to get the panels returned—can't you just see them running around matching panels to subway cars and welding them all back into place?—but then he had to bow out of the case because he found out his sister-in-law had purchased one of the sculptures and there was no way she was having her high-end art dismantled for the cause. And now the city is looking into training a team of homeless citizens as spot welders—which should get the city about five minutes of glorious PR until it's discovered they don't give their trainees safety suits, goggles, or ventilation (aka air).

And they think my culture is mad.

The Ring Bearer is staring at me now without break and thank God it's my stop. It's not that I take it personally. Allison told me they don't do anything to Glads other than make intense eye contact with us—hoping we'll change our violent ways. But it gets kind of freaky after a while.

Allison says she just looks on it—on her need to remain

aloof—as performance art. But I'm not in the mood to perform today.

I step onto the platform and his face rushes away into the next tunnel. A woman in a worn raincoat and natty hat puts her hand on my arm and that makes me jump of course. And she says, —My nephew was in the GSA.

That's the thing a lot of people don't like to admit, that they know someone, or are connected to someone, in the GSA— we practically all are.

—You're his daughter, aren't you? she smiles timidly. —Tommy G.'s daughter?

—I guess we kind of look alike? Some people tell me that anyway.

She assures me we do. I thank her and move on.

Tonight I'm the first to get to the empty storefront where we train. I've rigged some car-mechanic lights, since most of the lighting was gutted and the last tenants painted the walls black. There's a sink with running water and that's painted black too—thick with house paint. The only thing that isn't black is the red bathroom door. Lloyd and Mark pull up in the van in the alleyway, carrying cold drinks and bags of sand.

Once inside, Lloyd nails a ten-pound bag of sand to the wall by its edging, so none of the sand spills out.

—Okay, your job, he says, —is to try and slash the bag open, while Mark does everything he can to keep you from getting to it.

Mark gives me this playful look, and Lloyd hands me a

long sword. At first, Mark works me into a sweat, pushing me away with his shield each time I make an approach. But when he sees how frustrated I'm getting, he steps aside at the last second and I just rip the hell out of the bag and the sand flies everywhere. The sand simulates the beginning of an arena floor, which is fine. Lloyd wants me training in sand, but he yells at Mark to get serious.

Going over to his athletic bag, Lloyd rubs his stubbled chin and says, —Let's switch it up.

Now he throws both of us short swords that he's edged in white adhesive tape at the tips and down the length of the blades. I have one of Tommy's shields from when he started out and Lloyd tells me to pick it up. Then he puts an arm around my shoulders and leads me away from Mark for a moment, across the length of the room. Lloyd has this funny way of strutting—maybe the pride of a man who wishes he was still heading into the arena. In the bank of mirrors, I wonder at the image I've produced. I look fully Glad now, the black leather skirt and cropped top, the armbands and knee-high sandals, the armor and shield.

—Think of someone you really hate, Lloyd says, stopping in front of the mirrors to consider his muscles perhaps, the way they're articulated in comic book fashion by the lights.

—What do you mean?

—You don't have to tell me, just get someone in mind.

—The head of Caesar's?

—If that's what does it for you. When you fight, see his face superimposed over Mark's face.

—That's kind of creepy, Lloyd.

Mark is standing there with his arms folded across his chest, his hair hanging down over his eyes, his breast-plate still on from an afternoon at the Ludus, waiting, smiling at me in the reflection, no doubt trying to lip read.

—Maybe now that you're getting to know him, you might be thinking Uber's not so bad, Lloyd says. —He might be coming around to the house. He could bring you flowers, maybe take you out to dinner or the movies. These things happen. You end up fighting a friend or a colleague. I've been through it, it happens to lots of Glads. So you have to know how to function in that kind of fight.

Now I'm looking away. I sure don't want to talk about Uber. I've been feeling pretty bad knowing if I do arrange to fight him, it's going to turn the guy inside out. But then there's Tommy of course.

—Can we just spar for a while? I ask. —I can work on the hate thing later.

—*Just* spar? Like *just* fighting and *just* losing a body part?

—You're right, but . . .

—There won't be tape on the blades in the arena. So if you don't plan on beating Uber, I'm the wrong person to train you.

—Well, I . . .

—You know, I wouldn't be doing this if I didn't think you stood a chance, he says.

Then Lloyd begins to rub my sword arm to limber me up.

—I want you to go at Mark with everything you've got. Remember he's a little weak on balance ever since that diving incident in the Bahamas. The more you have him shifting about, the quicker he's going to fall. And use your helmet today so you get used to it.

—You're telling me about your own son's weaknesses, I laugh.

—That's what I'm saying. Right now, he's your competitor. Not your best friend, not my son. Your job is to take him out of the game.

It's never a straight line if you want to be Glad. You have to be able to make a lot of twists and turns in logic.

—Are we doing this or what? Mark calls impatiently. I'm not sure if he overheard us.

My helmet is one of Mouse's lightweight prototypes that polishes up well, covers my forehead and cheeks, and leaves my eyes uncovered. There's some narrowing of peripheral vision but I have no trouble watching Mark as he holds his helmet in his hands and decides to let it drop back into his bag. He's looking at me now, like he's not sure. Like maybe this storefront is too full of wrong ideas. I know he'll fight me because he's Lloyd's son, because I've asked for his help. But I also know, looking at his expression, that he feels squeezed on all sides.

—You sparring without your helmet? Lloyd calls over to him.

—It's too hot, he says.

I've seen people spar both ways—with and without. Lloyd doesn't press him.

We walk to the center of the room. Mark smiles at me and I try to see the face of the Caesar's man. But it doesn't work. All I can see is Mark's wistful look. We get our swords ready, our shields up. Lloyd blows the whistle for us to begin.

The first minute is about clashing, and I hear Lloyd's voice, telling me to move right, left, dodge, weave. Mark hits my shield with his sword, narrowly missing my diaphragm, but I'm able to turn at the last second. His eyes widen and he calls, —Time.

—You okay? he asks me.

—What's going on? Lloyd says.

—I think she needs more padding, Mark says.

—We've only got another twenty minutes, Lloyd says, looking at his watch.

—I'm fine, I tell Mark.

—Then let's do this thing, Lloyd says, and blows the whistle again.

I've noticed that Mark tends to start by moving to the right today so this time I counter and move in quick with my sword. Maybe the tape is more for show than anything else, because I open up a line of blood along his sword arm. I realize I'm staring at his cut, and in a moment of combat, this is when Mark should take advantage. But he's waiting for me.

—What the hell? Lloyd says.

—Sorry, I say. —The tape isn't working.

—I was talking to Mark.

—Everything's cool, man, Mark says.

—It's my fault, I say, but I give Mark a look, like he has to stop acting so lame.

Lloyd goes over to his kit and adds more tape to both swords. When we're back in position, he says, —This isn't a social club, in case anyone's confused here. Let's see some fighting.

This time he blasts his whistle.

The minute I raise my sword, I feel like I can't get any traction. It's hard to explain, but watching Mark, the way he moves, it's like he's swimming in molasses. Each time I thrust, Mark meets me with a lethargic response, just enough to avoid injury. He makes almost no effort to use his sword and I know Lloyd is about to yell at him again. And as much as I try to throw a mental slide show of hated creatures up on my mind's screen, I just keep seeing how ambivalent Mark looks and I finally shout, —OKAY!

Everything stops.

—LOOK, I say. —I'M GOING TO FIGHT *UBER*. So you have to get over yourself so I can do that. I need you to actually *fight* me.

—But you get how crazy this is, don't you? Mark asks.

—So it's fine if you want to fight, and not me?

—I'm not saying that.

—You're not?

—I'm saying, his voice drops, —I'm saying I'd like you to stick around for a while.

—Then show me how to fight, damn it, so I can do that.

And in this moment I start to think about what Lloyd said. And I honestly don't know if this should be about hatred. I don't want to hurt Uber, and yet if I cave and marry him, and keep this Gladiator Wives thing going not just for my family, but for *girls everywhere*, as the ads say, that's guaranteed sorrow at my door. I look at the black walls of the old dance studio, the black sink, and I wonder how the impulse came one day, to cover every last thing in black. Maybe they were listening to that early Stones song "Paint It, Black."

I raise my shield and shout, —NOW!

The sounds of metal strikes begin in earnest. I can feel each vibration through my bones and into the floor. I hit his sword arm again, and this time there's only a red mark, a welt, and I go for his stomach. Mark holds nothing back now. I feel the blows to my legs, my armored chest. And when he hits my throat for a quick second, barely grazing it, I feel it close up as I try to catch my breath. When he pauses momentarily to make sure I'm all right, I strike him across the brow. I see I've hit him pretty hard, the way he reels back. And I have this realization that all of us have too much power where life and death are concerned. But I don't like to think about that much. And I'm about to go at Mark again before he gets his bearings when Lloyd shuts us down.

Maybe it's the look I have, I don't know, but he blows his

whistle and I stop, breathing hard. He goes over to the cooler now and hands Mark a chill pack for his forehead. Then he throws me an orange Fanta. He tells me we'll work on shield technique tomorrow. Zipping up his bag, he looks at both of us and says, —You make me proud.

# CHAPTER

# 22

*Like an ancient Roman column, the gladiator's daughter is an essential support, holding up the structure of the Glad family,* Bylaw 82.

I once asked Allison, when she recited this to me, if she thought I was more Doric, Ionic, or Corinthian. She didn't think I was all that funny.

A couple of weeks before he died, I was down in the kitchen cutting up vegetables for salad when Tommy walked in. I had just gotten home from work and was starving for something fresh. He pointed out that I was still wearing that dopey paper hat they make us wear.

After I pulled out the bobby pins and tossed it his way, I realized that Tommy looked pretty keyed up. He had his computer open and he wanted me to see an online encyclopedia page. The subject: the Kali Yuga. He set it down next to the tomatoes to show me.

—Mark has that game, I think.

He laughed. —It's not a game. Yugas are periods of time. See, it says here they're defined in an ancient astronomical treatise.

—You're reading ancient astronomical treatises these days? Mostly he liked to read competition magazines and weapons catalogs.

—No, I just found this in the encyclopedia.

—You just found it?

—I've decided to read the whole encyclopedia.

—The good, the bad, and the make-believe?

—Just expanding my mind a little. So this treatise is how they came up with all the Hindu and Buddhist calendars.

—O . . . kay, I said, putting my knife down to give him my full attention. I begin to think this was his second unravel, the first one at that hotel in Rome.

He explained that the Kali Yuga is one of four stages of development the world goes through, each one lasting about four hundred thousand years.

—You're already into the *K*'s? I asked.

—I skip around a lot. So it looks like we're *in* the Kali Yuga, right now, he said. —The dark age. That's what they call it, not me.

—The dark age. Nothing would shock.

He leaned near my shoulder, eager for me to read the entry aloud so we could talk about it.

I pushed the finely chopped carrots aside and read to him.

*—Rulers will become unreasonable: they will levy taxes unfairly. Rulers will no longer see it their duty to promote spirituality or to protect their subjects: they will become a danger to the world. Avarice and wrath will be common, men will openly display animosity toward each other. People will have thoughts of murder for no justification, and they will see nothing wrong with that mind-set. Family murders will also occur. People will see those who are helpless as easy targets and remove everything from them. Men with false reputation of learning will teach the Truth and the old will betray the senselessness of the young, and the young will betray the dotage of the old. People will not trust a single person in the world, not even their immediate family. Even husband and wife will find contempt in each other. It is believed that sin will increase exponentially, whilst virtue will fade and cease to flourish. Alongside death and famine being everywhere, men will have lustful thoughts and so will women. People will without reason destroy trees and gardens. There will be no respect for animals, and also meat eating will start. People will become addicted to intoxicating drinks. Men will find their jobs stressful and will go to retreats to escape their work. Teachers will no longer be respected and their students will attempt to injure them.*

—The whole thing's kind of spooky, isn't it? I said.

—Maybe we should stop eating meat.

—You better talk with Allison, I said. —The freezer is half cow.

—We could give it away.

—Before she gets home? I joked.

He got another knife out of the drawer and began to cut up the tomatoes.

—Sure, why not? he said earnestly.

I had this picture of the two of us carrying armloads of wrapped meats out to the sidewalk. Cutlets and ribs, sirloin and rump. Setting up a table and a couple of chairs like a lemonade stand. Handing out everything to passersby. As if we could give away our whole violent culture. Allison would pull up to the house from her shopping trip and scold us fiercely, dying a thousand deaths of humiliation as the neighbors looked on. As he handed a shank to someone, Tommy would try to explain by saying we're in a bad Yuga.

—She's at the store buying pork chops for tonight. You might disorient her, I said.

Never being one who wanted to disorient Allison, or even trouble her as far as I could tell, Tommy stopped pursuing this line of thinking.

—You ever wonder if this whole thing, this business . . . , he began.

—What?

—Gladiator sport . . .

I knew what was coming next. I had seen my fifth father, Larry, go through this—the Vietnam vet. He had had that sudden gaping doubt about what he was doing, about the very nature of Glad sport, Glad culture. I was younger then and probably didn't understand that he was going through a breakdown. I do remember, however, the way Allison talked him down and kept him going long enough for him to die a flawless death in the arena. I don't mean she wanted him to die, just the opposite. She was worn out from losing husbands by then. But she always held out hope that they would serve out their time and be released to her.

—Some people say Uber's heart is as dark as iron, I said.

I had no idea really. But I was trying to think of something, some way for Tommy to get his nobility back. Tommy stood there for a long time, his knife poised, slit halfway into a tomato, the juice and seeds on his cutting board and fingers.

—There's a lot to consider, he said vaguely, ready to drop the subject.

He was nervous about the match—I finally got that. This whole business about time, his sudden obsession with civilization, he was trying to distract himself from thinking about the fight with Uber. I got a pencil out of the drawer and after I put a fine point on it, I wrote on the grocery list: *Vegetarian foods ONLY for Tommy while in training.*

—We'll tell Allison your trainer wants you eating this supercharged Indian diet. We'll buy lots of cilantro and chutney and chickpeas, I said.

Then he seemed to relax a little and lit up a cigarette.

—Thanks for getting it, he said.

I laughed.

—What? he asked.

—After your next fight, you and Allison should retreat to

Paris. Maybe there's less Kali Yuga going on in Paris these days. And, I understand they've banned smoking in their restaurants.

Tommy smirked, took a last drag on his cigarette, and put it out. I brought the salad over to the breakfast nook with two smaller bowls. There we could look out at Allison's orange poppies and white irises. While I shook up the dressing, he asked if I was doing any secret dating, if I had a new boyfriend. He understood that it's necessary, with Allison, to go underground if the guy isn't Glad culture.

I sat down across from him and opened my napkin.

—Did she ask you to spy?

—Well . . . yeah, he said, stabbing a strip of red bell pepper. —But you know she'll never get anything off me.

I didn't want to go into the whole thing about Giancarlo. I said, —I think I just need to be alone for a while. I'm trying to sort some things out, you know?

—Such as?

—You really want to hear this?

—I really do.

I drizzled dressing over the salad, tossed it, and filled our bowls. Then I sat there so long, my fork in midair, he probably thought I had become a living statue.

—You're not going to like it, I said.

—That's okay.

—You know, neo-Glad culture is your life. It's Allison's. It's what you do. And I'd die if I lost the people I love, but

I . . . I think Joe Byers won't talk to anyone because he can't live with himself. Or the rest of us, for that matter. And I'd like to be able to live with myself before I get old like him.

Tommy just nodded, like he got it. Then we both got pretty quiet. I think that's as far as he could take it—and I honestly don't think he minded my trying to express the things he couldn't or wouldn't.

A couple of months ago Mark and I saw *Hamlet* on TV, an old one. And I kept wondering why Hamlet was pushing Ophelia so hard to go mad. And then I realized he had to get her to hold his madness for him, because as much as he needed to go stark raving lunatic, he had to keep one foot in the game in order to exact revenge. I sometimes wonder who Allison is holding for. But I didn't say anything about this to Tommy. I might have eventually if he had lived.

Tommy and I ate our salads and looked out at the garden because it really is a place of tranquility. When we were done, I went upstairs to see what Thad was up to and Tommy and I just kind of went about our day and neither of us brought the subject up again. That was just two weeks before he fought Uber.

# CHAPTER
# 23

Benefit matches are held at night and that's when you see the best advertising. People come just to watch the way the ads glow above the stadium, every fifth image about the contentments of the Glad life. They look more and more like they've been ripped off from Marine recruitment ads.

Uber gets full use of the emperor's box for a couple of months now that he's champ. He asked if I'd be willing to use the box tonight in his honor in that overly polite way he has with me. There's red silk drapery on all sides except the one facing center stage and the couches are Roman style. Grapes—you get those if you tell the waiter that's what you want—but thank God there's no one standing around peeling them for you.

Tonight's benefit has been promoted as a novelty night, so no one knows what to expect. Neither Mark nor I remember seeing a novelty night before, so we think this is something new Caesar's has gotten up to. We have seen a dozen stall acts so far and we've listened to soft-soap commentary from Glad analysts. Now it's ten at night and Mark is growing impatient. He's got his hands up underneath his T-shirt, punching his fists around, looking bored. The tattoos on his arms flex with each jab. I'm aware, though it's not visible, that he has a tiger on his chest that moves when his pecs move. Of course he doesn't want to feel used, who does, so I was clear over the phone when I invited him that I was meeting Uber after the match.

—I can't tell if you're going to marry the guy or fight him, he said.

I knew he was busy gaming as we spoke. Mark is always gaming. I explained that I was going down to New York in a few days, to talk with Caesar's about setting up the match. Lloyd thought I was ready. Meanwhile, I had to keep Allison on track.

But Mark didn't get it.

—Meeting Uber after a night match is called surrender, not figuring things out. Of course we can always hope he eats it.

Suddenly Julie's voice was in the background. Julie is always ready to promote a good Glad alliance and I knew how worried she was about Allison. She was quite verbal about this idea, that a marriage to Uber would get the log out of the saw's way. So I heard her through the phone when she told Mark to chill. Not a word from Lloyd, who is strictly a corporeal man and stays out of his wife's pursuits.

In the emperor's box now I watch the bloody sand on the

arena floor as it's raked for the next event. Mark and I are each sipping a Fire Eater, a nonalcoholic beverage distributed free to the crowd. It does things to the lining of your stomach if you drink too much, so I always try to stop at slow burn. Mostly it makes you incredibly thirsty so you buy bottles and bottles of water afterward and that's how the concessionaires make their money, and the stuff's pretty addictive if you ask me.

Mark brought his computer so he can be on Second Life between acts. He's trying to get his alter ego, Cron, into New Rome without getting offed. The place is so well guarded Cron could get incinerated the minute he's spotted by the guards. Mark wouldn't mind except it takes days to build a character if you want to get the skin right, the hair, the clothing—especially the boots if you add things like knives to them, otherwise you've got the generic characters everyone comes in with and you're marked as a *noob*.

Mark opens his phone and starts texting me. It's the only way to have a conversation in the amphitheater without worrying about someone eavesdropping. He writes: *I hate the New Romans.*

I nod in agreement.

*The GSA hasn't said a word about Children's Hospital tonight,* I write back.

*Weird.*

*Whereas my BLACK DRESS has been captured on the monitors from every angle except the floor up.*

*We'll see those inner thighs on late-night television, no doubt.*

He razzes me each time my fashion ratings are thrown up on the screens—updated every twenty minutes or so with comparative stats against a running list of young actresses and models and their wardrobes—and it's possible I begin to see why Allison built such a fire under this dress. Like she says, if they're going to make a statement, better it be yours, not theirs. The only thing is, I don't think it's mine.

*I have to be more my own person,* I write.

Mark doesn't mind when I get random.

*That's what I've been saying. You can't be dating Uber. Come on, let's destroy the moment and go over to Harvard Square.*

Just then on one of the jumbo screens a photo montage begins—a sequence showing me from the time I was born up to this nanosecond. No mercy here. We have my naked bum at six months, braces complete with head gear, acne, squinting, too-thin dress showing off my figure in the sunlight, exposed breast as I came up from a rough dive in a municipal pool, the stupid things I posted on the Internet in high school, and of course plenty of shots with my ever-molting family. A lot of the pictures look Photoshopped and I don't even remember half the images. I am shown with guys, the caption *Early Romance* across their bellies, though most are friends like Mark or just acquaintances. And there's a pet monkey I never had, sitting on my shoulder in one shot. That would be okay except it makes my shoulder look as big as Lloyd's.

*A pet monkey?* I write.

Mark's fingers fly and I read his energized scrawl.

*Who's that guy sitting on your front steps?*

I look up at a man in a plain gray suit, a small valise by his side.

*Maybe he was selling magazine subscriptions?*

*So you're telling me there's something a little unreal about this version of your life?*

*I'm telling you.*

I see Mark's mouth moving now though I can't hear anything because sixty thousand people have started to cheer. Uber has entered the arena, in one of those short Roman skirts and full sterling chest plates expressing his contours—which is a style more about high-ranking soldiers than gladiators—but he looks buoyant and the outfit suits him. He takes a mic from one of the officials and shouts, —FOR CHILDREN'S HOSPITAL!

Fans stand on the benches and begin to stomp. And if you can't taste iron at a moment like this you never will, because Uber looks ready to go after the fair and the brave for the kids. It's rare that a fight is taken to the death in benefit matches, so you get a particular kind of crowd ready for fun, willing to stop at solid injury. Uber walks over to the emperor's box until he's standing directly below us, some twenty or thirty feet down, in his lace-up high-tops and leather gloves to his elbows that cover everything except his fingers. For all his gear, he looks exposed somehow, his expression somewhere between tough and shy, but I think it's probably confusion as he tries to read my face without his glasses. I finally had to ask and he told me his eyes swell up so badly he can't wear contacts.

The stadium quiets as he unsnaps his helmet and lifts it from his head.

—He's going to fight without his helmet? I say aloud, completely forgetting myself.

It's not like me to forget about the cameras and mics. There, up on instant replay on all the big screens, my worried little self repeats the same words over and over. —*He's going to fight without his helmet?*

The shaved head, the saucer eyes, I've become strictly mug shot. —*He's going to fight without his helmet?*

It's a rather benign question, but it expresses too much interest coming from me. And in this moment I'm someone else's daughter, not Allison's, because I know she's dying watching the match at home in bed, Thad curled around her feet. She wanted to come tonight and we got into it and I finally had to say, —*I can't take all of this on right now*, and left. You'd think it was enough that I was going, that I was dragging Mark along so she wouldn't worry. She's been driving me insane ever since Tommy died. So I get it, but she's still driving me insane.

Uber turns and watches one of the screens where I keep saying the same thing. And when I've finally grown quiet on the monitors, he swings round and throws his helmet up to where I'm seated.

I lean out over the rail and catch it before it tumbles back. Fans start to hoot and cheer.

*This isn't bullfighting*, Mark taps hastily once I'm seated again. *He's dedicating the fight to you. Shit.*

All I can do is shrug. Then Mark gets up and stands in that blind spot just behind my left shoulder. It feels odd that he doesn't put an arm around me as he often does when things are nuts, but I don't think either of us is prepared to answer for a small action that would become large news.

I place the helmet on the ledge in front of me and I can feel how annoyed Mark has gotten. Now he's up on the monitors, his unshaved face just behind my newly shaved head. The media speculations stream about Lloyd's scowling son, the very eligible bachelor who is training under his father. My whole body is full of heat now, a thousand pinpricks.

Thank God the horns sound.

Everyone watches the doors and gates that open into the arena.

Uber reaches up to adjust his helmet, smiles to himself realizing there's nothing there, and gets his sword and shield ready. He moves into the center of the arena and slowly pivots, his eyes tracking all the doors.

I have seen men fight in twos and threes and clusters. There were twenty-five at once one Christmas Eve down in Florida and I think that's the biggest match I've personally witnessed and I hope I never have to see anything like that again, live or otherwise. That was the first time I told Allison I wouldn't be coming to the arena as much. I've seen dwarfs engage dwarfs, two sets of conjoined twins fight each other, jungle and savannah cats, brown and black bears, pit bulls and roosters. The women's leagues seldom fight to the death, but many would prefer death to the way the human body can be maimed and scarred under torchlight by incarnate Amazons. For some, perhaps too many now, Glad sport has become strictly entertainment, just so much adrenaline and blood, the fighters a cash crop. But Tommy said people like that don't get it. They miss the larger mythology, the moments of Greek tragedy, the skill. He talked about repentance and loss and got me all the way to transformation. The way the psyche can know a match so that it becomes something beyond the physical. I wish I could weave it all together the way he did. I doubt it all added up—I tend to think it doesn't anymore—but you could see his passion.

The door on the far eastern side opens.

This one I have never seen: an elderly man, he has to be about seventy-five, and his wife, maybe in her late fifties, step timidly into the bright light. The woman carries such a short blade it's as if she's looking for a loaf of bread to slice and butter. She's five feet tall at most and her salt-and-pepper hair is wrapped in a bun at the back of her head. She wears a loose dress and an apron that covers her solid bosom and goes almost to her hem, and fuzzy shoes that make her feet look as if they're wrapped in small mice. As I look at the monitor, I see how very blue her eyes are, like Uber's.

Uber stands poised, ready to fight two blurred figures.

The man's suit is a little rumpled, shirt buttoned up to his Adam's apple, no tie. He looks particularly feeble. He's stooped and carries a shield that pulls him farther ground-ward. They've given him a pair of scissors instead of a sword. He goes through a complicated shuffle, trying to wedge the scissors into the same hand that holds his shield, and I feel concern for him, that he's going to lose his balance and fall. But he frees that hand so he can place it around the woman's shoulders, and they walk toward Uber. Finally the man, clearly overburdened by his shield, sets it on the ground.

The words SPECIAL GUESTS flash. Then: MEET UBER'S PARENTS.

Romulus Arena goes absolutely silent. There's an audio announcement as well.

I type, *He's supposed to fight his parents? Or are they supposed to fight each other?*

Mark doesn't know what to say any more than I do and just types his favorite swear. There is a close-up of Uber's face. His eyes express complete bewilderment at events.

—Mother? Father? Uber calls out, squinting. He looks incredulous as he starts walking toward them.

Suddenly the man begins to dance a little jig. His wife tries to get him to stop but he won't. He calls to Uber, like a child asking to be picked for a turn at a party.

—Kill me! he says. —Kill me!

*Tim Burton lives,* Mark writes.

Uber rushes over to help his mother subdue his father. He places his sword and shield on the ground in front of them and puts a hand on his father's shoulder. His father, who has started to tear up, stops his dance. Uber holds his hands out for the knife and shears and places them on the ground as well. He embraces his parents and you can see him whispering to them with great emotion.

Maybe this is the moment when my feelings toward Uber shift. Caesar's wants us to kill everyone we love, if not in body, certainly in spirit. I realize I'm going to have to find another way—that I'm losing my impetus to fight him.

A generic celebrity fills us in on how the parents have been flown all the way from Norway, where they went into retirement a decade ago. We see clips from a recent interview with them. The father was one of the first underground Glads. So Uber *is* a Born In.

—He was always a good boy, the father says.

It seems clear to me that he has dementia from the way he talks, the disconnected look in his eyes.

—He was a sweet child. A little awkward sometimes, but bighearted, his mother says. Her discomfort at being interviewed is palpable.

—His father, who was in the GSE at the time, wanted him to have an activity that would give him confidence.

They managed, the celebrity tells us, through long hours

of work and setting aside their pennies, to get Uber into a Helmet Wearers group after school . . .

I feel this deep sense of relief that the fighting is done for the night but I guess I'm alone in this as discontentment starts to build in the amphitheater. People jeer and demand a real fight. Uber, face wet with tears, guides his parents toward the door they came through, walking away from his shield and sword—a completely stupid idea—but I can only imagine how seeing his parents this way has screwed him up.

Some people gather their things to beat the rush to the parking lot and the T. They fold their cushions, seal their coolers. We hear a great deal of grumbling, see a lot of disappointed faces. Bad feelings about the Gladiator Sports Association are voiced.

—Let's get out of here, Mark says.

Just then a second set of doors opens in the arena but no one appears. Uber watches it for a long time, then turns back to his parents. Mark grabs his jacket.

—I'll have to tell Lloyd, Mark says. —He's been complaining about the doors. Ever since the layoffs, maintenance has gone to hell.

I stand and start to climb the steps to leave the emperor's box. But then something compels me to go back to the railing. Uber walks slowly toward his weapons, looking clearly unsettled. Leaning over, I call out.

—Uber. Uber!

What I want him to do is look at that door because I'm certain something is about to spew from its mouth.

—UBER!

The mics pick up my voice now and I'm on every screen in the stadium.

—UBER! my voice booms. —PICK UP YOUR SWORD!

Almost the moment I say this a tiger is sent into the arena. I watch its leg and chest muscles as it moves, the intense fixed look. People fight each other to get back to their seats. There's a rush of noise and then it quiets.

—*Bengal, Indochinese, Malayan? Can we get a feed on the tiger,* an announcer says on the overhead speakers.

—*One endangered species looks another in the eye.*

Glad announcers love to caption. And how many times have we heard that one?

—*I understand their large canines are used for tearing meat off the bone. Let's ask our resident expert.*

But I don't hear the answer of the resident expert because I'm thinking about the fact that Uber's shield and sword are closer to the tiger than they are to him—it looks like twenty feet or more to his gear. The cat begins to raise one paw, its shoulders elevated, rear legs hunched as Uber starts to make his way toward his sword, appearing to move as if he's not moving at all. His parents get through their door in time, and it closes behind them with a noise only those giant doors can make and the sound startles the cat. It runs toward Uber.

The technicians turn the strobes on so that when the tiger springs, as it does, it moves in what appears to be slow motion. Uber jumps into the air simultaneously. He kicks the tiger in the chest and they both fall backward, their movements split into ribbons of action. Both flip around quickly to avoid landing on their backs. Uber grabs the scissors before the tiger leaps a second time. He drives them into the tiger's chest just as the tiger claws his face.

The animal drops, landing on its side. It lifts its head for a moment, and dies. Its tongue hangs from its mouth and blood pours from its chest into the sand.

The crowd cheers with sweet enthusiasm. The medics rush out and huddle around Uber. I've never felt sick to my stomach like this at a match before.

In the great volume of noise, Mark and I can talk aloud.

—He had some moves, he says. —I'll give him that.

—His face looks really bad.

—Come on, I'll walk you down to the locker room.

—I thought you didn't like the guy, I say.

—Those scars are going to be beautiful.

—So he's cool now?

Mark touches the place on his T-shirt over his tiger tattoo in solidarity.

—I hope Lloyd recorded it. I loved the thing with the scissors. And the little old man, he says. —You look kind of bloodless. You okay?

—I have to sit down.

Mark offers me some water and when I take the bottle my hand shakes.

—I think you drank too much Fire Eater, he says.

—I think I've had too much circus.

# CHAPTER
# 24

We make our way toward the locker rooms, the paparazzi hooding us with light, eager to kidnap us if they can. I push against their vests and cameras, determined to get through, Mark in tow. As one guy rushes toward me and another pushes him out of his way, one of their cameras strikes me in the chest.

—Hey! I shout, thrusting a hand in the air for everything to stop. Catching my reflection in the glass pane of the next door, I remind myself never to look like I'm about to raise the dead in front of the media again. I take a deep breath and try to slip into press conference mode.

—I know you have a lot of questions. But at this time I can't tell you anything more about Uber's condition than you already know. I'm paying a short visit and I'll be returning his helmet to him. So I wouldn't call this a romantic visit unless you consider surgery romantic.

There's a short spell of laughter and then questions are turned on me like a fire hose. Two Glads who were in tonight's competition have posted themselves at the door. The tall one has buttery dark skin with a tattoo on his chest of a victorious gladiator, his foot resting on his slain opponent. He helps us get inside the locker room. He tells me the ambulance will be here soon, and that Uber is going for professional stitching, so keep it short.

—Nice tattoo, man, Mark says.

We find Uber flat on his back on a massage table, his breastplate off, and a large bag of ice against the right side of his face. I walk over and stand close to him so he can see me with his visible eye. Mark hangs back for now.

—Thanks for coming, Uber says, wincing as he tries to smile.

He takes the ice pack away and I see that someone has used an ointment over his wounds, and there are enough butterfly bandages to set off a small migration. The eye is shut, the lid badly swollen and cut. I set the helmet down on a table and put the ice back in place. I'm standing in a half inch of water. There are bloody rags in a bucket near my feet, coolers of ice, a table with first-aid gear spread out along the top.

—Are your parents here? I ask.

—They've gone back to their hotel room to lie down. My father gets confused about things. Alzheimer's. My mother will bring him over to the hospital later.

Then he speaks so softly I have to lean in close to hear. The smell of blood and ointment fills my nostrils.

—Thanks for the warning.

—That was terrible, what they did to your folks.

—The worst.

I'm aware of Mark standing by the door, straining to hear, and I gesture for him to come over.

—This is my friend Mark. I think you met his father, Lloyd, of the Ludus Magnus Americus.

—Hey.

—Fine work with the scissors. You knew right where to strike.

—I picked that up from one of your father's videos, actually.

—*The Panther*.

—That's the one.

—I'll let him know.

It's clear that Uber is tired.

—Hope you don't mind. There's something I have to tell Lyn before they cart me out of here.

Now the awkwardness between them surfaces. Mark bobs his head and says to me, —Call me when you're ready to go. I'll . . . check out the urinals.

Mark wanders into the room where I first met Uber. He slumps down on a bench and looks at me with an expression I haven't seen before. If I had to make a guess I'd say Mark wishes I was moving my bald head close to his mouth to listen to his every word.

—I know this woman in Legal at Caesar's. I called her this afternoon, Uber says.

He pauses to swallow.

—I asked her if I could write a letter releasing you from the obligation to marry me. She was nervous talking to me, he says.

Uber tries to smile again but he produces that same unnatural expression.

—She read me the articles in my contract. I'm afraid there's nothing I can do. I'm sorry—I mean for you. If I can think of anything else . . .

I'm sure he understands that on my end it's less straightforward but binds just the same. The daughter of a gladiator doesn't have a contract per se but if I don't follow a rule this large, this intrinsic, my family will be shunned. Allison will be shunned. And this would be more than she could hold. Her heart would bleed perpetually and I'd spend my days stocking gauze and medical tape.

—I appreciate that you took the time. Maybe when you're on your feet we could go for coffee or something, I say.

—My doc says I shouldn't be long at the hospital. And my parents go back to Norway day after tomorrow.

—Oh, well, then, that's soon . . . that we could have coffee.

I nod to Mark now, to say it's time to go. Then I make a small effort and take Uber's hand just for a moment and I'm struck by how warm it feels. When you're in the stadium seats, the competitors are often bigger than life, even cartoonlike. It's easy to imagine that their hands and faces, the waxy glow of their skin, that they're somehow made of different material than normal people. You sometimes feel they're going to leap into the air and fly around the city after a competition instead of just driving home, going over to their clubs, or stopping at the store for bread. You can even feel that about your own father at times. I can't help but wonder what things would have been like if Uber and I had met in a different place in time.

Mark doesn't seem to care if the fans follow us or not tonight, and pretty soon we're riding along Memorial Drive in a fleet. The air just right, the light on the Charles, the slick sound of the wheels because the street washers have gone through. He turns the radio to a random station and I put my feet up on the dash and slink down in my seat so I don't have to think about the paparazzi as they try to keep up.

—So Friday let's do something, Mark says.

He names this expensive restaurant that has all these Buddhas and tiny vases with things not entirely flowers, cool lights at the bar, water sheeting down one wall.

—Are you asking me out on a date?

—Why not?

—Because we're friends.

—Could be more.

—Sometimes I think you only get interested if someone else is interested.

—Are you accusing me of human nature?

—Yes.

—Girls like me, you know. He smiles.

—Of course girls like you.

And they do. Next year he's supposed to sign a contract with the GSA and I already know that lots of girls want to cage Mark—I've heard some of them talking. And in time he will make the perfect Glad husband. Julie's seen to that.

—I need to get my head clear right now, I say.

—You like me, don't you?

—Stop.

—Just let me know if anything changes.

—I'll let you know.

Allison gets over her peevishness about not being invited to the stadium that night when she learns I have plans to see Uber again. Though the ownership of the house is still as undetermined as the number of moods in her day, she goes out and buys flats and flats of new plants for the garden and has all the windows of the house washed, even the ones in the basement, which is her way of saying she can waste money again. She calls her tile man to get him started on the front steps, which already look perfectly fine to me. There are ceramic samples clustered around the house and out in the yard. I try to ignore this industry and work a little on *A History of the Gladiator Sports Association*. Thad is happy to have us both around no matter what we're doing.

On Saturday night, Thad and I are hanging out in the kitchen playing Chutes and Ladders. He has his own logic to the game and sometimes he takes my game piece and suddenly shoots it up a slide. When it's his turn he likes to dawdle, angling around so he can see through our gates out to the street. Suddenly he calls out, —There's a striped man!

Concerned that one of the photographers has climbed the fence, I throw the lights on outside.

Uber is walking across the lawn in a striped delivery shirt. He trips over a pile of tile samples out in the yard, a full half hour early. He's clutching a paper bag. I'm reminded of that guy in *The Invisible Man*, his head wound in bandages. Only one eye is exposed so I give Uber credit when he avoids a landing in the rosebushes. He rights himself and follows the light toward the kitchen.

Looking down at his chest, he tries to pull the two halves of his tiny shirt together. On the pocket the name *Dave* is stitched in carmine thread.

—A friend of mine has a brother who works for a delivery service, Uber says. —I was kind of hoping we'd be able to slip in and out without notice.

He explains that Allison gave him the code to the gate. I see the *CONSTANT BEAUTY FLOWERS* truck, backed in and pulled as close to the house as possible, almost shearing off Allison's border of small crescent-shaped bricks. I put on the shirt he hands me over my tank top. But the cap keeps catching on my bandages so I decide I'm healed enough and rip the bandages off and get the cap in place.

—You think I'll pass? I ask.

—You look constantly beautiful to me, Uber says.

—Groan. We better hurry, I say.

I go over and give Thad a kiss on the cheek and grab my purse.

—Lyn's going to figure everything out tonight, Thad says to Uber.

I don't know why this makes me blush. I excuse myself and call up the stairs to let Allison know we're leaving now. She wants us to wait so she can come down and say hello, but I shout that we're late and kiss Thad again and hurry into the garden with Uber. Then I look back for a moment.

Thad appears to be a little lost, motionless, already waiting for my return. Allison has rushed downstairs and is waving to us now in one of her Chinese robes. She swoops an arm of billowing silk fabric around him with great affection, the way she always holds Thaddy. And suddenly I'm aware of how old my mother looks standing there. I don't mean culturally old, throwaway old, liver spots and crow's-feet old. I don't mean that she should cut and shift her face around to be younger and therefore more *likeable*. She's a beautiful woman and always will be. But what I mean is she looks worn thin.

If grief comes in waves, Allison is standing inside one of those waves, completely submerged as her eyes follow me out into the darkness. She's learned to breathe water, to see through water. I think of telling Uber to wait, so I can run back inside to say something to her, to express anything, really, but I can't find the thing to say. I know we better get out of here before the media catches on, so I remind myself to get Thad out tomorrow so she can have some time to go to the movies or get her hair done. We have always been good at repair.

Keeping our heads down, Uber opens the back doors to the van and I climb in and crouch near the crates of empty plastic vases, some with water at the bottom. The windows in the back are blackened. Uber hits his head when he pulls the driver's-side door open to get in.

—Are you all right? I ask.

—I'm great. Great, he says.

He fires up the engine and gets the gate open. Despite his best efforts to fool them, the paparazzi swarm.

# CHAPTER
## 25

Once we're on the road, the water in the vases begins to crest and slop over the sides and I'm sitting in water and decide to take my chances in the passenger seat. Uber has his head cocked at an odd angle to see the road.

—Do you like bowling or pool? he asks.

—Sometimes, I say. —Maybe it would be a little tough with your eye tonight?

—It's not too bad but it does kind of cut down on my peripheral vision.

He's driving erratically, and I offer to take the wheel but he says his friend, the one who lent him the van, made him promise he'd be the only one to drive.

One of the photographer's cars, a small Dodge, suddenly pulls up on our right side. He has the usual complement of cameras around his neck, and he's holding one out, shooting lots of photos. I recognize him from the time we took Thad to exercise at the club downtown, when we almost hit a wall. Just as I fasten my seat belt, Uber pulls into the side of the Dodge, the two cars grinding metal. I grab the dash as we're pitched about.

—You want me to drive? I shout.

—No, that's okay!

Uber clips his opponent's front wheel, then swerves.

The guy tries to hold his car steady but a UPS truck comes to a dead stop in his lane. I hear the sound as the Dodge's front end hits the rear of the truck.

When Thad and I go to the movie theater, we test our skills at driving with a game called DRAG RACE out in the lobby. He likes it when I strap him in to the plastic seat, and I always bring lots of quarters. Although some people think the object of the game is to get to the finish line in record time without hitting other vehicles or signs, for Thad it's about the pleasure of crashing and burning, watching the way his Ford GT can launch into walls, partitions, palm trees, flag men, and desert landscapes. I wonder if Uber has the same feeling about the game.

—Don't hesitate to let me drive, I say.

—Sorry. He's been on my tail for months. I've tried to get a restraining order. So let's see. Would you like to see a movie? Hit the shooting range? Indoor rock climbing? Fortune-teller?

—I'm afraid I get my fortune told more often than I'd like.

I start to explain about my brother when a police car

overtakes us, sirens and lights, and Uber pulls over. The officer looks like he's done a little boxing in his time. He stands about five feet nine or ten. Cheerless. Uber hands over his license and starts looking around the glove compartment for the registration while the cop shines his flashlight on us.

I'm trying to see this whole picture through his lens. A couple in flower delivery uniforms that clearly don't fit, the woman with a bald head and the letter *T* stitched into the back of her scalp, the man with his head wrapped tighter than a mummy, with single-eye vision, and no flowers to speak of. The officer looks over Uber's license, studies his half-shell face, and just as Uber opens his mouth ready to launch into an explanation that I would have paid to have heard, the guy starts to crack up.

—Oh man, am I happy to see you. Do you have any idea what my girlfriend is going to do when I bring home your autograph? You don't mind signing something for me, do you? She's your biggest fan. And I've been in the doghouse all week.

Uber removes his delivery shirt and underneath this is a button-down shirt that he also sheds and drapes neatly on the stick shift. Below this is a T-shirt he strips off, revealing his many scars, his recent cuts, and that fine torso. He stretches the T-shirt carefully over his lap and pulls a black marker from a leather bag, and scrawls his name.

—Mind? Uber says, and hands the supplies over to me.

—You're her, aren't you? the policeman asks.

—That would be me, I say.

—Damn, he says.

I add my signature above Uber's. Meanwhile Uber fishes in his wallet and produces two front-tier tickets to his next competition.

—You guys need an escort anywhere?

—We're cool, but there's a Dodge back there that could use a little help.

After I've heard all the date offers again—water polo, night-time boat ride, hot stone massage—I tell him what I really want is to just sit and talk for a while. So we head over to Peking Duck. Peking Duck gets a number of personalities that eat there regularly, like talking-head attorneys and owners of large car dealerships who star in their own bad commercials. No one ever bothers them. They never bothered Tommy or Allison either, so I figure we can eat a quiet meal.

Uber buttons up his shirt and I de-uniform. Once we're seated inside, I watch Uber order cashew chicken, beef chow mein, spicy dumplings, and hot and sizzling soup with a side of sautéed eggplant and shrimp fried rice. He explains that his trainer wants him to bulk up for the next match. I try not to choke as I order mushu vegetables with thin pancakes and plum sauce.

—I was afraid you were going to take me up on one of those scary activity dates, he says.

—I was waiting until you got to apple caramelizing.

—I'm not very good at that, but I can show you something about napkin folding.

I laugh and say, —Prove it.

He tries to make a swan out of a napkin but keeps making a small tugboat instead, and when he starts anew he knocks the soy sauce over. He quickly rights the container and we both throw our napkins over the soaked spot in the tablecloth, and our busboy comes over and remakes the table linens and we start again.

—I don't think anyone has ever made me this nervous in my entire life. I've always been a little clumsy but this is nuts, he says.

—Why do I make you nervous?

—I like you. Which is, apparently, turning me into a complete idiot.

The food arrives just then. The waitress fills and rolls the pancakes and serves the other dishes in a way that makes you want to meditate on the food and not just wolf it. Once she's poured our tea, I look at Uber. I mean I really look, instead of veering off. I want him to see that I have every intention of staring right into his eye until he gets something or I get something that we've both been circling around.

—You know I've been . . . learning how to be an ideal Glad wife. And I can't blame all of that on Allison. When I was little, I really wanted to know how to act at a ceremonial dinner and how to maintain the swords if my father needed help. And I could sit here and recite every single rule and bylaw. For a while I was so particular about the way I dressed that if Allison slipped up and bought me a pair of bargain sandals with fourteen straps instead of fifteen, I wouldn't wear them.

—I sensed that about you, he says, stuffing a forkful of fried rice in his mouth. —I mean that you would know everything there is to know.

—Not everything, but I wanted to learn, that's the thing. Then I started to change and my mother began to push the idea of that Wives College on me and I looked at this introductory video and I saw how shallow the women were, because everything, every last little thing, was about their future husbands. I mean, I already knew this, but seeing so many women like that, all talking the same . . . They didn't have anything else going, they didn't want anything for themselves, for the planet. Then Allison began to have these complete panic attacks thinking she was going to lose Tommy and end up alone again. Maybe she knew.

Here it's difficult to look at Uber, and I don't even try. I just stare into my water glass.

—And suddenly, or not so suddenly, this thing she built, this whole life, was starting to kill her. And ever since Tommy died, I've been thinking about how I'm going to make sure Thad never has to see another fight. And how I really think I want to write about it, not be in it anymore. The problem is if I'm no longer part of of it, then my family suffers. God, I'm sorry. I usually don't talk this much.

Uber pushes his chow mein into his eggplant.

—So you're saying you'd make a lousy Glad wife?

—That's what I'm saying.

—Good. Because I don't want to be with someone who could pass Wife 101. My mother was her own woman. Always. They had their fights, but in the end, I think my father like⁴ having a real partner. And then when he got Alzheimer': it was a good thing that she's so resourceful. She used to read a ton. We had a big library like yours. She had first editions of Faulkner, Wharton, Steinbeck . . . I think that's how she made the whole thing bearable. I'm sorry you didn't get to meet her.

I express my anger again that Caesar's used his parents that way.

—Caesar's told them they were surprising me with this special day in my honor. It wasn't until after they arrived and a rep talked with them in the car on the way over to the stadium that they learned what was actually planned. They were then told that my competition load would double if they didn't go along. My mother knew I was eager to get out, so she went along. I didn't find this out until afterward.

—They're like the worst of the government now, the worst of the military, I say.

—What I was trying to say the other day, about taking off, I think you could say I have renewed conviction.

Uber fills our cups with tea and pushes a fortune cookie my way that I decide to take home for Thad because he loves the way they snap open. We talk for a while about growing up Glad, the strange mix of admiration other kids some-times expressed and the feeling of never fitting in—the con-stant need to defend what our parents did—the times we wanted to be like everyone else, the times we didn't, the fights people picked with us just to see if we'd do something crazy and pull out a sword on the playground. And when we didn't produce those weapons we were liars, we weren't real Glads.

He tells me about his first memory of seeing a fight in the arena and I tell him that most of that was erased from my brain except for the blue benches and my mother's slow undoing. We had both known mean teachers at our schools who treated us differently than the other kids. We had both tried to date non-Glads but never found it worked very well.

I think he's holding up better than I would with all that bandaging. But we finally start to wind down and he says, —I'd really like to see you again, and he reaches out and takes my hand. And for some dumb reason, I don't pull away.

—Even if Tommy's death wasn't between us . . . Allison married seven men and each one of them told her they were eager for the time they could stop fighting and lead a normal life. I think . . . I won't go there.

—If I could get out of my contract early, say, if I were done, you might consider seeing me?

—I have to take care of my family and get my head on straight and that's all I can think about. God, it sounds like I'm holding a press conference. But I do have to take care of us. My mother's always been a little wobbly. She's really a mess now.

—I'll work on my end. Maybe we can check back in a while, see how it's going?

I don't say no, and then we both agree that we're going to have to put Caesar's off for a while, so they think we're considering a Glad marriage.

When we leave the restaurant, it's really pretty late and we decide to drive over and take a walk by the Charles. It's a relief to feel the cool evening air.

Eventually we get back to the van and circle round to the cabstand so I can avoid showing up at the house again with Uber. He puts the transmission in idle and I thank him for dinner. And then I just kiss him full on the mouth, the taste of gauze and aftershave and spicy dumplings and strong tea around the edges. And if we were in a crowd of reporters they'd ask if he tastes like my father's blood and then I'd probably just go home and maybe I'd cry a little but probably I'd look for Thad and see what he needed, because it's a whole lot easier to think about his needs than anything else.

But we didn't have any witnesses and I said good night and flagged down a taxi.

# CHAPTER
# 26

On the ride home I'm thinking about Uber and how it was too easy to talk with him and how much I don't want to be grilled by Allison tonight. I have the driver pull up to the back gates with his headlights off and I start to think I should carry a baseball bat. I hope the paparazzi aren't waking Allison as they swarm and shout at me, and tonight I have absolutely nothing to say.

.One of the guards escorts me and sees that I get in through the kitchen and I go upstairs and tiptoe past her room, the lights blazing under her bathroom door, the TV on full blast in her bedroom. She's been waiting up the way she always does when I go on a date. I have to break her of that habit.

I decide to check on Thad first.

He has plenty of stuffed animals tucked under his covers, some dropped to the floor. I can tell he's had his hair washed by the smell of his shampoo and the slight dampness on the pillow. I bend to kiss his temple. He will sleep for hours. I turn his TV off and shut his door, and brace myself for Allison.

Outside her bedroom I realize I'm staring at a photo of my first father, Frank, with his plastic trident and the padding of a hockey goalie. That's how he dressed in those early Glad days. I touch the glass over his face. He had the slight cleft chin I have, and we shared the small gap between our front teeth, as if we both had something that was trying to split us down the middle. There are no audio recordings of him, and I have no memory of his voice. He doesn't speak directly to me in that way that dead people sometimes offer persistent advice or ridicule once they're gone, a little comfort. And I suddenly have this feeling that I haven't asked the right questions about him. So I don't know if I got my rebellious nature from him—if there's a logical excuse in the blood. Maybe he got lost in history books the way I do. I decide I'm going to quiz Allison for more details. She loves it when I ask about my fathers. I think those nostalgic moments assuage a lot of guilt. And maybe it will keep us off the topic of Uber for a while.

I think I hear her calling me from the bathroom but maybe it's the TV—it's SO loud. I knock on the door and when she doesn't answer I knock a few more times. After a while I push on the door and it comes open.

She's slumped near the toilet, head down, her back to me. All I see is the form of her curved spine in her lemon-colored nightgown and her legs sprawled out. My heart drops away, my head, my stomach, everything drops, and I think she could be doing one of her faux deaths, so I'm calling to her loudly. Maybe she's taken a small combination of alcohol and prescription drugs that have put her in a stupor. She did that once before, and she slumped just this way.

I don't even see the blood at first. Everywhere and I don't see it. I don't know how that can happen. The lights are those kind that last for months. And I wonder, did I just think that, about the lights? I can't imagine I'd think about that.

And then I realize a phone receiver is pressed against my ear. It occurs to me that I've dialed Tommy's private number like he's working out at the gym or took his car in for a wash where they have brushes the size of small fir trees and soap that changes colors as it activates—things Thad loves. Maybe I was thinking if Tommy heard my voice pushing to get out of my chest—trying to tell him about Allison—that he would rush home from wherever he is and cover her up so I don't have to be the one to do this.

But I've got it now. Tommy's dead and he can't do a thing about Allison.

I'm still here holding the receiver against my ear, right outside Allison's bathroom now, thinking I should find some Kleenex and blow my nose and maybe go downstairs and wash my face and put the receiver down, all of those things in some logical sequence so I can get the dial tone to stop ringing in my head. I don't think I'm trying to call the police. I wouldn't do that unless she had a pulse.

The walls that she had once painted a mushroom color, the white sink and ceiling, the toilet cover she has washed and bleached by the woman who comes in to do the twice-weekly cleaning, the towels Allison has made sure to replace as soon as one thread comes loose or the smallest drop of makeup won't scrub out, those things are all covered in blood. I can see that now. When I crouch down, I say her name softly so she won't get mad at me. As I move around her, I finally see her face.

I have to step into the sticky blood to hold the wrist without the gun and feel for a pulse. I realize, as I back out of myself and float up to the ceiling, that there is no hurry to call anyone. I take a clean towel from the shelves and cover her head. Another towel over her legs where her skirt has risen up.

And I think about how every three or four months she gives those imperfect towels to the woman who cleans— the woman Caesar's sends—it seems they're always changing these women, and before they change we send them off with everything we've got: old towels and clothing, toys and magazines, plastic containers, old television sets.

Sticking out of the wastebasket is one of her personal note cards with her embossed initials at the top. It's a letter she's started to me. So I pull it out of the trash even though my hand is crazy with shakes. And I look at Allison and I tell her I'll read it later. I tell her Thad and I are going to be all right. *You'll see. We're going to be all right.*

Putting the letter in my pocket, I step out of my shoes and go through her bedroom and lock the bathroom door and I'm standing in her bedroom barefoot. I look in that wastebasket and there are two more letters she started and I take those and fold them and put them in my pocket as well. That's how I find the first three suicide notes. And I still haven't called the police because I need to take care of Thad and I need to think. That's one thing she'd want me to do for sure, to think about how I'm going to handle this with the media and Caesar's Inc. and Child Protective Services if they show up.

I find one letter in her lingerie drawer facedown. I find two in the highboy. Back downstairs. Three in the office, one in the kitchen trash. I find fourteen in all. None of them complete. Just starts, just intentions of letters, none of which had apparently hit the mark.

I wash up at the sink. I wash my feet. Then I call Julie.

Julie tells me to turn on the kitchen monitor to Thad's room, so I can hear him if he wakes up. Lloyd and Julie will be here in a few minutes. She directs me to the hall closet where I should get a warm sweater or jacket.

—Anything. Take anything, she says. —And put it on.

She tells me to put my arms in the sleeves of anything. I am to go back to the kitchen and open one set of French doors onto the patio, it doesn't matter which set. I turn the lights out in the kitchen.

—You need to sit outside and get some oxygen.

She wants me to stop hyperventilating. Julie instructs me to sit in a chair on the patio with the French doors wide open so I can hear the monitor.

—Whatever you do, she says, don't turn on the outside lights. That would only draw the paparazzi. Just sit out in the night air and whisper with me. Just listen to my voice if you can't talk. You're going to get through this, Lyn. Lloyd and I are here for you, baby.

So I sit in the dark and look at the phone I'm holding.

—Who's calling? I ask.

I notice it's a mild night and I wonder if it's going to rain tomorrow. No one has been able to figure out how to turn the timer off on the sprinkler system since Tommy's death.

—You're still talking to Aunt Julie, dear. Now really listen. It's important that you don't go back upstairs unless Thad wakes up. Don't talk to anyone if the other phone should ring and don't answer a knock at the door. We'll come the back way. I'm on my phone and I won't put it down for a second until we get there. We'll just stay on the line and keep talking together.

—Julie? Did you say you're coming over?

—We'll be there before you know it. We're on our way. You let Lloyd and me handle everything, sweetheart. We'll take care of every last thing. You're going to be all right, I promise. Thad and you are both going to be all right.

There's enough of a moon out so I can see the dark

outlines of Allison's plants. Maybe she planted too much narcissus this year, the smell is very intense.

—Julie? I didn't know you were on the phone.

—Yes, Lyn, this is Julie.

—You're crying, I say.

—I'm just feeling sad, Lyn. But we're on our way over right now. We're in the van. I'm going to stay on the phone with you the whole way. I don't want you to think about anything except taking deep breaths.

I look at the phone in my hand.

Maybe I had been trying to call out.

# CHAPTER
# 27

Thad holds my hand during the entire memorial. If Allison could come back from the dead long enough for the service, he would hold her hand the whole way. She was, after all, the one who got him through everything.

Although I still don't think he understands that Tommy is gone, I believe he knew even before he woke up that morning that Allison had taken her own life. Julie made certain he came nowhere near Allison's bathroom, and she helped to specify a closed casket, not that anyone wanted it to be open. But the image of Allison's face, the blood, I think those things streamed through his brain though he didn't see her in that bathroom even once. I think he *saw* what I saw in the way that he captures the unseen. I hope I'm wrong. I feel completely wrong now about everything. About my inability to tell her how much I loved her in those last days.

No mention of *Uxor Totus* is made at the service. Nothing about it in the memorial booklet, and I'm relieved about that. Instead they remember the young Allison. At the entry to the funeral parlor her full-color photo on a large poster board. She was around thirty then and wore a cool gray Oleg Cassini knockoff, her hair swept up and off her neck, and she looked remarkably happy.

Caesar's arranged everything, with Julie's help. Lloyd told me he heard they were going to bury Tommy next to Allison eventually—but so far I have no idea where Tommy is.

Periodically, Thad leans into my side and cries against my dress, which isn't like Thad. Often he has a detachment that worries me, but today he leans into me. Thad's the one who keeps bringing me back from that place I went to when I found Allison, because I had to come back for him. It wasn't a choice. It isn't. At least it isn't for me.

The flowers are almost as remarkable as the ones she grew in our backyard. They are as abundant as her efforts to make life full and pleasant despite all. So now I'm crying with Thad, and that's just the way it has to be, I guess.

I look around the room at all the mourners. I see that Sam and Callie are here. They sit side by side, drowning a little, Sam's eyes bulging with remorse, using up a box of shared Kleenex—no doubt thinking about their own parents. They're wearing black like everyone else. This is still a ritual that Glads cling to—the intense identification with the color of mourning, because in many ways, we never stop mourning. Callie reaches her hand partway into the air, as if to wave, but stops short. Maybe she realizes that waving is not the thing to do at a memorial. Sam looks at me apologetically. Perhaps she wants to apologize for everything. I honestly don't care to invite her in or push her away. These are not my enemies.

We take a limo out to the gravesite in Lexington. It's hard for Thad that we move so slowly. He rocks forward and back, as if his movements could propel the vehicle to pick up the pace.

Allison is buried with full GSA honors. One hundred and eight horns and drums sound. And every gladiator present stands in a circle surrounding the gravesite and the mourners. They have their formal shields today. There are six sleek tour buses that brought most of them here from other cities and will drive them away, the way firefighters or policemen come when one of their own dies.

At first looking around at all the arrangements, I wonder what has softened Caesar's heart—why this sudden extravagance—until I see the casket as it's pulled from the hearse.

I realize that the black shiny top is actually inlaid with a forty-inch flat-screen set right into the lid. We watch as the casket is lowered into a metal liner in the ground. Once it's in place, there are two feet between the casket and ground level. Instead of filling this in with soil—everyone looks about, waiting for the soil, at least I do—a crew of technicians comes in and they mount a Plexiglas lid on top, sealing it in place with cordless screwdrivers, so it's flush with the ground. I ask Julie to take Thad's hand and then I stand directly over the grave.

A young woman, a representative from Caesar's, approaches me. She is strictly Roman culture, the long fluid tunic and *stola*, the braided hair up on her head, the sandals. She carries a small leather pouch over one shoulder. From this she removes a remote control and aims it at the casket. In a flood of panic, I wonder if she's setting off a bomb. But I can't move to save myself.

I quickly realize that the casket monitor has started to show in sequence a million pictures of Allison. Each shot fades into the next, carefully separating her life into seven periods—each period represented by a neo-Glad husband. As if she didn't exist before she became a wife.

The Glads thrust their swords above their heads and hold them in the air for a good long while, until the horns sound again.

The woman gently pulls me aside. She hands me a brochure. She explains that visitors and mourners will be able to sit by the side of Allison's grave—benches will be installed next month—and they can view Allison in perpetuity. Technicians are working on the sound system. She apologies for the equipment delays.

I can think of a hundred things to say, none of them about equipment delays.

Then she touches my arm and looks me in the eyes, while I look at Thad, who's trying to break free from Julie, and she says, —No one will forget Allison.

I make a signal to Julie so she'll go ahead and let Thad sit down on the ground to watch Allison. It's an overcast day that opens up to a slight drizzle. The light from the screen beams onto his face, rising and falling as the pictures change, and he gets his handkerchief out that I folded and tucked into his suit pocket and he cleans the screen off. Neither Julie nor I have the heart to pull him away, poised as he is for the next set of images no matter how many times he views them.

—Look at all the fathers, he says.

I finally crouch down and tell him we'll come back in a few days. —We'll come and have a picnic and watch Allison and all her wonderful outfits, and all the fathers.

—I love Mom's clothes, he says, wiping the glass again.

—I know. I love them too.

I show him in the brochure that the images will play forever. —So it's okay to leave and just fine to come back, I say as I try not to choke up. I have to be strong for him now.

I tell him he may have five more minutes. I shake people's hands, I accept Sam and Callie's condolences, and I slowly watch all the people in black, umbrellas up, drifting back to their cars.

Before I can gather oxygen, the Roman culture woman

pulls me aside yet again and I let Julie talk Thad into going back to the car.

—As a representative of Caesar's Inc., I want to express my condolences.

I look at her, wondering what's up now.

—And I want to make sure you understand that Caesar's has invested heavily in this technology to honor your family, she says, nodding to the casket. —And you might be interested to know that we've purchased several graveyard properties around the country.

—Is that right, I say.

—Your mother should expect a lot of visitors.

—Is my mother actually . . . in there?

—Well, yes, I assume so, she says, looking a little doubtful.

—Just so I understand, is my mother like the demo house people mill around when a new real estate development goes in?

In a world of people suddenly not knowing what to say, I've caught one.

—You should be receiving a formal letter with all the details.

She looks over at Julie, who is trying, trying to get Thad to come to the car.

—It would be best for a few months if the family didn't come out to the gravesite. Visitors will want an uninterrupted experience.

—I am determined, I say, —that my brother, Thad, and I will have a beautiful life.

Then I turn away from her and together Julie and I coax Thad back to the car.

Survival can sharpen the mind if it doesn't obliterate it. During the daylight hours I insist that Julie and family go off to their jobs and activities and that Thad and I will be all right, though nothing is all right and I know this. I remind Julie that Caesar's has posted a bodyguard near the two main doors, so no one is about to storm us. Though I get plenty of calls from them, asking me to grant interviews to various media outlets, I do my best to put them off. Right now I feel like one of those people who can pull a car off a child—I just have to lift. I have to lift for Thad.

I get boxes from the local stores and start packing up the bits of the house considered to be personal items, though I'm not sure where we're going yet, and I will admit that I put Thad in front of the television until his eyes saucer. That way I can cry for a while and he doesn't have to watch.

I look into government. There are some social security funds for Thad, so I put in a claim there, and I take a phone shot of the administrator's eyes when she notes *father's former occupation*. They hate neo-Glads over at the SSA, but she indicates the modest sum he's entitled to, and how many weeks this might take. Then Julie warns me to curb my enthusiasm for assistance—she knew, apparently, about Allison's inquiries into a place for Thad and was, like me, vehemently opposed to the idea—so both of us worry about officials coming out to the house. There has to be another way.

When Lloyd and Julie come over, she tells me I am wasting away, that I need to eat. It's possible the paparazzi eat every pound I lose as if I'm shedding fruit. She begins to cook extra meals, which she brings over for us as soon as she realizes I won't go anywhere near the freezer.

After a hard, soaking rain one night, the kind that used to seep into the basement until the French drains were put in, I stand in the upstairs hallway near the photo gallery just outside my mother's door. I've thrown open windows now that the rain has stopped, and I feel this breeze pick up and circulate through the house. I say, to no one at all, something about the way the air came up so suddenly. Thad has gone to sleep and I go into Allison's room. She liked to entice me to come into her room to talk with her a little by saying: *It's such a beautiful night, isn't it?* Recently, I said something disparaging in answer. I regretted that the minute it came out of my mouth.

I lie down now, on top of the covers where she liked to nestle, and allow my head to sink into her pillow. I can hear the way her thoughts turned to beauty and the way mine were unyielding. I said something about it having no future, that a steady diet of violence cuts it out at the root. But she just touched my face and talked about the garden a little, as if that was the subject.

Too often lately, we seemed a long way from repair. I can't help think if I had been nicer to her in the last three or four years, in the last three or four days, she might still be here.

There's a light on in her closet now, the door wide open, all of her clothes there—to view, to try on if I want, to bag up and give away. I can do anything I want with her clothes. I can have everything taken in to make them fit. I can shove everything aside and move my clothes into this giant closet. I'm at complete liberty. Maybe that's what death does, puts everyone at liberty.

Thad and I, we're absolutely free, I tell her.

I know the shears she used to make alterations are up on the highboy, along with the tin of buttons and the box of threads. I get those shears down and I rip into her clothes with the blades. Her creamy white silk blouses, her rayon dresses, the carefully tailored jackets and tunics. All the tunics. I cut into her favorite clothes the way she cut us out so deftly.

When I wake up it's two in the morning, and I pull myself from the bottom of the closet. I realize what I've done and how upset Thad's going to be about Mom's clothes.

So I set to work, removing the outfits I've torn apart. I haul them over to her sewing machine. From an early age, she wanted me to learn how to sew, but I never advanced beyond making small quilts for doll beds. So that's what I do now. I cut neat squares from her clothes, and I sit up all night and make a small quilt for Thad. When I'm done I bag up all the remnants and take them down to the garage, where I stash them so Thad will never have to realize just what I've done.

# CHAPTER

# 28

Representatives from Caesar's wearing monogrammed blue jumpsuits have already come out to tag furniture and items that will be in their possession soon. I'm trying to keep Thad shored up by the hour. He's spending too much time beneath his train table, though sometimes he gets a burst of energy and goes around removing tags with a pair of kiddie scissors.

—Good man, I say with each snip.

I check the mail chronically but I have noticed a general lack of cash flow. I have now forged three postdated checks in my mother's name, taking them over to that store in Cambridge that sells War Tickets, where the guy is a little sloppy on his check-cashing policies. I think he thinks I come in to spend time with him, but now I don't have to worry about this because, as of yesterday, her accounts have run dry.

I have, therefore, formulated a plan.

I'll need Mark's geek skills, but if I pull this off, Thad and I are going to come out of this in one piece. I tell myself this when I'm not stretched out on my bed quietly falling apart.

The first thing I have to do is sell the emerald necklace. And here's the punch line: when I take it in for an appraisal at her jewelers, I discover that Allison has popped out and replaced one stone after another over the years with fakes, I guess in order to make her own ends meet. Most of the necklace is paste and I take a thousand for the rest, no questions asked.

The Chinatown bus that runs from Boston to New York is fifteen dollars. It's had only three reported shootings and a couple of flameouts—one bus burned to the undercarriage—which makes it a fairly good statistical value for the money in my worldview. But I need help with Thad in order to break away to New York. So here's the lie I cook for Julie one evening, when we're sitting around our kitchen, taking a breather from packing.

—Caesar's called and asked me to come down to New York to discuss this wedding idea. They're up for a giant televised event. I heard the word *global* in there somewhere. I haven't even accepted Uber's offer. Crazy, huh? But I think it's better to do this in person.

—Absolutely, Julie says. —It's a wonderful idea to connect personally with them. I know they've put us through a lot of changes this year, baby, but they're still family, you know?

Lloyd, who's guessing at my real reason for going, says, —*Mano a mano.* That's the only way.

Then he turns to the fight channel on the TV.

Julie grabs the remote and mutes the volume.

—You don't have to make any decisions yet. Just hear them out, she says.

When I stare into the center of her eyes, I see small white cutouts of wedding dresses floating in her irises.

She has no idea that she's making my guilt a permanent thing when she surprises me with a round-trip ticket on the Acela the next day. She and Lloyd bring this over to the house tucked into a greeting card with an image of a young woman who lived and died in ancient Pompeii. I know she's trying to reinforce my ties to all things gladiatorial, but in this moment all I can think is: lava—what a horrible way to go.

—The train is more suitable, Julie says, —for a woman of your rank.

—I don't think I have a rank now.

—But you're Allison's daughter, she says.

She tries to pull me into her arms, but I slip free and say, —I'm all right. Really, I'm just fine.

Then I clear my throat and blow my nose and get on with the work at hand.

Lloyd gives Julie a signal so she'll leave me be. And pretty soon they're hustling Thad into their Suburban to take him over to their apartment so I can pack my bag. I hug him and kiss him lightly on the cheek. It chokes me up to see his face, the raised and waving hand, Julie's arm around him in the backseat.

—Give my love to Tommy! Thad calls out.

I'm a little winded by this, much as I understand his confusions.

—I'll be back soon! I say.

Julie shouts, —We've ordered the Funamation station on

cable! He'll have total anime access. Call us when you get there!

As soon as the van's out of sight, I go back into the house and up to my desk. I dig out that scrap of paper Tommy gave me the day before he died.

LeRoy Gastonguay
New York, New York

*If you're ever in a bad strait, this is the guy.*

I tuck his number into my wallet and quickly pack a small duffel.

The train is weirdly empty—there were only six other people in my car when I got on at South Station, only a few more now. I have four seats to myself with a table, and I watch the snacks I purchased as they vibrate and move slightly across its surface. Maybe it's this part of Connecticut, the way the boats shift in the water, the rundown industrial buildings, the over-amped sky, but I pity everything that streams by.

And then I remember the unspoken bylaw: *Learn how to be an orphan if you're young; learn how to breed an orphan if you're of age.*

Maybe Caesar's thinks I'm at that perfect time of life when I can do both at once. Because surely, if they convinced me to marry Uber, they would nudge us to have a child—offering handsome cash incentives, the way they do. We could produce a Super Uber, or in celebrity-magazine parlance, the child of *Luber*—how horrible would that be? And clearly no one can question my status as an orphan, though I keep thinking Allison is going to pull back the train-car door and drop down in the seat across from me, and start giving me advice on how to talk with Caesar's.

I lean my head against the window, and see her face streaming across the blurred landscape. She's the sliver by my side now: the braid of long hair, part of an eyebrow, half an eye, the confused part in her hair. She can't move fully into the frame anymore or shift completely out of it.

I pull my raincoat up over my head and summon my discipline to be completely still as I cry, not making a sound.

I knew she was unhappy, but I can't understand why she took her life that night, that particular night. I went out with Uber. I did everything she wanted. Maybe if I could bring myself to read her suicide notes. Someday I'll be able to do that, I guess.

When I jerk awake there's too much light pouring in from the windows and I realize we're twenty minutes outside Penn Station, my raincoat down around the floor. I pack up my things and wash up in the bathroom, where I apply a fine layer of makeup. It's essential that I make a good impression.

I'm not a suit person and I don't want to go insane here, so I've settled on unripped jeans, a clean T-shirt, a short jacket, and my best sandals. I run a hand over the quarter inch of hair on my head and look at the stitches in the back using my hand mirror. Though I appreciate her needlework, I really wish Julie hadn't gotten carried away.

After the train gets in I decide to walk for a while, worried that someone in the crowd at the Penn taxi line will recognize me despite my sunglasses and hat. When I do flag a cab down, I tell the driver he should go AROUND Times Square, NOT THROUGH IT, but it's possible he doesn't hear me over the blaring radio that's trapped between two stations—maybe it's Senegalese and the traffic report listing places to avoid like Times Square—and now here we are right in the heart of it, gridlocked in midafternoon.

I pay the driver and pry myself out of the cab. You can't fight everything—even if you feel stalled out, crushed or pick-pocketed, and inundated with bad souvenirs. So I start to look around at the neon, the videos, and think: okay, my heart belongs to *Blade Runner*. But when I turn all the way around, I'm looking at a sixteen-story filmic projection of . . . *UBER*.

His muscles giant-sized, baby smooth, highly moisturized, ready for action. Yet the poor guy looks miserable. He's a thousand feet tall, looking right at me. And I find myself engaged in a mute conversation with him, listening to the cadence of his voice, listening to my own voice as I apologize for what I'm about to do to him. Because everything has changed, now that Allison's gone.

I start jostling people and nudging and shoving until I twist my way out of the square. Then, as I brush past a group of young preppy teenagers, they start shooting me with their phones.

They don't say anything, certainly don't ask permission, just keep laughing and shooting. Once I turn the corner onto Fifth Avenue, I start running and they start running after me, and they're still taking my picture, and I can imagine the captions, depending on the rag:

*Lyn Flees Marriage* or *Glad Girl Mad with Grief in NYC* or *How Lyn Keeps So Slim.*

Then I stop long enough to say, —Look, I've just lost my mother and you should go figure out something else to do.

But they probably just switch to video mode and I have to keep running.

For blocks the duffel hammers against one hip until I shift it so it hits the other, and eventually I'm looking up at the Flatiron Building, sore and breathing hard, and I just have to stop and put my hands on my knees, looking for air. When I turn back, I see they've finally dropped off. I grab another taxi and head over to NoHo and the driver lets me out in front of this Revivalist building where Caesar's Inc. is located, and it's all kind of weird because it looks, except for its particular architecture, more or less like any other building in New York, and I don't know what I expected—a statue of Caligula out front?

I enter the doormanless entry and note that the whole operation takes up four floors, starting on the tenth. I take the elevator. The reception area for the Caesar's suites is all about gold and black walls and busts of rulers past: Pompey, Julius Caesar, Augustus. . . . I want to jump over the desk and move their heads about on their pedestals to put them in proper sequence, but I know that's my obsession with history, and Caesar's is strictly about business, not allegiances.

I look at the woman on the phone in her trim summer dress and tiny sweater, her head shaved more or less like mine. She's busy, busy talking, and she barely looks up at me, and she's chattering away, maybe talking with a friend, something about the new Glad Club Med down in the Bahamas, when she suddenly gets it, gets me. That I'm there, not some stream on YouTube.

—Wow, she says, leaping to her feet.

—I'm here to see Mr. Gastonguay.

She starts to tell me how much she loves my hair, then catches herself and asks me to wait right there and walks down the hall at a clip in six-inch erroneously called gladiator heels—it's amazing to watch the angle of her. She ducks into a large black door and I walk around an odd assortment of almost Roman chairs—no one ever gets the shape right— and trim leather couches and on the tables small crops of grass, which I nervously run my hands over and back.

—Right this way, she says, suddenly looming into view again.

As I follow her down a long hall, hoisting my duffel, I realize that she has a *T* tattooed in the back of her head as well, and I want to say something. But what do you say other than *I think you're out of your mind*? I do have to wonder if this is getting her in trouble around the office, now that Tommy's reputation has been so eliminated—or if this is somehow cool because this is how I'm branded, and I am a unique entity now, not my fathers' daughter, not my mother's child.

We go past a long row of offices and cubicles, windows and water coolers, the sounds of corporate work, people churning away at unknown tasks, and I'm glad that this is not my life. *So glad.*

Mr. Gastonguay has one of the larger offices with an impressive view of the neighborhood. He is a short, slender man with a thick head of hair, I'd guess early thirties. As he springs from his chair behind his desk he rushes over to shake my hand, and I realize he's bowlegged.

—I was so sorry to hear about your mother, he says.

Then the receptionist distracts us with beverages while he offers me a seat on the couch. He takes a chair across from me.

—Your father and I lived in the same neighborhood growing up. There was no one like Tommy. He was a stand-out from the beginning. Really the nicest guy you'd ever want to meet.

When I realize I'm rubbing my wrist back and forth where my dowry bracelet used to be, I stop.

—But you know this more than anyone. And you've come all the way from Boston. How can I be of help?

—Well, Mr. Gastonguay . . .

—Please call me LeRoy.

—I'm aware that Caesar's is banking on a marriage . . . LeRoy.

—Should I offer my congratulations? he asks.

His attitude seems more about genuine curiosity than the promotion of a concept.

—He didn't realize he was picking up *my* bracelet, though I get the rule. But you should know I have no plans of marrying him, or anyone else for that matter—not now or in the immediate future.

LeRoy seems to take this in slowly. He pushes his lower lip out, nods his head up and down.

—I'm sure you've given this a good deal of thought, he says.

—But I *will* fight him.

He suddenly lists in his chair, as if he's about to pitchpole.

—What? he says softly.

—Uber. I'm willing to fight Uber. I'm aware that a marriage could be a large moneymaker for Caesar's, but . . .

—Go back to the beginning.

—When I fight Uber, when the daughter of seven gladiators steps into the arena, I say, sitting up straighter now. —I will be there to gain my freedom. I will be there to help my brother, Thad; to win back my family home; to retain our possessions. I will be fighting for all of this and a guaranteed tax-free award of three million dollars from Caesar's, with no future contractual obligations.

—You're serious, aren't you? He almost laughs.

—Can you imagine what you're going to be able to charge for a one-minute advertising spot on your station during our match if we fight to the death?

I start to rifle through the papers in my duffel.

—I will do a month of promotion leading up to the match, of course, including TV, radio, print, and blog, as long as it doesn't interfere with my training schedule.

I give him some credit that he isn't already on the phone to someone, either to push the idea or have me carted from the building.

—Do you think Tommy would want you to put yourself in that kind of jeopardy? I know with my own fifteen-year-old daughter . . .

—If I survive, Caesar's pays out directly to me, immediately upon leaving the match. If I die, the payment will go to my brother's estate within twenty-four hours. I'll have an account set up in advance to take care of that possibility.

—Uber grew up fighting trained gladiators. The *best* trained gladiators. Of course, I don't need to tell you that.

—I've been training for a while now, and I'm willing to take the risk.

I don't tell him it's only been a couple of months.

—I know Uber's weak spots, I say. —And I think Tommy would want me to take care of Thad in any way I see fit. He was very concerned about Thad before he went into his last match.

—You've been training?

—If you have a sword lying around, I'd be happy to demonstrate.

—Ah, no, he says. —That won't be necessary.

—Then I'll leave a DVD.

I dig this from my duffel and hand over a twenty-minute training session I did last week. LeRoy takes this and locks it in his top desk drawer. Then he goes over to one of his large picture windows, so I'm looking at only one side of him as he thinks things over. Maybe we're both aware that this could mean a significant promotion for him.

—But if you lose, what about Thad? he asks.

—Lloyd, the head of the Ludus Magnus Americus . . .

—I know Lloyd and his wife, Julie.

—They'll take care of him.

I pull out the document I've spent the last week creating, going through my fathers' old contracts, borrowing legalese with impunity. I even had it vetted by the family attorney, though he was opposed to the idea, and angrily said there would be no charge when he handed it back to me with his corrections.

—I'm going to sign and date these, I say, putting three copies of the contract squarely on the coffee table, accepting the pen he reluctantly pulls from his suit jacket.

—The contract is nonnegotiable. If Caesar's won't sign the contract in this exact form, my brother and I will essentially disappear. As you know, I'm not under any contractual agreement at this point since I am now of age and haven't married into the GSA, and have no living parents in the GSA. The rules no longer apply to me. If Caesar's decides to sign, I'll need a copy right away. You can send it by courier to the house.

He takes one of the framed photos lining his desk and hands it to me.

—My oldest daughter, Alesha.

Alesha has a pretty tennis look, her teeth whalebone white (whoever started that trend?—and why don't we go for blue teeth, crimson, emerald green?—it's like the days when all linens were white, all underwear), each strand of her hair in place. A girl who has arrived, I guess. I have no idea who Mr. Gastonguay is, really, but I have Tommy's endorsement. I imagine he's trying to convey . . . a fatherly concern.

—She married a Glad just last year. They're expecting their first child in the fall. The thing is, Lyn, you would be a rich woman if you married Uber. You could hire a full-time caregiver to help with your brother. Have you considered making it easy on yourself?

I just have to laugh.

—My mother illustrated that there's nothing easy about widowhood. It only seemed to lead to more widowhood.

—I don't have full authority to make this happen, but I'll start the meetings on it right away. I'll hope to have an answer for you by the end of the day. Are you staying in New York tonight? Can my wife and I take you to dinner?

—I'm going to see the superheroes exhibit at the Metropolitan.

—See if you can get some ideas for a fighting outfit?

—Something like that. Then I'm taking the train back.

He goes over to his desk again, picks up a piece of paper and a pen and says, —Could I get your phone number?

As I recite it, he seems to write this out, then he hands me the pad.

—Is this right? he asks.

I read: *I think you should see something.*

—Yes, that's right, I say.

As I gather my things to leave, my eyes wander around the office. Maybe I'll find a mic popping out of a flowerpot, a hidden camera. When he opens his office door, staff members are lined up in the hallway, waiting for a look at me.

—Everyone get back to work, he says with a broad smile.

Though they shift a little, they remain essentially in place, whispering among themselves, until we go through the large doors back to the lobby. Here he summons the elevator and then asks the receptionist to go on some errand that I sense might be bogus. Once we're inside, he puts a key into the control panel to get us up to the fifteenth floor, which is one more floor than I understood Caesar's to own, given that there is no thirteenth floor. I start to open my mouth to say something but he shakes his head just enough to make me wait. Before we get out of the elevator, he punches a button to send the car back down to the lobby. We step out into a large space with a wet bar along one wall, chairs stacked in high towers. It appears to be a kind of banquet room, with a small stage and a wooden floor, perhaps for dancing. Again the windows onto the city. The sun has just crested the high-rises.

He leans in toward me and I flinch.

I can barely hear him when he says, —If I turn on the lights, someone might find us.

—Okay, I whisper back.

There are two doors leading to another room, maybe a closet. He unlocks these and pulls the doors open into another dark space, this one windowless, I can't tell how deep. I'm not sure what I'm looking at at first. It seems to be some kind of tank. There's a strong chemical smell. Even when my eyes adjust, it's just too dark. He turns on a tiny penlight and hands it to me, standing just behind me.

There he is. There's Tommy.

*tommy.*

He's floating in a sealed glass tank, a vitrine full of formaldehyde. All of his parts have been sewn back together. His eyes shut, he's still wearing his gladiator costume. They have made Tommy into something like Damien Hirst's *Tiger Shark* once displayed in an art exhibit titled The Physical Impossibility of Death in the Mind of Someone Living.

I gasp and LeRoy gently covers my mouth. Then he whispers, close to my ear.

—They're trying to sell him to a foreign collector.

I shake my head back and forth, tears run from my eyes and over his hand that he gently removes now. I turn around and face him. We both whisper now.

—*They?* Not you?

—If you learn that Tommy's body has disappeared into an unmarked plot, long before it's sold off, you'll know there are more than partyliners around here. But it might not be safe for you to come here again.

I nod in agreement.

—I'll do what I can to get your contract through, though I wish you could see some other choice. I almost died when my daughter married her gladiator.

Then I ask him to give me a moment.

I touch the case and tell Tommy that I don't want him to worry about Thad.

After a while LeRoy takes out his handkerchief and wipes my fingerprints away. He tells me we are to take the stairs down to the ninth floor. From there we will both take the elevator down to the street and then he'll travel back up to the office. He tells me where I need to walk to catch a taxi and wishes me Godspeed.

It's good that I take the last train back. It's dark and quiet now and I'll get home to Thad soon. At the speed of the Acela, I get out the superheroes catalog. It's so much easier to think of oneself in a comic book.

The costumes are broken down into eight basic types: *graphic, patriotic, virile, paradoxical, armored, aerodynamic, mutant,* and *postmodern.* Although some might consider me paradoxical, or even a little armored, I think postmodern will suit my time in the arena. *Adorned with skulls, hellfire, and other symbols of mortality, they embody . . . the postmodern body of both fiction and fashion and the darker terrors of our contemporary world.*

I don't know what comes after postmodern, which is already turning old when five-year-old girls can go into local department stores and buy tights with skull and crossbones all over them. Maybe the next phase is to crank up the particle accelerators, rev up the nuclear reactors, peel the ozone away, spew oil from the offshore platforms, take Russia or China on. But I would like to imagine something else. I don't know. Something.

# CHAPTER
# 29

Thad waits for the first pancake off Julie's griddle, his jaw tipped open. She's made it the size of his face and plans to decorate it with Thad's basic features.

I see he's wearing a new gladiator costume. The work is so good it looks almost like one of Tommy's outfits. His wooden sword and shield, painted bronze, rest next to his chair as if he's going into battle as soon as breakfast is over. They've even purchased a new pair of sandals for him with the right number of straps. I know there's no discouraging Julie in this kind of gift, and God help me if I try and take it away from Thad now.

—Would you like tiny marshmallows or little bits of butter for the mouth? Julie asks.

Thad furrows his brow. —Lyn's going to lose everyone, he says in his point-blank way.

—He really missed you. I think that's all it is, Julie says, but she looks away, clearly worried.

Just once I wish my Thad would say I'm going to win

something or take a pleasant trip or meet an interesting stranger.

Now Julie steps away from the stove long enough to kiss me on the forehead. Then Mark leans into me with that look like I need a distraction. One eye on his computer, he starts to whisper to me about just how bad things have gotten in Myanmar, about the things they do to albinos in Tanzania.

—I was only gone for a day, and I read those articles online, and I'm really getting this, that the world is going to hell.

—Sorry, he says, rubbing his goatee.

—I'm just tired, I say.

Lloyd, who's probably only caught a little of our conversation, begins to shake his head, his eyes fixed on the sports section. —A lot can happen in a day, he says vaguely, more to himself than us.

I want to tell him that it already has. I got the call last night from LeRoy as soon as I got in. Caesar's is sending signed copies of the contract today.

—Jesus, since when did the army get into Ultimate Fighting? Lloyd says, smacking the paper.

—Since they figured they could make a buck airing it on primetime, Mark says.

—No shit.

—Lloyd, Julie scolds, nodding toward Thad.

—Sorry. Cute pancake, Thaddy, he says. —Looks just like you.

—I'm the most famous person you'll ever meet.

In a low tone I say, —Tommy used to compare ultimate fighting to cockfighting.

Lloyd folds the newspaper back. —Listen to this from some Major Crigger.

—Crigger or Trigger? Mark asks.

—I quote: *The Ultimate Fighting Championship provides a great venue to get the Army name into the minds of millions of young Americans.*

—Why don't they just brand us at birth? I say.

—Right on the frontal lobe, where my sense of humor is, Mark says.

During the conversation Thad has picked up the uncapped maple syrup bottle. He holds it in front of his right eye at a slight angle until his T-shirt is spattered syrup. I realize how much he loves the amber view but I know in time he'll drop the bottle. I gently nudge it away from him, saying, —My turn.

Then I look through the glass at him and say, —You're my favorite person, Thad.

He watches Julie set his starkly happy pancake on his placemat, and I know he's hungry. But when I get up to wash my sticky hands at the sink, he jumps up and moves to the floor next to my legs, as if he's there to catch the tiny drops of water that splash against the stainless steel. He hums to himself while I wet some paper towels and crouch next to him, washing the syrup off his hands and face and T-shirt.

—I'm sorry I had to go to New York, I say. —I missed you.

—Let's go home and see Mom now, Thad says.

Lloyd gives me a sympathetic look.

—Julie would feel very sad if you didn't eat your pancake. And I have to talk with Mark a little. Then we'll go home.

I signal Mark to meet me in his bedroom, then I lead Thad back to the table, where I cut up his pancake for him. He watches, tapping his index fingers against his thumbs as if one hand is talking to the other hand. Once he starts eating, Julie tells me to go on.

Sometimes Mark's room is barricaded, but rarely on purpose. It's just that the dirty clothes and dishes and cereal boxes and things end up by the door like he's planning on taking this stuff out to the kitchen eventually. But he gets caught up with the computer a lot and he trains every day, and I don't think he realizes he's creating burial mounds. I have to lean my weight against the door to gain entry. Once I do, I slump down at the bench press, close to Mark's desk, where he's already signed on.

He offers me a Coke out of his mini fridge but as I told Julie, I'm just not thirsty, not really hungry. He forces it into my hand, saying I look too thin.

—He doesn't understand that Allison's dead, I say. —And he still hasn't figured out what happened to Tommy and he was right there in the stadium when he died. He saw everything, but nothing sunk in.

—Maybe it's better if he can't remember?

—Maybe. But then he asks for them and I can't produce them, and then he runs and hides under his train table for hours.

He gives me one of his long, considered looks, like he's about to doctor me.

—I'm worried about you.

—Me? I'm okay.

But I can never bullshit Mark. He pulls up the latest photos circulating the Internet. There I am, running down Fifth Avenue.

—I do look rabid.

I tell him about the kids who dogged me. And then I tell him that I need his help. Mark puts his hands around one of my knees.

—Anything, babe, he says.

I tell him about LeRoy, and outline the business about the contract. He drops his hands and tips back in his desk chair. He says, —I'm going in for you. You get that, don't you? I'm taking this fight.

—I appreciate that. More than you know. But I have someone else in mind.

—That stings.

—No, listen. Do you remember that woman in Sacramento who projected her avatar into the courtroom where her divorce proceedings were taking place, because she was too nervous to personally attend?

—That woman's going to fight for you?

—You know, she rigged the avatar to a Living machine.

—Shit, you can't be serious.

—If she could that, why can't I put my alter ego into the arena?

Mark cracks up.

—Didn't they catch her? he asks.

—Only after it was in action for ten full minutes.

—And wasn't her avatar a troll? Okay, but the thing is, I'm not sure if we can get your alter ego to lose a limb or bleed if she's hit—without making her look really stupid—like a gushing fire hydrant. And what if she goes crazy and tries to take one of your arms off? But hey, I'll bring my computer over tonight and we'll see what we can do. What the hell.

—I've already started to build someone. I'll tweak around with her, see if I can lose the wings and spear.

—Spears are good. Keep the spear.

—It's going right through the center of her chest.

—Yeah, well, lose the spear. And look for a current face shot of yours that we can patch in.

—Just so you know, I'm fighting if this doesn't work—and you're not responsible for anything.

—I told you I'm going in for you.

—No, I'm serious. Just help Julie with Thad if I go down. And loan me your electric razor. This stubble is driving me crazy.

—I love your bald self.

The paparazzi's in my hair, though I have none. If I did I'd be pulling it out, strand by strand. After Thad tucks his share of pancakes away, Julie checks my stitches and says they're dissolving nicely, and encourages Lloyd to see us home. Lloyd explains that he decided to camp at our house while we were gone, and he caught one of the photographers trying to break in. Lloyd made the man strip and he hosed him down with the garden hose. That's when he decided to send tag teams from his trainees over to the house to keep guard—one by the back entry, one by the front—round the clock, in eight-hour shifts. They love Lloyd, otherwise there's no way they'd stand around in the heat, glaring down the paparazzi all day.

The van is swarmed. We can't even pull round to the back.

After Lloyd leaves his van in the middle of the road, he and Mark clear a route to the front door. When we're almost inside, I let this slip to one of the female reporters:

—Caesar's will be making a big announcement within the next forty-eight hours.

Of course Lloyd wants to know the second we make it into the house what the big announcement is. So after I get Thad settled upstairs, I spell it out for him. Not the part about my alter ego. With Lloyd, you either fight or you don't fight. He'd rather we all burn in hell than send artificial life into the arena. But then Lloyd's a pretty straightforward guy. And there's no way I'd bring up the thing about Tommy's corpse. God knows how freaked he'd get about that. So I stick to the essentials, and tell him that I've settled on my fate: *No* to the wedding, *Yes* to combat.

Lloyd hugs me and once he's out the door, I turn on the TV, where I watch him get through the crush of people until he can pull away. Our house is being broadcast round the clock. Helicopters chop the air.

I make up a stack of sandwiches, all with the crusts trimmed off the way Thad likes, and then I realize we've got these guards now. Today they are Slade and Dave, and I better call them in for lunch. They both like the intensely caffeinated beverages that Tommy liked, and we still have some in the fridge. Dave keeps asking me things, like do I always cut the crusts off the bread, and can he see where Tommy worked out, and after a while I leave them in the kitchen, telling them to help themselves if there's anything else they want. I take the rest of the sandwiches upstairs for Thad on a tray, garnished with chips and carrot sticks, anchored with a cup of orange juice. He's up in Allison's room of course, curled at the end of her bed. He's been waiting for me to turn the TV on. I remind him that Allison's bathroom is being renovated so if he has to go he should give himself enough time to make it down to my bathroom.

Then I announce, —Today is *ANIME MARATHON DAY!*

We will, I explain, be tuned in for hours. He seems very

content with this idea, once I get my laptop and bring that onto the bed to work.

My alter ego, Eos, has wings, a short lace-up top, leggings, a small skirt, rabbit slippers, and yes, a spear through her chest. My goal is to make her battle-ready. The clothes are the easy fix. I make a new skirt using a wide leather belt from which I hang other smaller strips of leather. It sits on my hips and hits where a short tennis skirt would fall. When I walk, the strips of leather swing back and forth against my thighs. At the bottom of each strip I attach a silver coin with a peace symbol stamped into it.

I go for bronze chest armor shaped with strong pecs and well-defined breasts and the word *egalite* over my breastbone, in a circular pattern. I create pads for the legs and sword arm that I think are fairly authentic but have a titanium lining. The belly is exposed, because that's regulation, so I spend some time working on my abs and though I consider a belly button ring, I decide they're overused and could be an easy target in competition. I've seen what happens when a ring is suddenly ripped out.

I'm tempted to leave the bunny slippers, but I'm afraid people won't get my sense of humor. Sandals are never worn in the arena. Tommy preferred Nikes, but I've decided to go barefoot since it will be an evening match and the sand will be fairly cool by then.

When I walk, I move in an almost fluid way but I'm concerned that my eyes are too scary so I go for sunglasses, for now anyway. I select the mirrored type, hoping Uber will have a narcissistic moment and forget about me.

I have to call him. But I keep putting it off because I don't know how to tell him yet. He's left lots of messages on my phone, most of them pretty nice but the last one a little despondent.

It's hard to know how to approach him. Maybe a couple of years ago, I would have taken this up with Sam and Callie, and we would have sat around like complete idiots, trying to strategize. And they probably would have given me plenty of bad advice, so I'm better off with my own sense of cluelessness.

When I first created my avatar, the makeup streamed down her face. I don't cry a lot so maybe I wanted to express something I tend to stuff. But Tommy said, *You have to be tough to decipher when you fight.*

It's not hard to make her bald, but it's putting the *T* in the back of her skull that takes forever. In between, I run up and down stairs getting beverages for Thad, watering the security force, checking on the paparazzi, dawdling by the library.

Thad sits up for a while and I fluff a bunch of pillows behind his back. He asks to see what I'm doing.

I turn my computer around so it faces him.

—There's a spear in your chest, he says.

—Oh, yeah. It's just a decoration.

—I want a decoration.

—Later, I say. —Later we'll make you your very own avatar.

And I'll make some wings for you. And you understand that real spears don't belong in our chests, right, Thaddy? It's always very important that we take good care of our real bodies.

—Our real bodies, he says, and curls up.

—And after that, we'll go on the treadmill down in the basement for a while. I'll let you do all of the walking.

—I'll do all of the walking, he says, slowly drifting.

I'm down to the wings and spear now. Those wings took me three days to perfect. I know that sounds lame, but I got lost in the beauty of engineering. I threaded each strand like tatting a fine French lace. So I have to unravel them strand by strand.

I think Thad's on his seventh anime show when I lift that last feather from my back.

The spear looks dangerously close to the heart but it's actually running through the breastbone—lodged firmly there. I can run, fly, use a hover board or jet pack, and that spear remains fixed in place. I do not bleed. If I went into a state of convoluted metaphor, I could try and make something out of this idea that I'm walking around with a spear through my chest. Or I could keep it simple: it's just a form of adornment, like scarification or piercing. It's something you get up to in another state of mind. I realize the afternoon is getting late, and I should clean up and get ready for the changing of the guards, dinner, and Mark. I'll work on the spear tomorrow.

Thad snores lightly now. He'll nap for a couple of hours. I slip the remote from his open hand, putting a wrap on the marathon. I get up to stretch and go over to Allison's garden windows that look down to the backyard and out along the treetops and neighboring homes. I often found her standing by the windows like this, taking in the view, sometimes shaking her head as if she couldn't believe this was something she owned. I wonder if she stood here and considered the way the light slips through the trees the night she suicided. But then I realize her mind was too dark to see more than a foot in front of her.

# CHAPTER

# 30

I flick on the kitchen lights.

—Uber. *Jesus.* What are you doing here?

—I knocked but no one answered, he says. —Should I come back later?

—No it's okay. I just . . . wasn't expecting you.

—These are for you, he says, handing me an armful of sunflowers.

I set them on the counter and go over to the cabinet where the vases are kept. I fill a large blue vase at the sink, staring at the swirl of water, trying to avoid his look. He's gone to an eye patch now, the stitch marks visible across his check in four even rows. Upstairs with the AC going it's easy to forget the heat and humidity, but here with so many windows and doors onto the yard, it just pools. Uber wears a pair of shorts and a T-shirt, looking like a guy ready to grill or knock a birdie around a badminton net. I watch a bead of sweat leave one of his temples and travel down his cheek until he wipes it clear.

I set the flower arrangement on the table and flick on the oscillating fan.

—I have some really good news. But I wanted to tell you in person, he says.

The fluffy hair on the top of his head rises and falls with one complete oscillation.

—You want something to drink? I've made one ton of lemonade for Thad.

—Lemonade would be great.

He starts to pull out one of the chairs at the table and manages to knock himself in the knees. It never seems right to say *You okay?* to a gladiator when he knocks his knees or stubs his toes. So I just set the cold lemonade pitcher and two glasses on the table, but then I realize it would be a mistake to let him pour. We would soon be drowning in spilled lemonade. I laugh to myself.

—What? he asks.

—It's just strange, our sitting here like this, the paparazzi outside, the guards, the quiet house . . .

Before he can say anything, I go over to the pantry and set some macaroons out on a plate. I watch his hair rise and fall again.

He picks up a cookie and considers it.

—Will this make me smaller or larger? he asks.

—How about . . . human scale.

If there's any space between my waterlogged thoughts and his sputtering intentions, I realize I've sort of missed his company, if that makes any sense at all, which I know it doesn't but there it is.

—That's fine with me. How's Thad? he asks.

—He keeps thinking that Allison and Tommy are off on a trip somewhere.

—I'm sorry, he says.

—You have some news?

—I've talked Caesar's into reducing the number of matches I have left to one. I'll have to do more promotion, but in one match I'll be a free agent. And then, well . . . I'll be a free agent. I fight in about a month and then . . .

—You'll be a free agent, I say, trying to veer around the unstated.

—Exactly. I really couldn't believe how easygoing they were about the whole thing. I was actually suspicious but then they told me I'm more valuable to them alive than dead now.

—Uber, there's something I need to tell you as well.

I grab his glass just before his elbow knocks it over.

—Before you tell me, could I . . . kiss you?

I jump up, and now he's the one who has to grab my chair before it falls. I start to pace.

—You and I . . . how can I put this? You and I, you see . . .

—Yes? he says, smiling broadly now.

—I'm your last match.

—Wow, that's exactly how I feel.

It's like we've just wandered into one of those *NYT*'s Weddings and Celebrations videos by mistake. He starts to get up but I motion for him to stay seated. Then I line the potholders up on the counter, straighten the salt and pepper shakers, consider the rubber band collection in the drawer, all the time with my right hand in the air as if to say: *wait*.

—I don't mean . . . I'll start over. You know your last fight, I say.

—Oh God, don't worry about that. They have me fighting a rookie. They kept saying they don't want to lose any more of their heroes. Not that I feel like anyone's hero, but . . .

—You wouldn't kill your rookie, would you?

—Nothing that couldn't be stitched back together. I mean I do have to make it look like I'm trying.

—Good to know. This rookie . . . it's not a guy, Uber.

Uber stands and comes over to the counter.

—What are you talking about?

—I'm the rookie. You're going to fight me. That's what I've been trying to tell you.

His face suddenly busts a gasket and he laughs, —Very funny.

He wipes a tear from his good eye; then he begins to tuck in his shirt though it looks tightly anchored already. He moves his flattened hand all the way round his waistband, my dowry bracelet rising and falling as he goes.

—Call Caesar's if you need to verify it but you and I are fighting each other in Romulus Arena next month. Your last match, my one and only. They're going to make an announcement.

—That's crazy.

He stops laughing.

—I know. I know it's crazy. But the thing is, it's really okay.

—It's okay? What's okay about that? 'Cause I don't see anything okay about that. Who told you this?

I give him the bare bones story including the virtual punch line, about my plan to send my avatar into the arena.

—*You* arranged this?

—I'm not ready to get married. I have things I need to do, a brother to take care of. And I barely know you.

I want to say something about this feeling I have when I'm with him, the ease despite it all, the attraction I'd rather not think about. But I stop myself.

—And what if your avatar doesn't work? he says.

—Then I guess you'd have to fight me.

—You guess I'd have to fight you? But I'm crazy about you. I don't want to fight you.

—Then you'll go easy on me. You know, nothing that can't be stitched back together.

—You can't do this, he says, practically choking on his own words.

—I signed a contract with Caesar's. The house will be returned to us, which is the best thing for Thad. And I'll have money to take care of him properly while I go to college.

—I'll sign up for ten more fights in exchange for this one. I'll buy the house for you. Just don't do this.

—I have to be the one to take care of us, that's the thing. I'm . . . sorry.

Just then, a sound like a bird hitting one of the picture windows. It's Mark screwing around outside, as if he's been thrown against the glass. I motion for him to come in. He picks up a cardboard box full of electronic equipment by his feet and joins us. When Mark shakes hands with Uber, there's that admiration thing all over again.

—I better head out, Uber says.

—No, stay, man, Mark says.

But Uber comes up with some excuse for leaving. Our good-byes are strained, confused. Mark watches us and I notice that deep line he gets between his eyebrows.

—I'll call you, Uber says, and heads into the yard.

Mark wants to know what's up. I click on the TV. We watch Uber as he moves into the crowd outside the gate.

—I told him the plan, I say.

—Dude.

—He doesn't like not being able to rescue me.

—Good man, he says.

—Don't start, I say.

—Shh, listen, Mark says, taking a bag of cookies over to the tube.

Uber is surrounded by the media now, the fans.

—I've just seen the family, he says. —Lyn is a remarkably strong woman. I hope you will allow her and her brother to have some peace, so they can get through this difficult time.

—Have you set a date? someone calls from the crowd.

Microphones press in toward Uber's face.

—I have no further comment at this time.

We watch him battle his way into his car. I don't know if everyone else understands how troubled he looks.

Mark turns off the set, stuffs a large cookie into his mouth and says, —The man's a pro, what can I say?

—I've really screwed up here.

—But if you pull this off, you'll be the woman who beats the system. And he'll be done with competition for good, he says, offering me the cookies, which I turn down.

—But you're the guy who's signing up to fight *in* the system.

—I can live with this dichotomy. He smiles.

I punch Spider-Man emblazoned across his T-shirt. —You're so strange, I say.

—That's why you can't live without me. Okay, let's see what we can do.

I tiptoe upstairs, take a peek at Thad sleeping soundly, and grab my computer. Back in the kitchen, I show Mark my fortified avatar. I've glued in one of my face shots.

—Nice. But you couldn't get the spear out?

—Not really.

—We'll deal with that later. I was up all night figuring this out. Where's the Living machine?

—I got a couple of the security guards to help me bring it downstairs. I locked it in the weapons room so Thad wouldn't mess with it.

—Perfect.

I unlock the door and I'm almost blinded by the light streaming in through the windows, glinting off the wall where the shields hang. Mark has two computers and a bunch of cords and cables and extra hard drives and God knows what all. He begins to set things up. Within an hour, we have my virtual self standing by one of the sword racks, swaying a little at the hips as if she's trying to get her balance for the first time. She blinks several times and then tries out a variety of expressions like an actor warming up for a performance.

—She's so disconcerting and wonderful, I say.

—Good outfit, he says, running his palm along his goatee.

—*Hello*, she says, in a voice designed to make us feel like complete idiots. —You can talk directly to me, you know.

But I don't know where to start.

—We brought you here for a mission, Mark says, like he's prepping 007 for his next assignment. He's just eating this up.

—I don't do *missions*, she says, and takes a seat where Tommy used to fasten his sandals. The spear that goes through her chest comes out the back of the chair.

—Right, I say. —What Mark is trying to explain is that you'll be fighting at Romulus Arena, as part of a Gladiator Sports Association event next month. We appreciate your help.

—I know what the GSA is, but I didn't realize you wanted me to *fight*. I'm a pacifist.

I bite my lower lip and look at Mark.

—You want me to get all the glitches out in twenty-four hours? he asks.

—If anything happens to you, we'll simply put you back together again. So you don't have to worry about that, Mark says.

—So it's okay if I get sliced and diced. Great. And my opponent? she says.

—We just want you to spar a little. We're going to try and keep you in the match the whole time, and we'll do everything we can to protect you, I say.

But once again I'm feeling queasy about the whole thing; inauthentic . . . virtual.

—That doesn't tell me *whom* I'm fighting.

I ask Mark, —Am I always this difficult?

—You think I'm taking that bait? he laughs, tipping back in his chair.

—She asked a pretty straightforward question, *Lyn* says.

—I have an idea, I say, addressing her. —Why don't you see if you can pull the spear out of your chest.

She looks down at the spear. —I think it gives me a certain . . . I don't know . . . it's like an outer manifestation of my internal wounds.

—This is definitely not me, I say.

—I'll make you a deal, *Lyn* says. —I'm willing to lose the spear if you give me back my wings. I'm not kidding. I feel naked without them.

—They're too . . . lingerie ad, Mark says. —No one will take you seriously.

—You think so? she asks, giving this serious consideration.

—We're getting off track, I say. —Why don't we go out to the living room and see if we can spar?

—Good idea, Mark says. —*Lyn*?

—Can I have my pick of swords? she asks, eyeing the racks.

—Uh no, I say. —Mark and I are going to supply you with a Living sword and shield.

—Which means I can't really hurt anyone . . . which means I'm still a fully-aligned pacifist, which means this is a completely stupid exercise, which leads me to this question: why are we doing this?

—To save a couple of lives, I say.

—Oh, well, she says soberly. —Then I guess I'm your woman. I've always wanted to save lives.

Maybe she feels some alignment with superheroes? She puts her hands around the spear, as if she's gripping a rope for tug-of-war; then she rips the spear from her chest, and lets out this agonized sound.

I watch the blood ooze from the open wound.

—It should spurt more when she does that, Mark says. —We can work on that later.

—Can you get me some paper towels? *Lyn* asks.

I direct *Lyn* out to the living room, where I bring paper towels, which of course absorb nothing since there's nothing to absorb, and while I'm at it I grab one of the lighter swords with a small shield for myself.

Mark figures out a way to transport a sword and shield to *Lyn*, and both of us begin to look the part.

—We better keep the volume down, I say. —Thad's sleeping.

I go off to the library and change into an outfit identical to *Lyn's*. The real difference, again, is something in the eyes. That's what Mark says. I think he's kind of freaked the way I am, though freaked for Mark is a cool thing.

As *Lyn* and I face each other, the blood continues to trickle down her abs and runs down one leg and seems to drip into the carpet, but leaves no mark. We take up our swords.

*i know not what i do.*

—You sure I can't get hurt? I ask Mark.

—As sure as I'll ever be, he says, typing something into one of the computers.

—That's reassuring. Um, *Lyn*, would you mind making a small cut on one of my fingers?

*Lyn* draws her sword over my outstretched index finger. The only thing I feel is warm air, as if someone has just blown on my finger. No blood.

—When I get this right, fake blood will appear where you've been cut. So, let's see you mix it up, he says.

Before I get my shield up, *Lyn* whips her sword into the air in a circular motion and slices right through my neck. If she had had a real weapon, and kept it as sharp as Tommy's blades, I would now be headless.

—You have to let Lyn have the upper hand, Mark says to my avatar. —And if you have to cut, go easy.

—I was just kidding, *Lyn* says. —You should have seen your expression.

I'm starting to feel queasy, but I know we have to make some progress and get her back in the machine before Thad wakes up.

—You're going to be fighting Uber, I say. —He's left-handed, so you have to be prepared for that. Maybe I should use a left-handed shield and sword so you can get the feel of this.

*Lyn* flops down on the couch. —I can't do this.

Mark and I give each other a look.

—I have feelings for Uber, *Lyn* says. —Though I know I shouldn't, because of Tommy and all.

—You programmed her to have feelings for Uber? I ask.

—Don't you? Mark asks, tucking his hands up under his T-shirt.

They both stare at me, waiting for an answer. I can't believe Mark is doing this.

—He's actually a decent guy. It's just . . . well, you know.

Mark gives me this look.

—Stop, I say. —Look, *Lyn*, if Uber and you fight, and don't *really* hurt each other, it will be his last fight and you'll never have to fight again, and we're doing all of this for Thad. So you see, you want to fight but not *fight*.

—I'd do anything for Thad, she says. —Wow, I'm getting such a bad headache.

—Maybe your armor is too tight around your neck, I say.

—Just try working with your shields for a while, Mark nudges.

So Lyn and I stand again, and we make an effort at shield strategy. Only the strange thing is, there's no sound when her shield hits mine.

—This is too weird, *Lyn* says. —It's so noiseless.

—But you look great. I'll get the audio portion going, Mark says.

Just then, I hear Thad call out.

—Mom! he shouts down the stairs. —Mom, I'm hungry!

Two days later Caesar's spokeswoman, Sappho, appears on a round of talk and interview shows starting with Jon Stewart to let the world know Uber and I will be squaring off in the Romulus Arena in a little less than a month. She says that we are both in training and will not give official interviews until a few days before the match. She emphasizes the choice of combat over marriage. She goes on at length about Thad, his special needs, and his sister's desire to take care of him at any cost.

Jon says, —Sounds like Juliet is turning on Romeo.

—Well, Jon, it is a fight to the death.

—But didn't Juliet fake her own death? Jon points out.

—Maybe we're taking the metaphor too far, she says with a smile. —Glad fans aren't looking for irony. They're looking for a fair fight, they're looking for skill in the arena.

—Both of your opponents are eighteen or older, that's right, isn't it?

—Yes, Jon. If you can join the military, you can fight for the GSA.

—So you have two young, fit, and I assume, bright people—though some question their smarts in entering this competition—who have their whole lives before them, and your organization, Caesar's Inc., thinks it's acceptable for one of them to die, maybe the other to be crippled for life.

—I don't need to tell you that gladiator sport is deeply embedded in our culture as an acceptable form of competition. But you might not recall that the founders hoped it would someday replace military combat. We still hold out this hope for the future.

—The pundits I'm hearing from say this will be more watched than the Olympics. But it's also the most contested fight Caesar's has ever presented. You've stirred up activist groups around the world. It could mean, ultimately, the end of gladiator sport. I quote this from the *Los Angeles Times*: "This may well be the maiden voyage of Caesar's very own *Titanic*."

—Great way to sell a newspaper, don't you think, Jon?

—So you believe this statement is more about hype than reality?

—You know what's real for most people, Jon? That we have steadily rising unemployment, people are losing their homes, and some say we're in an economic depression, and now some excitable types want to take away their right to see legalized entertainment.

—But is it fair? We now turn to . . .

I can't imagine a worse feeding frenzy. If Thad were to go into a supermarket with me, he would find himself on all sorts of magazine covers. If I'd let him watch the general fare on TV, he'd realize that everyone knows, or thinks they know, a young boy named Thad G., Tommy and Allison's son—the world's new orphan.

Along with the guards the Ludus sends over and the two bodyguards Caesar's posted a while back, Caesar's threatens to provide even more personal bodyguards, but I decline, worried that they'll make it their business to spy on us as much as protect us. I try to leave the house as little as possible now. I hire a nanny named Sheryl to help with Thad. She seems like a perfectly nice woman in her early thirties, slim and poised, though her tweed skirts annoy me. After a day, I realize she's constantly chipper and chronically making suggestions about changing Thad's schedule, what he eats, how much exercise he gets. She tells me she had a cousin with special needs growing up, so she *knows*.

But Thad wails like a factory siren if I try to do anything without him, so against my better judgment I let him dress in his gladiator outfit and sit in the covered bleachers of the Ludus Magnus Americus while I spar with Mark or one of the female Glads. Sheryl, peeling the wrappers on his Free-way bars up in the bleachers, makes sure he keeps his fluid intake up in the heat.

Julie is barely talking to me now and doesn't have much to say to Lloyd, for that matter. When Mark isn't at the arena, he devotes himself to the world of my alter ego, and though Julie doesn't know what he's up to, he reports that she seems pleased to have him around the apartment more.

One night I arrange to have Sheryl stay over so I can get away. When Thad drops off, Mark and I drive the Living machine over to the stadium in his van. It takes two hours to lose the paparazzi with a friend of Mark's driving a decoy van. But we have to try *Lyn* out in the arena. We set up the machine in an old storage room just a few feet from where the competitions occur and Mark rigs up this miniaturized modem in some kind of protective shell under the sand where we'll be fighting, so she'll have the strongest possible signal.

When *Lyn* appears and the icons above her head light up and then hide themselves, it's as if she's just woken from a long nap, stretching and yawning. One of Mark's little touches.

We both gear up and get in position. She strikes first and our swords clang loudly.

—Good sound, I call out to Mark.

But while I'm turned she delivers a blow to my sword arm, and Mark tells me to look down. Some strange almost phosphorous red substance stains my arm.

—Weird, I say.

—Not as weird as you, she says.

—No, I . . . , I start to say, but she's coming at me again. I cut her right cheek.

Soon I understand that *Lyn* will appear to spurt or slowly bleed in proper measure depending on the injury. Again I see something like blood sprout up from my wounds, though there's no actual wound.

—The blood is amazing. You've done an incredible job.

—But? Mark asks.

—I wasn't going to say anything.

—There's something about the way she pivots at the hips, he says. —And the way she raises her arms and the turns are more like rotations.

—Everything else looks pretty natural, I say.

—She's as good as she's going to get, I'm afraid.

When we pause between trials, I notice that she flirts heavily with Mark and that he doesn't seem to mind this too much. In fact you could say he laughs easily with her.

Once we've shut down the equipment and she's back in the box for the night, I say, —You better not be thinking about keeping her around.

—Jealous?

—No, I'm just saying.

Uber has not called and the fight is next week. The TV appearances are just starting to crank up. Caesar's makes sure we're never in the same room together. Mostly, the crews come and set up in our living room or library.

Where before we had only the paparazzi to consider

when we backed out of the driveway, now we have protestors of every stripe. There's been some buzz that I should lose guardianship of Thad. As far as I'm concerned, this fight can't get here fast enough.

While Thad takes an afternoon nap, to the syncopated sounds of helicopter blades overhead, I sit down with Sheryl and tell her that the day I fight, she's to keep Thad away from the Romulus. So far, to the best of my knowledge, he has no idea about the match. Like a post-9/11 parent keeping their children from the horrific details of that day, I don't watch the evening news, I don't even discuss it within his earshot.

I mention a long list of activities Sheryl might do with him.

—Where should I tell him you'll be? she asks, not looking wholly convinced this will work.

—It's best not to lie to him too much, he's so intuitive. You can say I've gone to the stadium to accept an award for Tommy.

—I'll do my best.

I tell her she has to do more than that.

Julie has us over for a vegetable lasagna dinner two nights before the match. She knows I'm strictly vegetarian now. I imagine it broke her heart to alter her family recipe, but she's more cheerful than I've seen her in a long time.

Over dessert, she starts in.

—I saw the way the two of you looked on that morning program. You can't buy chemistry like that, she says, referring to the spot Uber and I did from our individual homes at the beginning of the week.

Mark laughs but Lloyd ducks, moving straight into the kitchen to get an early start on the dishes. He asks Thad to keep him company over a scoop of chocolate ice cream, since Thad seems troubled by the tiramisu. I watch my brother as he puts his hand in Lloyd's, and they head off.

—Maybe she doesn't *want* to marry a gladiator, Mark says, scooping the creamy pastry into his mouth. —Wicked dessert, Mom.

—Maybe she just needs some *understanding* of the benefits, Julie says.

—Maybe she's just a modern woman, he says.

—Maybe, as a man, you don't have a lot to contribute to this conversation.

Julie throws her napkin down. I've never heard her speak to Mark in quite this way, and I can see he's decided to stop.

—I hope you'll understand, eventually, I tell her.

—But would your mother understand? Julie says.

—Mom, Mark scolds.

—It's better that she think about this stuff now, than regret it later.

I wasn't keeping track, but Mark indicates the empty wine bottle, raising his eyebrows. And now that I think about it, she's probably on her third or fourth glass.

—Allison couldn't live with her decisions. With any of them, really, I say.

When Julie breaks down, Lloyd, who must have had his ear to the door, edges out of the kitchen. He sits Thad down at the phone table in the hallway and helps him with his sandals. Then he gets my jacket from the closet.

I want to go over to Julie and try to comfort her but Mark makes it clear that I should wait for another time.

Thad takes my hand now and we slip through the door to the garage. Once he's in his seat belt, Lloyd puts an arm around my shoulders and says, —Part of the training in a way. Look, you just have to be able to put everything, even tonight, from your mind. I don't want you doing anything tomorrow but resting up. Watch a funny movie with Thad for a while when you get home and then go straight to bed.

—You're a funny movie, Thad tells Lloyd.

It's hard to say how many hilarious movies and whacko shows we've watched in the last thirty-six hours. Thad and I burned through some Woody Allen and Marx Brothers, and then he just loves that one with Steve Carell and all those animals, and I insisted on *Stranger Than Fiction*.

When I couldn't sleep, and I haven't slept since that lasagna dinner, not really, I began to surf stations that know how to wring the last bit of dopiness out of a day. Candid footage of people hurting themselves and their relatives (but not *seriously*, the disclaimer says) is always good for a late-night belly laugh; talk show hosts that can't stop mining the beaches of dysfunction and stupidity in the celeb world; the cheesiest stars from the worst reality shows back to savage each other. Unsuspecting people who think they've lost their cars, their wallets, their dignity, *ha, ha, you've been punked!* will get you through a full two hours. Or those people who dress horribly and they're told why, in excruciating detail, as they stand in front of a thousand mirrors, or the one where parents try to pawn off their ugly daughter on some new guy because her current boyfriend is chronically calling her mother a whore. And people worry about the impact of television.

This morning—the morning of our competition—I wake up and quickly feel just how suffocating the air is. The AC churns so slowly I realize we're in a brownout and the LED display on the clock is blinking so I know we've lost power at least once during the night.

I call Sheryl to make sure she's awake. She plans to come over while it's still dark out. As soon as I get her on the phone, she complains heavily about the sudden heat wave. At least she's there so I can slip out of the house before Thad gets up. She knows to keep him fully occupied, and far away from the stations that carry the match, or anything on popular culture. She knows to call Julie if there are any problems she can't handle.

Mark and Lloyd retrieve me from the media circus so we

can travel over to the bread and circus. Lloyd has rented a fancy car for the occasion. I'm running on raw nerves, no sleep, and strobe lights everywhere. If the seats are plush or scratchy, the ride smooth or rough, I can't feel a thing.

# CHAPTER
# 31

I shift about now, my feet cold on the damp stone floor. I'm aware of the thunder of people overhead as the last of them enter the stadium, find their seats, and purchase their food and souvenirs for the big match.

I've been here all day, checking my weapons, getting a massage, doing limbering exercises. I had a quiet lunch with Lloyd.

Mark is up in the emperor's box. He's hiding behind the curtains with his computers. Once the horns sound, he'll put down his burger and fries and Rock Star, and activate *Lyn*. She will suddenly appear next to me, identical to me, eager to be me in the dark passage leading into the arena. I wait behind an iron gate, breathing, hardly breathing, considering my sins, my digressions, my lineage, my reasons for fighting, where I'm going, and how insane is this?

There's something about Mark being planted up there that makes me think of assassination attempts, only this assassination is about my identity, and even though he's turning the dials, I made it clear to him that I'm the one squeezing the trigger.

Last night, in between all that funny stuff, I drifted down to the library for a while. There *The Bhaghavad Gita* jumped out at me, the way books often do in our library. You can look at the same shelf a thousand times and suddenly a title pops out. It's not like I know Sanskrit—ours is an English translation—but as I read I was thinking about this guy Arjuna who had to go into battle. As he wrestles with the moral implications of what he's about to do, he talks with this god—this *real* avatar—who helps him understand his destiny.

There are certain people I could talk to in my head who might try to convince me that I should or shouldn't fight today and that this avatar idea is frantic or clever or chicken-hearted or right. I could reach out to Tommy's spirit, I could wrestle with Allison's, but that's just battling myself in a way. And I have to stop doing that and get a clear mind. And I have to accept that even if I pull this off, people, a whole lot of people—maybe tabloid-reading millions?—will have opinions about me, most of them pretty whacked.

I can see most everything through the gate, except for the stadium seats above and behind me of course. The night sky is overly dark and with the lights, it's impossible to find the moon or stars. The air is muggy. I know from being in the seats that no one can see me in my corridor waiting for this gate to lift. Standing here, I'm thinking passages of birth and death, water bottles and alter egos, the screwed-up life I've lead—when someone grips my shoulder from behind. I quickly spin round and grab my heart to stop the pressure. Uber's in gear, in his part.

—Don't creep up on me like that, I say.

—I have to talk fast, he whispers. —I know you've gone to a million matches, but it's a little different when you're in the arena. You've got to be ready for anything.

The one eye is still covered by a patch, gauze visible around its edges. He touches my arm and his hand is warm. I'm aware that he's taking a huge risk being here. There are rules about opponents conferring before a match. There are *rules*.

—They could send a lion out, another warrior. Watch the gates, he says.

—But the contract states . . .

He shakes his head.

—Caesar's doesn't care. Just assume that anything that enters the arena is there to take you, or your avatar, out. I never wear glasses in the arena, but I'm great with shapes. If I see something coming your way, I'll signal. I've told Mark if that happens, he has to be quick and aggressive. There's no time to stop and think.

—No time to think, I say, suddenly aware that I am trying

to memorize his face. The marks in his face. If I had a mirror, I would memorize my own. We are fleeting at best.

—If you end up in the arena, he says, and hands me a small vial.

—Poison? You want me to take poison?

—Rub it on your arms and legs. It's an anesthetic. It will numb your skin, but it won't last long.

I feel pinpricks in my feet now, as if they're going asleep.

He leans in and kisses me on one temple, like I'm his sister or his girlfriend. And I go with this momentary impulse and grab him by the armor and hug him briefly, kiss his unscarred cheek.

—It'll be over soon, he says.

I almost say, *That's what worries me*, but just then *Lyn* walks up behind Uber, pats him on the back, though he can't feel this, I know. But he can see I'm staring at something, and he turns.

—Wish me luck too? she asks.

He looks from one to the other of us. I should have asked her to wear the sunglasses. Her eyes still have that unreal quality and she's a little too bright in the corridor.

—I'll try to go easy on you, she says to Uber.

But Uber appears to have lost his sense of humor. —I hope you know what you're doing, he tells me.

—Probably best if you don't say anything in the arena, I tell her.

She just laughs. —But this is my big moment.

—Please, I say. —For Thad.

*for thad.*

Uber gives me a concerned look and says, —I have to go.
He takes off at a run through the passageways.

It's hard to express how completely disconcerting her look
is, especially since it's almost my look. It's like standing in
front of a mirror, only the mirror walks and talks and goes
into battle for you.

—We're just sparring, right? *Lyn* asks.

How can I feel remorse over what I'm doing to her?

—That's the idea, I say. —Take your time. Pace yourself.

Just then the horns ring out. We see Uber step into the
arena from a gate opposite ours. The crowd goes manic. Popcorn and crazy hats are tossed into the air, banners unfurled,
everything airborne.

—*UBER, UBER, UBER.*

I realize in this moment that they're just as much in love
with Uber as they ever were with Tommy, maybe more. The
boards are lit with all manner of photos of Uber and me from
childhood on. Romance played up, enhanced, expanded,
and enlarged. Commentators speculate, dissect, scramble, talk
Shakespeare's *R and J* in that prepackaged commodity way,
consider our horoscopes, our statistical chances, what our colors mean, and so forth. My legs are numb. My teeth.

I watch *Lyn* intently as she stretches her arms out in front of her, then behind. She moves her head from side to side, cracks the vertebrae in her neck, adjusts her armor, then looks at me again.

I think she's finally lost her comic self.

She reaches out now to take my hand in hers, which is only that sensation of moist cool air.

—Don't let me die, she says.

Before I can find anything to say the gate lifts and she only waits until it's halfway up before she ducks under it and enters the arena to cheers that eclipse even Uber's. And then I see it, the odd way she walks, the hip action—it's only slightly better than before, and my stomach seizes up.

Uber and *Lyn* move into the center of the arena.

I have this sensation of being very small and very large all at once. There's a moment of silence as they stare at each other. Then Uber secures his helmet and takes a stance.

*Lyn* suddenly swings her sword over her head and with a sound that seems to push out of her throat, she drives the sword toward his stomach. It's met by his shield. The first sound of metal on metal resounds in the stadium.

I have to give *Lyn* credit for the beauty of this first move, the exact articulation. For one second, Uber glances over to where I hide and then he lifts his sword and they begin to fight, which is unlike fencing because the swords are too heavy, but one blow seems to match another. As she dodges and strikes, I realize there's something too syncopated, her actions are too repetitive. And maybe this is what seems to be making the crowd so restless. Suddenly she leaps into the air, higher than one can leap, really, and I am reminded of those movies like *Crouching Tiger*.

When she lands her legs go almost transparent and just as quickly regenerate, as the lights in the stadium dim and then brighten. Another brownout.

An uncomfortable murmur goes through the crowd.

Uber, who looks very pale, tries to get things back on track by making the first cut. The blood trickles down *Lyn's* sword arm, which brings good spirits into the amphitheater. But instead of fighting back, she stares at the blood, mesmerized.

I know Uber is backed into a corner now, trapped by *Lyn's* confused efforts to fight and simultaneously consider her wounds. So he draws more blood, this time from her left leg. Then I lunge at him, I mean she does, and maybe he's afraid she's going to try and run him through. He moves back too quickly.

When he trips I see the edge of the black modem pop out of the sand. I doubt anyone else will know what that small bit of black is, but I know. Uber knows.

He lands with one foot caught on the edge of the power cord. I swear he falls to the sand in slow motion. And the lights, the entire lighting system, in the stadium go down and we're all pretty much in the dark now except for the toys the vendors sell—those small handheld lights that whirl about and turn different colors, the glow-in-the-dark necklaces and pop beads.

There's a long minute or two. The crowd begins to stomp their feet.

The lights come up in the top tiers.

I see Uber's dark shape. I think he's untangled himself.

*Lyn* has disappeared.

Mark, I'm sure, could rectify this situation in short order but we agreed in advance that if she were to disappear entirely it's just too risky to make her reappear. This has to do, in part, with the way she glows into existence and the icons that might appear around her head.

I try to get the cap off the vial of painkiller, but it slips from my hands and shatters on the stone floor. I understand that rubbing glass shards into my skin is counterproductive at this point, and I know I have to get out there.

Heart accelerating, I pull out the short blade I have tucked in my belt. I cut my arm where Lyn's arm was cut. Then I reach down and knick my left leg where her left leg was nicked.

I step into the arena.

And something kicks in that I haven't known for months. Maybe I've never known it. I have an almost unbearable sense of peace.

As the rest of the lights return, I see that Uber has pushed the modem back into the sand along with the cord. There's a resounding noise as the crowd sees Uber and me facing each other again. I wonder if it's actually a jeer. Maybe it's a feeling about the management, or the wish for blood and death to make up for the management, but it's a rousing sound nonetheless.

I never understood just how bright the lights in the arena really are—how invisible the crowd becomes—how much I could use a pair of dark glasses. But unlike my avatar, I can't manifest them or fight with my eyes closed. I'm aware of all the calls, the chants. My head is filled with chanting.

I secure my left hand in the shield's strap and grasp the sword tightly in my right hand and looking Uber dead in his visible eye, I give him a slight nod to say: *I'm ready.*

He lifts his chin in acknowledgment. He waits for me to begin.

If I were at the Ludus with a sparring partner, I would start with a blow to his sword arm. But Uber is left-handed, and I feel less confident here, despite all the practice. His face is guarded by his helmet. I could try for his stomach—always the gut—he stands with his shield slightly off to the right. There's an opening if I'm quick enough.

But in thinking over Lloyd's coaching, I aim high and suddenly swing low and make my effort at his knees. He's very fast, deflecting my sword, which prompts me to raise my shield and right my sword again, but I'm surprised to see that I've drawn blood with the tip of my blade, just below his left kneecap.

You might think this would bring a certain satisfaction to the crowd but I'm aware of their impatience, especially the ones that hang around the edges, who almost reach in and try to fight for you. I've always thought the stadium is an odd design, the lower seats so close to the action that some people fall into the ring each year. Guards have certainly had to chase down the enthusiasts, the streakers, and so on. Accidents have occurred. Some fanatics actually try to do battle with the Glads in the arena.

Now the catcalls, the egging on. They're like generals and senators—always carefully removed from the action but chronically propelling it.

Withou waiting for me, Uber strikes his blade against mine as if to say: *fight.*

We go to blows again. And I think I'm holding my own until that second in which my mind steps out of the action and I realize I'm thinking about what I'm doing. And what I'm doing is feeling a stinging pain and my sword arm starts to bleed.

Then the stupid thoughts stream. I'm not my double. I could die, actually, truly die. And the only twisted antidote I can see, in this moment in time, is the knowledge that I'm capable of wounding and maiming and killing in real time, in the real world, without restraint.

I am everything I am not.

Uber rams his shield against mine now and in the impact my sword flies to the ground. I thrust my shield as hard as I can at him, and I'm surprised to see him trip. Maybe later I'll learn he lost his footing as a way to buy me time. But for now I have my sword in hand again and he's righted himself and we are fighting, harder now.

I cut his left leg, he slices my left arm. I rap my sword

against his helmet, he cuts me below my chest plate. I hear the ten-minute signal.

And just as we raise our swords again, Uber is suddenly looking behind me, wide eyed, his mouth streaming terror as he calls out, —*NO!*

*you can't stop to think.*

My feet seem to take off from the ground as I turn. I thrust my sword out with all the force I own, at the tiger, at the lion, at whatever Caesar's has set free, covering my face with my shield, all in one motion. And I think, *This is it, I'm going to die.*

Then I hear his cry.

I pull my shield away.

I see Thad drop to the ground in his gladiator outfit, his arms and legs splayed, blood spurting from beneath his thin chest plate, down his torso, into the sand.

—Lynie, he says, barely pushing my name from his lips.

I get his chest plate off and press my hands over the wound.

Sheryl, the nanny, is running toward us now, as if she could still catch him in time to prevent what's happened.

Julie and Lloyd are running into the arena behind her.

I keep telling Thad he's going to be all right.

Uber shouts for the medics, the ambulance.

Julie tears a swath of cloth from her dress and kneels next to me, pressing the cloth against his chest.

—I told her not to bring him! I scream at Julie, through my tears.

I look at Thad's confused face.

He can't catch his breath.

I think he's starting to turn blue.

—You have to hold on, Thaddy, I say, kissing his forehead.

The ambulance pulls up close. They apply a dressing and strap an oxygen mask over his mouth and nose. The bed is popped out of the back and they hoist him up.

They tell me to stand back.

—*I'M HIS SISTER!* I shout.

—You have to stand back so we can save him, a female medic tells me.

Julie pulls at me, saying we'll follow them over to the hospital.

I watch the ambulance doors shut, the ambulance lights go on. The siren pierces the absolute stillness. I watch it pull out of the stadium.

The nanny is crying. She tells me he wouldn't stay home, that he got under the train table and kept hitting his head against the wood until he was bleeding, that she didn't know what else to do.

I tear myself away from Julie and pick up my sword.

With the handle in both fists, I drive the blade into the sand as hard as I can so it penetrates the wood below and stands straight in the air.

—*NO MORE!* I shout.

Uber throws his shield on the ground and brings his

sword over next to mine and drives it into the ground as well.

And the last thing I see as I rush out of the arena is the rain of plastic souvenir swords.

Thousands and thousands of swords as they're pitched into the arena.

# EPILOGUE

I'm crouched outside a hotel room in Harvard Square. I have my tape recorder, and a notebook and pen in case technology fails me. While I think over my questions to Joe Byers, I get a call from Uber telling me he and Thad have arrived at Singing Beach. It's funny the way he'll go off with Uber and be perfectly okay with this—they haven't known each other long. Maybe Uber reminds him of Tommy in some way.

—Make sure Thad doesn't go in the water above his knees, I say, —unless you're right there with him. And don't let him oracle too many strangers.

I include cautions about sunblock and a hat. People recognize Thad everywhere he goes now, and he tires easily because everyone wants a personal reading

Another inch or two and my sword would have gone through his heart. That's what I'm trying to live with. Whenever I change his bandages, Thad gives me his manga look, his eyes large and wide and eager to get the tape pulling over with. Predictions trickle from his lips as if this might make it easier to deal with the tug at his chest. I've begun to write down as many of them as I can.

I don't know what it means that Thad's wound is in the same spot where my avatar had her spear, but I try not to focus on this because it makes me nervous, and then I think I make Thad nervous and the important thing now is to look forward and put our world on solid ground.

I fired Sheryl, the nanny, outside the ER that night. And once Thad was on the mend, I retained an attorney to get my funds from Caesar's, along with the deed to the house. They claim, since it wasn't a fight to the death, Uber and I are required to have a rematch. They gave Thad and me an initial sum to live on for a while but nothing close to the contract. My attorney claims that Caesar's created an unsafe and hostile work environment, and that the amphitheater facilities put my brother at risk since he was able to climb down to where we were fighting without much effort. Getting legal help is a completely unacceptable thing to do in Glad culture. We never bring in outside counsel. And once this hit the news, I was made out to be some kind of hero to young Glads and an enemy to the old guard, and the truth is I'd rather not be either one.

Mark comes over all the time. He hangs out with Thad so I can work out or grocery shop or have some time to work on *The History* uninterrupted—that is, when he can make it in or I can make it out—because the paparazzi have just about tripled in numbers around the house. Mark and I are tighter now than we've ever been. He really goes the limit to make things cool for Thad. And sometimes I think he's met someone but if he has it will take him a while to get around to telling me.

We're getting a lot more foreign press now, and thick outcroppings of protestors and supporters, and God-knows-what-all people hanging out in the streets, including all those oracle seekers, so I've had to start looking for a place to move to with Thad, and that has me thinking about colleges in different areas. I don't know. Sometimes I think Europe, the Netherlands. Sometimes I just want to write the *History*.

Once things settle down, I want to do whatever it takes to give my parents a proper burial, even if that means breaking into Caesar's headquarters for Tommy and robbing the graveyard where Allison is photographically interred—or inhumaned, as some call it. Both Uber and Mark say they're up for that, and they'd be happy to recruit some friends to help out.

I've had a stream of offers coming my way, so I don't answer the phone much. Movie deals, clothing line, TV series, a tell-all book, my own column in *Glad Rag*. I know Thad would like it if I'd accept the gaming offer because they told him they'd put him in the game as the Living Oracle, before I grabbed the phone from his hands.

Thad doesn't ask for Mom as much now, or maybe I should say not in the same way, as if she's stepped out to the store and he's expecting her home any minute. But I'm not sure if he'll ever understand that they're firmly anchored in two different worlds now. Sometimes after I've washed his quilt we just sit with our backs against the dryer, the fabric going round and round, and I tell him all the stories he wants to hear about Allison and the fathers. I don't say this to him, of course, but sometimes I think we'll always be in mourning.

Most of the time the house is drowning in quiet, no matter how I blast my operas, and Allison's bathroom door remains locked. When Thad goes to bed, I move from one area of the house to another as if one of them might contain a room with sleep, which they rarely do. Even though I dismantled the Living machine, a couple of times I've imagined Allison moving from room to room looking for her unfinished letters so she can tear them up and start over. I like to think that if she had stuck around, we would have talked about how stupid and selfish we were, how lost. I think we could have gotten through all of it and laughed at the total inanity. But who knows.

Uber has his own troubles. His mother had to put his father into a managed-care facility shortly after the trauma of charity night. And Uber has also hired attorneys, who sometimes work in conjunction with mine, to see that we don't end up back in the arena together. His contracts, including the ones for endorsements, are absolutely contradictory and will keep his team busy for some time to come.

When Thad went upstairs to get his beach ball this

morning, Uber dropped the lid on the picnic basket and said, —Maybe we should go out to dinner sometime, just the two of us.

I continued to wash the dishes as if I hadn't heard him over the running water, because I still feel pulled in two by the whole thing. Finally, I dried my hands and then I showed him the stack of college catalogs I've been poring over, including the low residency programs and those abroad. He seemed to accept this pretty easily, I mean, all he said was, —Okay, I understand.

I watched him open the basket again to nestle the soft drinks around the sandwiches without looking up at me.

Only then did I say, —Well, maybe next week if I can find a sitter for Thad.

You know how it is when you get something you want and then you have no idea what to do with it? It's kind of that way with Joe Byers. He agreed to come all the way from Akron, Ohio, despite his hip and knee problems. He rarely travels now that he's in his seventies, but he actually wrote to me after he heard about what had happened to Thad.

I sent him a plane ticket and got him a room at the Charles. He agreed to an interview as long as I guaranteed his anonymity while he's in town—which meant a serious coordinated effort with Mark to outwit the paparazzi.

So now I'm crouched here in a hallway of the Charles, thinking about what I really need to ask Byers when he opens the door because this might be my only shot at him.

Maybe I need to say: just tell me the facts as you recall them, Mr. Byers, the plain truth about how Glad sport started. I'll put things down exactly as you dictate them so people in the future can dissect and misinterpret, and psychologize and generally mangle your words until no one knows what you said anymore, but at least I'll know what I heard from you.

I know you can't push the plant back into the seed, but if I'm going to sit around dreaming, I'd like to imagine there's a way to put an end to Glad sport someday. They ended it in Rome, and the war in Vietnam ground to a halt, and the Berlin Wall came down—that kind of thing.

And then maybe I could go on a tour, because I'd know I gave *A History of the Gladiator Sports Association* a decent ending, and I could talk with young people, young women in particular, about how we once lived in a time of blood. Blood and money and lots of publicity.

## ACKNOWLEDGMENTS

My thanks to my amazing daughter, Sienna, who helped me navigate virtual reality, reminded me of the teen world, and opened up a window so I could understand the only way this wild book could possibly end; to my editor, Melanie Cecka, my agent, Charlotte Sheedy, and Meredith Kaffel— the divine team who lived Lyn's world every step of the way; to the Briggs-Copeland Lectureship at Harvard University that made Rome possible; to the Burdicks, who gave me respite so I could toil by the surf last summer; to Daniel J. Quinn, who designed and created my Web site; to my students, who rock; to my intrepid family and friends; especially to my father, Norton Kay, who is the salt of the earth.